# DON'T LET ME GO

## Jamila Mikhail

KEEP YOUR GOOD HEART
Ottawa, Canada

# IN MEMORIAM

## Grandma Gertrude
## 1937 – 2018

This book is dedicated to my late grandmother Gertrude who is the only person who never stopped supporting me when I decided I wanted to be a writer and most importantly, the only person who never let me go.

# CONTENTS

# ACKNOWLEDGMENTS

Above all, I want to thank my grandmother Gertrude (1937-2018) for everything from raising me to always encouraging me in my writing endeavors despite that she couldn't read any of my works. You were my life in more ways than one and I'm still trying to figure out what the hell I'm going to do without you. I hope they have books somewhere between the sky and heaven.

Secondly, I owe the greatest gratitude to my loyal friends who have also been by my side through the many trials of my life, most notably Julien, Leo, and Daniel. A big fat thank you is also in order to Team Golfwell for their support and entertainment (despite that I really don't care for golf) and Dave for our long conversations, the periodic intellectual stimulation for always filling my mailbox with postcards and vintage photographs, among many other things.

Thanks to my cat Squeaker for being both my best friend and the love of my life and for sitting by my side for hours on end while I was typing up this book. I am proud to call myself a cat lady because of you.

Thank you as well to all the people who have somehow contributed to making this project a reality, in both big ways and small ways. You are numerous in number but you all know who you are. I could not have done this without all of you. It takes a village to write and publish a book, any author can testify to that.

It would be erroneous not to thank my dolls as well considering the subject matter of this book. My two favorite little guys dutifully watched over me from the shelf above my desk as I typed each word of this book.

Last but not least I need to thank my snail mail penfriends who have been with me for many years. I know that I've been a handful at times but I've shared some of the best friendships of my life with you, particularly Beth, Jenni, Duane, Joel and Andrew.

# ONE

The water splashed up against the rocks as I looked at the civilization in the distance. On the other side of the river there was a small factory and a water treatment plant on the industrial lot next to it. Passed that there was a lot of greenery with only the tip of the skyscrapers poking the distant skyline. The water was especially blue considering the fact that it passed through industrial land, but then again the town wasn't called Bluepond for nothing.

There wasn't a single cloud in sight and it was a beautiful day but I lacked the capacity to appreciate it. The cars going Nascar fast on the highway behind me were nothing but a dissonant hum in the background of the day. Some birds sang somewhere in the full scope of things too, but I couldn't see them as I kept on looking at the buildings in the distance. I couldn't believe that things had gotten to the point they were currently at. I couldn't wrap my mind around my own life anymore, if I had ever been able to understand it in the first place.

I got down from the railing I had been sitting on for hours and hours and walked back towards town before my mother got some idea in her head that I ran away because I hated my stepfather and stepbrother. I wasn't exactly on good terms with any of them, but I also had nowhere to run away to. I didn't really know where I was going to begin with, and I didn't want to get lost either. I especially wasn't looking forward to starting school in a new town either, albeit not a completely unfamiliar one. I'd spent a couple of my summers in Bluepond with my grandfather when I was younger, before he passed away.  I also knew that a few former schoolmates from Redmont had also relocated to Bluepond but that brought me no comfort. I hated school and I'd never made any friends there.

My only friends were my dolls. The only friends I'd ever had were my dolls. I began making action figures a couple of years ago after venturing out into a flea market being held in the basement of an old church and finding arbitrary parts. I thought it might be fun to recycle neglected and unwanted action figures and turning them into handsome little men again and it certainly was endless creative fun. What started out as an experiment became a steady hobby, and that hobby eventually turned into a passion. I ended up crafting everything from movie characters to soldiers of the Second World War to real people in my daily life.

As sad as I had been to be forced to sell most of them during the move, my talent had made me a small fortune. My stepfather thought it was stupid that a thirteen-year-old girl would want to spend all her time in her room playing with children's toys as he called them instead of going out and having a social life and my mother always took his side.

My actual father was nowhere to be found after the divorce and my stepbrother was the equivalent of a ghost. I literally only had my dolls, and even they seemed to be in jeopardy. Aside from them I only really had myself, and I wasn't good at being all by myself. Ironically the only person you really have your whole life is yourself.

That was abhorrently depressing to say the least. All you'll ever have is yourself, but what if you aren't a good person? What if you're good for nothing and nobody likes you? What if, no matter how hard you try, nothing ever changes? What if you're just a dunce and there's nothing you can do about it? What was the whole point of living then? Thinking about such things brought me no comfort as I approached nearby civilization.

I dreaded walking into that tiny pink house on a hill by the outskirts of town regardless of anything else. It didn't matter what I felt inside or what was going on around me, I simply didn't want to go. No more, no less. I was only a pawn in a game of chess greater than I, or so it seemed to me. The worst part was that it seemed like I couldn't even do a damn thing about it, and that feeling of powerlessness was probably what upset me the most in the entire thing.

The lawn was pretty much evergreen as my mother took great pride in that and her huge flower garden. There was a little paved driveway leading to a small shed in the backyard and my mom's little green Ford Fiesta was usually backed up all the way over there but there didn't seem to be anyone home despite that the lights were on in the kitchen and it was still daylight outside. The sun was just starting to set over the valley, beautifully illuminating everything in various shades of red, orange and pink. I sighed loudly and walked in through the side entrance.

In front of the side entrance there was the spiral stairwell to go upstairs and underneath on the other side there was the stairwell to go downstairs hidden behind a door. Then there was the living room taking half of the first floor, and right next to it on the left side there was the kitchen mingled with the dining room. And that was the entire main floor. *That small.*

My room was on the second floor along with my mother and stepfather's room as well as the bathroom that was no bigger than a closet. My stepbrother lived in the basement and he didn't just sleep there, he *lived* there in every sense of the word. Aaron was supposed to be my sibling, but he was really nothing more than a stranger living with the rest of us.

My existence was consumed with sadness and grief as I walked up to the bathroom to clean up a little bit. There had been a certain degree of mud involved with going to the waterside to clear my thoughts but it turned out that I hadn't cleared out anything from my head at all. The bathroom was small and claustrophobic but it was cute.The ocean blue walls were decorated with paintings of fish and seashells and other aquatic things that my mother had made in order to create a little life in the place.

The shower, the toilet and the sink were all incredibly white and shiny without a single stain. The bathroom floor was of a light golden brown, kind of mimicking sand, just making the small room even more beautiful. On the east side of the room there was a large stained glass window covered with a blue and white chevron curtain that was handed down to my mother from an old relative, among other things she had received.

Over the sink there was a large mirror with bare bulbs over it of various colors spicing up the room just like my mom liked it. She had always been so vibrant and eccentric but her artistic side had declined since the divorce, and I greatly missed that about her.

Nowadays she was an entirely different person. Since she shacked up with Mike she had become a stranger to me. The bathroom was the only indication that she was still in there somewhere, or at least I believed that she hadn't vanished completely. I looked at my ugly face in the mirror and pushed my hair out of my face. I had never like my auburn hair too much so I had tinted it red, which was more to my liking, but I still wasn't completely satisfied.

My hair extended down just passed my shoulders with my overgrown bangs going down just passed my ears. Letting my bangs grow out was a futile attempt at hiding my cheeks which I thought were too chubby for the rest of my face. In the middle of that my nose was too small and my big round eyes were placed too closely together. My olive eyes were nothing more than something else I didn't like about myself on top of the mountain of things that would've been different if I could rule the world.

My face was too round and my top lip was too big for the bottom one. I wasn't morbidly overweight, in fact my BMI said I was *normal,* but my stomach could still have been flatter. All in all, I had absolutely no self-esteem and even less with my stepfather constantly being on my case about my appearance along with just about everything else.

I tied up my hair into a ponytail since it had been a victim to the wind by the shore during the last few hours and went into my room to work on a doll I'd started a few days ago. I was almost done but couldn't really decide which military uniform he was going to wear. I knew he was a soldier and I instinctively knew that he was a good man but I kept on going back and forth on other details.

Was he going to be an American or a British soldier of the Second World War? Or maybe a German. If so he would've been part of the German Resistance. Or, alternatively he could be half British and half German, I already had a few American soldiers standing twelve inches tall. I didn't really know what I wanted to do with him so I went downstairs and got a snack before resuming my work on him.

Eventually I decided that he would wear a Wehrmacht uniform and gave him the rank of lieutenant. I added a few finishing touches to his face and gave him sparkling stereotypical blue eyes and sandy hair. I also put some miniature 1940s round glasses on him to give him an extra touch of elegance and to stand out from my other soldiers standing on my shelf.

One of them had a missing hand that I hadn't been able to repair after finding him in that condition at the thrift store so I'd added an eyepatch to him to give him more of a hero returning from battle type of look. He had been my favorite until I'd just finished my first German, a good German. He had been a savior to the most vulnerable during one of the worst times of their lives. He was sort've a metaphor for what I wanted in my own life, or more like *who* I wanted to enter my life.

"Welcome to the world Adler," I whispered to him as I placed him on the night table next to my bed, "welcome to war."

My new home was indeed a war zone. My mother and stepfather fought constantly and I could not understand at all the appeal of staying with a person who always disrespected you and put you down. My stepbrother was seventeen and there was no telling him what to do or not do, he did what he damn well wanted and he was always in trouble both at home and at school. I sort've simply fell in the shadows but I also got my dose of being yelled at for not doing chores on time or not doing them according to standards.

Mike also thought I was stupid when I asked for help with a homework question that was supposed to be easy. I'd resorted to not doing my homework anymore which caused an entirely separate truckload of troubles and I'd made it into high school hanging by a hair.

As I looked through my bedroom window I saw my mother pulling into the driveway so I decided to go downstairs and have her be the first person, and probably the only person aside from me, to meet Adler. Unlike Mike, she never had a problem with me making dolls and action figures and before she divorced my dad she had actually taken great interest in my collection.    Together we had spent many hours imagining the lives of the little men and women I made. My dad had even helped me make a little military base for the soldiers and a little beauty parlor for the divas so I could put makeup and accessories on them while I played. I missed those days so much.

"Hi there Joanie," my mother greeted me as I came downstairs.

"Hi mom," I replied joyfully, "I want you to meet someone."

"Oh?"

"His name is Adler."

My mother took him in her hand and examined every detail carefully and smiled as she did so. It had been a while since I could show her something I'd made that I was proud of and that she could be proud of too. I knew that she liked him from the obvious look on her face when she gave him back to me.

"He's very handsome honey, good job."

"Thanks mom."

"Mike and Aaron will be home soon so I'm going to make dinner. It'll be ready in about half an hour."

During that time I went back up into my room and I dug into my box of arbitrary doll parts to see how I would recycle them and what I would make next. Maybe I would make one of my grandmother that I'd never met, or maybe dolls in the likeness of both my grandparents on their wedding day in 1953.

I had so many good ideas swirling around my head but not enough materials to make exactly what I wanted. I'd either have to get some more or make something else with what I had. I ended up pondering for a while because before I knew it my mother called me down to come and eat. Once again I brought Adler down with me because he had turned out really good and I hoped that for once Mike might realize my talent.

Adler was by far the most beautiful and most detailed action figure I'd ever made. He looked just like a real person, had he really been one. I imagined him being a tall and strong man with big arms but gentle hands and a good heart. He was intelligent, charming, fluent in many languages and multi-talented. He was in his mid-thirties but the war had made him look older despite his good looks. He had been a brave man and was highly decorated even if he wasn't a high-ranking officer. He had also helped save people during the war, and I somewhat wished that he could miraculously come to life and save me too.

My mother had made pork chops despite that she knew very well that I absolutely *hated* any and all pork products with a passion. But of course they were Mike's favorite so Mike had whatever he wanted regardless of what everybody else thought. When she was around him she was a completely different person. She almost physically changed too. He had convinced her to give up our previous house even after my dad had voluntarily given it to my mom before he moved out of province.

I missed my big old room and the big bookshelf I had in there. I barely had any books at all left and the library was too far away for me to go by myself so the most I read was the newspaper during the months that I was out of school. I really liked the crosswords section and had learned a lot of new words that way.

The sky was now pitch black outside once I sat down in my usual spot at the dinner table. We often ate late but it generally wasn't *that* late nonetheless. My mom worked long hours as a nurse and usually didn't come home early and Mike never cooked no matter what.

He would have preferred to go without food than to actually have to make it himself. Aaron always ate takeout and I didn't have very many cooking skills myself so I mostly ate delivery or junk food I bought from the corner store until my mom arrived to feed all of us.

"What the hell is that?!" Mike grumbled angrily when he saw that I had Adler in my hands at the dinner table and violently ripped him away from me.

"His name is Adler! Look how great he turned out to be!"

"If you're doll hobby wasn't stupid enough for someone your age now you had to go and make a doll of a Nazi!"

"He's not a Nazi! He's just a Wehrmacht officer and he's with the German Resistance just like Claus von Stauffenberg! He saved people during the war and he's one of the good guys!"

"You dumb cluck don't you remember that my great-uncle gave his life fighting these damn Germans? I never want to see another one of these things in my house again!"

Just as he said that he began to dismember Adler in a belligerent yet so trivial rage. I protested and begged him to stop but that only seemed to fuel the fire. I got up and tried to physically take back Adler but all I managed to get were half a leg and a few torn pieces of fabric from his uniform before Mike positioned his elbow in font of me and turned away so I couldn't get to Adler which in turn hit me right in the ribs and I went down on the dirty floor immediately and hit my head.

It was a legitimate accident, he hadn't tried to hit me but he wasn't sorry that he did either. My head was spinning as I hit the cold hard floor but I clearly saw him destroy the doll that I'd been the most proud of by crushing it with his boots he never took off so I wouldn't be able to glue it back together. I hated those boots and the sound they made when they crushed the plastic and little pieces of what used to be Adler scattered everywhere across the floor.

Mike always wore those dirty old cowboy boots in the house and only took them off to take a shower and go to bed. It didn't matter how filthy they were, he didn't take them off and it was my chore to clean up whatever traces they left behind when he came in. I had politely offered to clean the boots themselves so they wouldn't look so faded and disgusting but I was accused of being judgmental and lazy.

That was the first and last time that I'd ever made a suggestion to Mike but I still wanted his approval so badly. I wanted to feel like he was proud of me and that he loved me. I wanted that from everyone; mom, Mike and Aaron. They were my family and families were supposed to be united by love.

I cried profusely when I saw Adler, or whatever was left of him at least, sprawled out on the floor like that. He who had been so beautiful was now completely unrecognizable and beyond repair. Nobody at the table had any sympathy for me and nobody uttered a single word once Mike's outburst was over.

The three of them ate quietly at the table and once I managed to collect myself a little bit I got up and I ran upstairs without eating anything or saying a word to anyone. I ran into the bathroom as soon as I made it all the way up and threw up whatever was left of the junk food I'd eaten earlier in the day. I was too stressed and filled with agitation and despair to keep the food down despite my best efforts.

I was sweating profusely just by thinking and having a full-blown anxiety attack about what had just happened and despite my best efforts to keep my cool I was losing my battle. When Mike tuned in to his evening TV shows my mother came up discretely and asked me if I was okay in the bathroom. I dismissed her saying that it was just diarrhea and that I was fine. She left and went back downstairs without incident and I laid on my back on the bathroom floor looking at the ceiling blankly.

The more I tried to think the less I could function and the less I tried to think the more I wanted to puke again. I needed my *mom* so badly in that moment. I didn't just want the mother that lived with me now, I wanted my *mom*. One second she wanted to be close to me and the next she pushed me away and I didn't understand why. What had I ever done that was so bad to deserve that? I felt like only a pawn in a game of chess without any voice of my own. I felt worthless to put it mildly.

After about an hour of being borderline passed out on the floor I collected myself and went to my room which was just a few footsteps away at the far back of the top floor of the house. The only thing on the second floor of the little house was the bathroom, my tiny room, my mom and Mike's slightly bigger room and a small closet in the hallway.

The walls were painted a dark blue with a dark brown imitation wood floor. It was a beautiful little top floor. My room was a little more wacky with my walls painted a mixture of red, yellow and white with a black carpet covering the whole floor. There were road signs on the walls everywhere mimicking a racetrack or a highway. When we moved in I had insisted that the room stayed that way because I loved it and my request had been granted. Why not? It saved both mom and Mike a ton of work and money having to repaint it anyway!

There was only enough space in there to fit my small bed, a black children's dresser that matched the wall and a small square table to place junk on it along with several shelves mounted on the walls. Under my bed I had some colored plastic containers with drawers holding my clothes that didn't go in the dresser or the closet. It was claustrophobic but that little room had really become my own personal sanctuary over time and I would honestly have no idea what to do with a room that was any bigger.

There was a little window on the side with no curtains through which I could see across the valley. I could see the top of buildings in the distance, about a fifteen minute walk away on foot. As I looked outside I noticed that it had rained a little bit since I'd come in and the atmosphere had cooled down considerably.

I knew that my mother and Mike would be going to bed soon so I decided to wait a little bit before going to venture outside at night. I climbed into bed and hugged my Pokemon plushes for a while until I knew that everybody was sleeping soundly and then I put on some warm clothes and tip-toed downstairs.

I took a shoebox and a checkered cloth and wrapped Adler into it like one would do with a dead house pet, put everything in my green backpack and walked outside quietly into the darkness. The night air was cool but not particularly cold, it was just the kind of weather that I liked actually. I walked over to the bus stop not too far from the house and hopped onto the bus that would take me down by the water.

I was the only one on that particular bus going down to the riverside and it was a somewhat eerie experience to be completely physically alone despite that I was a professional at being emotionally alone. When the bus came to a halt, I got off and went to sit back on the wooden railing by the water, looking at the illuminated industrial establishments shining dimly in the skyline in the distance. At night it was beautiful to look at the water.

All the industrial lights reflected on the surface of the water creating flickering patterns that almost looked like liquid fire. I caught a chill and for a moment I looked back almost like I could feel somebody behind me but there wasn't anybody. Nobody was there. It was just me. Just me and my thoughts amidst the darkness and the lights in the distance somewhere I couldn't reach.

Once I gathered my courage I got down on my knees and started digging in the dirt with my bare hands until I made a hole big enough to bury the box that contained Adler's remains. I wanted to cry but I couldn't bring myself to do so. The tears simply didn't come out. What had I done to deserve that? Once upon a time I'd had a happy family but now it was like I was surrounded by strangers.

Strangers who didn't have any consideration for me. My relationship with my mother seemed like a tug-o-war that I could never win because I was the rope. One minute she seemed to be on my side and the next I was worthless in her eyes. How could she love a man like Mike? She had become a completely different person since he'd come along.

I gingerly deposited the box containing Adler into the hole and covered it with dirt. It took me a long time to cover it completely because I couldn't bring myself to do that either. By the time I was done the starry sky had become covered with clouds and I saw occasional flashes of lights in the distance.

A thunderstorm was rolling in. I knew from watching the forecast that one was supposed to pass during the night, how long had I really been out? I did not feel tired. I did not feel the need to sleep either. Generally I enjoyed sleeping, it was sort of an escape and I probably would've enjoyed sleeping for eternity on your average day but I felt different for some reason unknown to me. Something inside of me had changed.

I walked over closer to the water and carefully crawled in between the fragmented barbed wire fence so I could rinse off my hands in the current. The water was freezing cold as I dipped my hand inside and chills ran through my entire body. I hadn't needed to be woken up as I was running on my second wind at that point but the sensation certainly made me more aware. For the first time I felt the humidity by the water and the added dampness brought on by the incoming storm.

I had to come to terms with the thought that I'd have to go back home soon even if I didn't want to. I hid my freezing cold hands inside my pockets and carefully went through that fence that was falling apart again. I randomly noticed a single drop of water hanging from the wire just above me, waiting to fall. The moonlight reflected in it in an explicably beautiful way. It seemed so insignificant but heavy at the same time. It was so small but carried so much weight.

I stayed by the waterfront and sat on the wooden railing again until way passed midnight because I'd missed the last bus at eleven o'clock. I didn't mind walking back home though, the night didn't scare me. I wasn't scared of what lurked in the shadows. I was truly apathetic to everything really. Somewhere along the way I had become that way.

Not only had everyone around me turned into strangers over time, so had I. I had become a stranger even to myself. It started to rain shortly before I had started to make my way back home slowly. I was soaked by the time I got there but at least the most of the storm had gone and dumped itself elsewhere. Thunderstorms didn't scare me but I hated them anyway.

I creeped back into the house and tip-toed back into my room, hoping that I wouldn't leave a trail of water for someone to find out exactly what I had done. I had successfully slid into my bedroom unnoticed by anyone, mission accomplished! I took off my wet clothes and jumped into bed.

"Joanie!" my mother's voice echoed from behind the door, "Get up, it's time for breakfast!"

"Okay, it'll be just a moment," I muttered and rolled over to the other side of my bed.

I felt unbelievably homesick as I sat up in my bed, and I really meant *sick*. I put my head between my knees and took a series of deep breaths to calm myself down. I zoned out and thought about a happier time, back in Redmont, with my entire family happily together.

I even longed for the little old lady that lived next door to my friend Andrea's farm. We hung out all the time since our moms were friends and I loved being out in the country and riding horses or even running after chickens.

One specific cow from the elderly couple's ranch next door always wandered off the land and came to eat in Andrea's family's garden. It actually did very little *eating* but a lot of shredding plants and that was particularly upsetting to my friend who dedicated so much of her time to caring for beautiful flowers that she'd planted and grown all by herself.

Finally, one day we decided that it was time to put this to an end once and for all and we both angrily went stomping over for the old couple's house about to yell at them to build a darn fence or at least do something to stop the cow from coming over but when we got there we couldn't possibly be angry at the sweet old lady who opened the door.

We politely asked her to deal with the cow in a soft whisper and before we left the old lady had even given us a blueberry pie to take home. Whatever had been done about the cow, it never came back to destroy Andrea's beautiful garden. All the pretty flowers and the delicious produce had been intact since that day.

"I made you some bacon and eggs!" my mom went on to say, faking a joyous tone and bringing me back to reality.

"Thanks," I muttered, not really knowing what else to say.

I didn't like bacon, that was never a secret but apparently it was never a factor either. How I wished for a piece of that old lady's blueberry pie in a moment like that! I would've loved to share it with Adler and all of my other dolls had they been real people.

If I had the chance I wanted to go to the thrift store later in the afternoon to see what I could find for my next masterpiece. I wanted to make a little guy in the likeness of Bernard Law Montgomery, or simply Monty for short. I still had a bit of money left and still plenty of time to kill before school started again. The days seemed to drag on forever in my life and I needed some entertainment.

For the moment I concentrated on getting dressed and gathering my strength for whatever hell I was going to face once I got downstairs and force-fed myself bacon mostly against my will because I didn't want to stir up any trouble by complaining that I didn't like it or by refusing to eat it entirely.

# TWO

Tossing and turning brought me no comfort. The voice of the wind moving through the trees brought me no consolation. Cars passed by and for a brief moment their headlights made the ceiling of my room just a little brighter. I felt as if the walls of my room were closing in around me as my breathing accelerated. My body ached with stress and despair, my mind felt like a bomb about to blow and my heart was crying out for help.

I wished that the sheets could just have suffocated me in my wake. My whole world seemed like it was coming down, crashing hard as it hit the ground. My soul shattered under the fire of pain and the absence of momentary hope. I buried my face into my pillow as I started to cry because I didn't want anyone to hear me.

They couldn't help me anyway. I didn't feel like I could be helped in the first place. I felt like nothing but a problem and a burden and although I knew intellectually those were corrupt and untrue feelings, that didn't stop me from *feeling* them.

I didn't know how to deal with what I was feeling so I stumbled into the nearby bathroom that was just down the hallway from my room and grabbed a razor from the room's junk holder cabinet behind the door. I brought it back to my room so I could have some privacy and I contemplated doing something that I hadn't done in over two months; cutting myself. I had been a cutter in the past. I hadn't adapted well to my new life in a new town with new people but I had met a girl named Rachel who had also been a cutter in the past.

She told me very gently about how she had found hope and had come to give up that bad habit and I found truth in her words so I began to listen. Quitting the cutting was something I was always proud of because it had been the first step in the right direction for me in my life. The ironic thing about that though is that that girl had ended up committing suicide a few weeks later. Looks like she hadn't found much hope after all.

My conscience was telling me not to cut myself again but my pain and my anger was telling me to do it. That desperate voice at the back of my mind was louder than a thousand hurricanes and I couldn't shut it out so I removed the blades from the razor and sliced my arm in a couple of places.

I then let the razor drop to the floor and shoved the blades on my night table as I buried my face in my pillow again and cried until I had no more tears. Only the streetlights in the street below gave off a faint glow just bright enough for me to see the fresh wounds on my arm. As more tears escaped from my eyes everything became a blur of faint colors as the dim light could not penetrate through the tears obstructing everything in view. Each vertebrate in my spine seemed to throb, begging my mind to cease the pain and my heart seemed to shake my entire core.

The cuts on my arm burned as the blood coagulated and sealed my skin together again. I thought it would've helped me forget the emotional pain but it didn't; my whole body was declaring a state of emergency.

One by one all of my hopes had vanished just the same. My erratic breathing seemed to slow as my mind gradually shut down. I felt like my pain resonated throughout the entire universe, maybe it did. I let out a sigh of relief as my tense body seemed to relax. It was almost like a hand touched my every aching bone and filled it with the essence of serenity.

I couldn't move onto my back, but I felt a presence behind me. As my mind became more aware of my surroundings I realized that something was indeed touching me, it wasn't just in my head. But I wasn't afraid, I felt a sense of calm and pure bliss sweep over me. The pain was gone for a moment and I indulged in the feeling for a while. Eventually I managed to find the strength to turn around and could not have been more shocked and surprised at what I saw.

It was Adler! Not just doll Adler either, but full size *man* Adler. He was just like my doll, but *human*. I turned on the lamp next to my bed so I could take a better look at him. Could he really be human like me? As I examined him further I noticed that he was breathing just like anybody else and that a certain warmth radiated out of him.

I admired every little detail that I'd put into making that doll, it was my masterpiece and now it had come to life. Everything I'd worked so hard on had materialized right in front of my eyes and he was the most beautiful person I had ever seen. I didn't understand how all of that could be but that didn't matter because I was in complete awe at him.

"Don't be afraid," his voice was just a soft whisper.

"Oh Adler, I'm not afraid," I responded, my voice cracking with a surge of mixed emotions.

I wasn't afraid of him, not after the good vibes his presence let off, but I was curious and thoroughly confused. How was *that* even possible? How could you go from being an inanimate object that was savagely torn to pieces and got buried inside a shoe box to being seemingly fully human and letting off such good energy?
I reached out and touched his hair just to prove to myself that he was real, and indeed he was! His hair was the softest thing I had ever touched and so was his flawless skin as I let my fingers trail down his perfect face and onto the collar of his uniform.

He was a masterpiece of a man, exactly like how I imagined him, yet I hadn't imagined the part where he would *actually* come to life and find me during a difficult time to comfort me. That part I never could've imagined in a million years.

There were also other questions, such as how he could've possibly gotten into my room. I'd buried a doll in the soil but now a person well over six feet tall was right here in my room. There was no way he could've walked through the locked door of the house or climb through my bedroom window on the second floor without being noticed at all!

I let my fingers trail down the buttons of his uniform and as my hand passed over his chest I couldn't help but feel his heartbeat. I let my hand rest there a little bit as I tried to make sense of the situation but all of my questions would have to wait because I got lost in his blue eyes that almost sparkled in the dim light as he looked at me compassionately.

Needing to be comforted and reassured, I latched onto him and he took me into his big strong arms. I laid my head on his chest and let some more tears escape from my bloodshot eyes. I was exhausted and worn out but his gentle touch relaxed my racing mind and brought it to a peaceful place.

The rhythm of his heartbeat soothed me and brought me to a place almost beyond this world. And that touch, it wasn't human, it was something else entirely. I'd always believed that only angels could take away your pain by simply stroking your shoulder with one hand.

He was a godsend! He was exactly what I needed, specifically what I couldn't get from anyone else in my life. I tightly latched on to him, never wanting him to leave. I let my mind drift away to the steady beat of his heart and eventually dozed off in his arms with my pain completely gone from my heart and soul, almost like it had never been put there in the first place.

As I closed my eyes and drifted away to another world my mind went completely blank and only woke up again early the next morning from a dreamless, exceptionally peaceful sleep. Adler was still right there beside me, still letting off an overwhelming aura of calmness and inner peace. In the early morning sunlight he looked more like a regular person instead of the luminous supernatural creature I had seen the previous night, however I knew full well that he was something more than a mere mortal.

"Good morning Joanie," he spoke with a German accent in a voice that was like music to my ears, "I reckon that you slept well?"

"Yes," I replied in a groggy voice as I rubbed my eyes, "it was absolutely heavenly."

"You didn't move an inch!"

"It's no wonder that I'm sore this morning! And now you've gotta tell me, what in the world are you?"

"So, I'm a *what* instead of a *who*, huh? Well, my name is Adler as you know and it looks like I'm your keeper."

"My keeper? What's that?"

"Pull out your laptop and I'll show you."

My body ached for a few moments as I sat up on my bed and stretched my legs but within a few moments all of that went away and my body felt very relaxed and all the pain disappeared. I bent down and reached under my bed to grab my old laptop that I'd gotten from a relative several years ago after they'd bought a new one.    It was slow and outdated but still one of my most prized possessions. I fired it up and waited for it to connect to the internet. That wasn't something I did very often because my machine couldn't handle high-powered video games and I wasn't allowed to go on social media. I then let Adler connect me to a page about keepers.

*Keepers are said to be souls of various different existences who come into the metaphysical world to provide guidance for fellow humans. Keepers are not guardian angels; they have not descended from heaven nor have they even been there. Keepers are unknown beings similar to childhood imaginary friends who may have several human-like attributes including bodies, hearts and minds.*

*The legend says that keepers can come in many forms; a faint presence, a glowing orb, or even in the form of a human being with flesh and bones. Not much is known about keepers apart from ancient legends written thousands of years ago. It is said that every person has a keeper, but many are unaware of this as keepers manifest themselves in various different ways and some people never acknowledge them at all.*

*It is also believed that each person creates their own keeper, much like they would create an imaginary friend as a child, and after being birthed out of pure love and genuine need stemming from a person's innermost being, keepers take on a life of their own depending on the aura of the person they belong to and the circumstances under which they enter this realm.*

*The legend says that keepers come to this dimension to guide us but are able to retreat to their vortex beyond this universe since their souls are not bound by mortal flesh and the binding laws of nature.*

*Since the atomic energy that composes their souls can vibrate at two places at one time, they are free to come and go as they please. Energy cannot be created nor destroyed, and our dimension is nothing but a transition phase for the soul; we come from nothing and we are nothing when we die.*

"That's amazing!" I exclaimed. "But how is this possible?"

"You tell me Joanie," Adler replied softly, "you're the one who created me."

"But I didn't create you like this. Where am I gonna hide you once I go to school and things like that? You're a big man, you don't just fit in the closet!"

"Here's the thing Joanie, you're the only one who can see me."

How was that possible? I was both in awe of him and thoroughly confused and was further perplexed after learning that he was also invisible to everyone except me. I reached out and grabbed the edge of the collar of his uniform, Lieutenant Adler's uniform, just to make sure that I wasn't dreaming or having some insane delusion. Adler wasn't invisible to me. He was angelic to me, some kind of flesh and bones ghost with a warm body and a heartbeat. He could not possibly be invisible!

"On the bright side Adler," I said as my more humorous side surfaced, "you can watch people in the shower and they won't even know."

We both cracked up laughing for a few moments but then reality came creeping back in all too soon and it was all too real.

"You can literally walk through walls and look at people right?" I asked with a more serious tone. "I mean, how else did you get in here?"

"Yes," Adler's voice was deeply thoughtful, "but I'm not exactly interested in doing that."

"That webpage still doesn't say much, and I still have so many questions. So, do you have some kind of supreme understanding over the universe?"

"Nope, no divine understanding of any kind and nothing beyond traditional human wisdom and what I can observe now, but with added clarity."

"Added clarity? What do you mean by that?"

"I suppose that those things were already inherently there when I was created," Adler was deep in thought and it was obvious that he too had many questions about his own existence, "like they are my factory default settings. In our human lives we get so distracted by everything that this clarity eventually becomes foggy. Since you created me and our souls are forever linked together in this way, I do have some insight into your life though."

"Can you read or hear my thoughts?"

Suddenly a cold chill ran through me. I didn't want anyone to know what I was thinking. My thoughts were shameful and depressing and I didn't want Adler to know any of the things that went through my brain. What would he think of me? Would he still care about me? Would he still want to be my keeper? I swallowed hard. I didn't want to lose him under any circumstances.

"No, Joanie." Adler replied in his usual gentle voice. "I cannot hear anything that goes on inside your head but I can feel every single thing that goes through your heart and I know you're hurting."

Hearing that didn't exactly made me feel any better. Okay, so, he couldn't hear me telling myself that I was worthless and better off dead but obviously he would still still figure it out because he *felt* it. Which one was worst? Either way, knowing that another person now also felt worthless because I felt worthless inside only made me feel even more worthless. Everything was worthless.

"I'm sorry to feel that you don't like the idea of sharing everything that passes through your heart."

"Do you have any emotions of your own that you can share with me instead? You know, Adler, I could really use to feel better inside."

"While I don't have any emotions of my own the same way you do, this is something that always makes us feel better."

He signaled me to scoot over to closer to him and he wrapped me up in his arms. Of course hugs always made everything better, plus a keeper's touch filled a person with sublime electricity that made all the negativity dissipate. Maybe it wouldn't be such a bad thing after all that he could feel my emotions. Maybe he could prevent me from feeling them to begin with or at least make them disappear in a heartbeat.

"Another question." I said after Adler let me out of his miraculous hug.

"I'll answer to the best of my abilities," he replied calmly.

"If I buried you, well, doll you, in a field far away from my house how did you find me?"

"That's the interesting thing about feeling your emotions. I may not know what's going on inside your head unless you tell me, but I can feel your heart from a world away Joanie. Finding you was as easy as following your aura of energy all the way here."

"That's amazing!"

"Now you should get dressed, you have a big day coming up today."

"Is that so?" I was curious to know what Adler had in mind.

"Yes, we're gonna go watch people in the shower!"

We both cracked up laughing again as I got up off my bed and dug around in my dresser for clothes that weren't too wrinkly because I knew I'd get a speech from Mike about that.

"Okay," I said giggling, "but now you can't look while I'm getting dressed."

"I won't, I promise," Adler replied in a serious tone of voice.

Once I picked out my clothes I looked around the room and saw that he had left so I took off my pajamas and put on a white

Pokemon shirt with Pikachu on the front and some stretchy blue jeans. I dug out a dark gray zip-up hoodie from the closet and completed my outfit with it. I looked normal and presentable and it was comfy for the entire day so it would have to do.

I specifically needed to wear long sleeves even if it was going to be a hot day because nobody could know that I'd cut myself the previous night. I then proceeded to try to fix my hair as I looked at myself in the long mirror behind my bedroom door but once it registered that it wouldn't work I decided to tie it up in a ponytail and fix up my bangs with a few flower-shaped hair clips. When I was finished I was expecting to be able to show off my look to Adler but as I looked around everywhere in my room for him he was nowhere to be found.

"Adler?" I called out suddenly feeling deflated about the situation, "Where did you go?"

"I'm right here Joanie," he said as he suddenly reappeared right next to me.

"Oh! You're right back here with me again! So can you simply disappear and reappear at will?"

"Yes. I must now explain to you how my aura of energy works so you can properly sustain it once it starts to get low. This energy can do truly amazing things, like wash away all your pain, but the downside is that is doesn't last forever. The energy needs to be sustained and renewed periodically if you want to keep me around."

"I'm listening."

I was enthusiastic to learn more about preserving the aura of energy that Adler let off because I never wanted him to leave. Part of me honestly still couldn't believe it. I couldn't believe that he was here and that he was real. I had my very own keeper. He was mine and mine alone.     In truth I would never really be alone as long as I had Adler by my side. I looked up at him in awe again for the millionth time just to remind myself that everything was indeed real because it still felt so surreal, so sublime, so divine. Adler's perfectly oval face didn't look like it belonged to a man weathered from war.

Maybe he hadn't actually *gone* to war, but that was the backstory behind the original doll. Unfortunately the doll had lost the battle. His sandy hair was also immaculate, his undercut hadn't gone out of style. His round glasses were a little dated but they still made him look very handsome.

"Admiring your creation," he said with a grin in the corner of his mouth.

"This is just amazing," I responded in complete awe at him, "unfathomable I could even say."

"Now let me tell you about the energy. Right now I'm completely replenished on it but when it runs out you'll have to summon me if you still want me around this way."

"And what happens if I can't or I don't? Where do you go?" I asked, now with a worried and sad tone in my voice.

"I go right back to where I came from originally: nonexistence. When I'm not in this dimension I literally don't exist, I can't feel, I can't see, I have no idea what's going on here. I don't die and it doesn't hurt, there's no concept of time or anything whatsoever. It's basically limbo. From the moment I disappear to the moment you bring me back there's absolutely nothing in between. You can be without me for extended periods of time but for me it'll only seem like a moment."

"That's amazing! So, does that mean you'll be with me forever?"

"That's the thing Joanie, I have no idea how long I have here. I don't know if keepers hang around forever or if they are only here for a little while. What I can promise you, however, is that you can open up to me about absolutely anything and I will *always* do whatever I can for you. I'll console you, guide you, comfort you, anything you need."

"And what if you want to leave? Can you leave on your own?"

"I can dematerialize, like this."

In that moment Adler disappeared and immediately reappeared in the other corner of my room.

"That's amazing!" I exclaimed.

"Dematerializing isn't the same as disappearing, listen

carefully," Adler went on.

"Yes, sir!"

"I'll still be within this dimension even if I'm not technically in human form so I in that sense I can leave at will, yes, but that's completely different than when the energy runs out and I disappear into nonexistence. Then there's nothing I can do. The energy you need to feed me if you want me around is called *agape* but it's not the same kind of agape that you'll find in the dictionary. It's the purest form of love that exists in the entire universe. Immerse yourself in it and my energy field will meet yours. Give it a shot right now."

I closed my eyes and tried to find the most unconditional love that existed inside my heart and for a moment a burst of the most amazing feeling in the world swept over me but it came crashing down within only a few seconds. It merely lasted an instant and I felt greatly deflated when I couldn't sustain it.

"Don't worry," Adler reassured me, "it'll come eventually. That agape is what us keepers need in order to keep existing in this realm. It's what gives me that slight glowing aura that contours my shape. It's not easily visible to the naked eye but pay close attention and you'll see it begin to dim when the agape gets low. Remember that I have an energy field too so you won't be alone sustaining this once I'm replenished. We're in this together Joanie."

"So you promise to not disappear on me if you get sick of my troubles?"

Adler must've had some idea that I wouldn't be too much trouble for him because after all he wasn't just a doll or a puppet anymore, he was in control of himself. He could remove himself from the situation if he wanted to or if he got tired of my problems that according to some people, weren't real.

"I absolutely promise Joanie. If I'm gone it's because the energy is out, not because I want to be away from you. You'll never have to be alone as long as I'm here. Of course if you get sick of me you can cut off my energy though."

"Well, you won't have to worry about that Adler. I absolutely want you around. Just the idea of one day maybe being without you if keepers aren't forever is devastating to me."

"Don't worry about that right now. I'm firmly convinced that I wouldn't be here at this precise moment if there wouldn't come a time in the near future that you would absolutely need me. And who knows? I might come back someday in the future even if my time here runs out quickly. Remember that it doesn't hurt me to not exist for a while. It does nothing to me. There's already enough pain and suffering in this world so don't trouble yourself over me. It's *my* job as a keeper to worry about *you* Joanie."

Nothing about Adler's existence had really sunk into my brain yet and I was still completely blown away but so overjoyed at the same time. Having to live inside a house that was filled with practically a bunch of strangers, I was grateful to have someone whom, in one way or another, was on the same level I was.

One top of that, I couldn't ever get enough of the energy that he let off. It was contagious and addictive. I didn't remember the last time I felt that good about myself. I didn't remember the last time I felt like I could breathe and that taking a single breath didn't hurt deep inside.

"If there's one thing that I'm sure of Joanie, it's that there's no situation that is beyond healing. Sure, you can't turn back time, but that doesn't mean that there's no forgiveness and moving on towards bigger and better things." Adler spoke softly almost like he could read my thoughts even though he was adamant that he couldn't despite his supernatural existence. "I know it sounds cliche and it's much easier said than done, especially when you can't see passed the situation you're trapped in, but there's still much truth in that."

"I swear you can read my mind Adler, I swear." I muttered, completely floored.

"Remember that everything that goes through your heart goes through mine too."

"I couldn't forget that even if I tried."

I walked over to Adler and gave him a huge hug. Standing well over six feet tall he was a giant next to me and my face was pressed into the many medals I'd delicately put on his uniform when I first created him. I'd made him a strong and brave soldier, but also a good man. A man who took a stand for the most vulnerable in the most appalling of circumstances. A man with a heart of gold. I put my hand over where his heart was supposed to be and felt it beat steadily in the palm of my hand. I could understand now what was meant when they said that keepers were a manifestation of something from deep within ourselves. Indeed, he was exactly what I'd needed.

"Oh, I'd almost forgotten about this," Adler spoke matter-of-factly as he rolled up my sleeve and exposed the cuts on my arm.

I tried to pull away because I was deeply ashamed of what I'd done but my keeper had quite the grip on me and he wasn't about to let me run away from my problems one more time. Adler brought my arm up to his lips and each cut disappeared with every kiss.

I watched in astonishment as the scars all faded away and completely disappeared one by one with no remaining evidence that I had ever put them there in the first place. He let me go and I touched where they had been because I couldn't believe what I was seeing. The scars were gone and my skin had returned to exactly the same state it had been in long before I'd ever taken out those dang razor blades.

"That's not possible!" I exclaimed in absolute shock.

"It is in my world," Adler replied with a grin on the side of his face.

"Are they going to come back?"

"Not if you don't make them come back."

"That can't be! This is unbelievable! You're nothing other than an angel, there's no other explanation."

"No dear, I'm not an angel. Angels are from God, I'm not. I'm from within you. I'm a keeper. These things exist in my world. I know that you have a lot of questions and I may not have many answers right now but we'll figure it out. We're both still here for a reason after all."

There were still so many unspoken things and so many

questions but I had the comfort of knowing that Adler had my best interest at heart. He was probably the only one who did. At least he seemed to be the only one who *still* did.

"Why can't we humans feed off of the same unconditional love that keepers do?" I asked blankly after a few moments.

"You tell me," he responded in a voice equally devoid of emotion, "I've never figured that out. The things you see in a war make you want to give up on humanity but at the same time there's still something inside of you that keeps pushing for you to do the right thing and make the world a better place."

"Did you die during the war?"

I was almost scared to ask that question because after all I was the one who had created Adler so I was also the one who had subconsciously written his life story at some point even if it was now highly out of my control, or so it seemed. Getting to know him was really like getting to know an unknown part of myself. A part that I didn't know existed. A part of me that had never been touched before.

"Yes," Adler spoke softly, "I was killed in combat."

"Is it scary to die?" I inquired after another long moment of silent contemplation.

"Yes, very." Adler responded in a low voice. "There's nothing pleasant about it, especially not under circumstances like that."

"I'm so sorry that I even put something like this on you," I grumbled as I removed a badge with a swastika on it from his uniform.

"Don't be sorry Joanie. I'm with the Resistance. I'm proof that nothing is black and white. Good and bad exist equally everywhere and it's usually in the greatest darkness that light shines the brightest. I wouldn't mind wearing civilian clothing though, it would probably be more appropriate for modern times despite that you're the only one who can see me."

# THREE

For the first time in my life I was actually dressed and out of bed before the alarm clock rang. That was obviously the *Adler Effect* because getting me out of bed was usually a war within. I desperately didn't want to get up and have to face reality. I wasn't happy in life. I missed my family and being carefree like before.

But at the same time I didn't want to loaf around in bed and make Mike or my mom angry. That would only be further contributing to the problem and not the solution. In truth though, I didn't really want to leave my room. I wanted to spend some more quality time with Adler doing nothing but contemplating the mysteries of life for a while. Doing that felt so much better.

My train of thought was cut short when my mom called me down for breakfast. I sighed loudly. Breakfast meant sitting across the table from my mother, between Mike and Aaron and not saying anything because we were supposed to listen to the early morning news on the radio. Adler felt the anxiety in my heart. It almost felt like I was having a heart attack. My chest tightened up, it seemed like I couldn't get any air in my lungs and I felt lightheaded. That's what they said heart attacks felt like on TV but the doctor had assured me that it was *just* anxiety that I was feeling, like it was nothing and it didn't cause me great distress.

Adler walked over to me as I was standing near the door and squeezed me tightly in his arms. All the anxiety suddenly left me like a breath of air leaving my lungs. I wrapped my arms around him and hugged him tightly too. That was exactly what I was needing. I listened to his heartbeat for a few moments before I let him go. I looked up at him and his eyes sparkled in the sunlight coming through the window.

He gave me a reassuring nod indicating that he was right there with me and everything would be okay. If only it was as easy to convince myself of that! Adler followed me downstairs silently where I loafed around, taking more time than necessary to get down because I hated bacon and didn't care for the stupid morning news.

"Do you have to eat?" I asked Adler in a low voice in the stairwell.

"I don't have to in theory but it's a little taste of being human," he replied, "I don't have to walk either but levitating near the ceiling is too weird for me."

"Will my folks be aware of anything, like that there's somebody else with me or something along those lines?"

"They shouldn't. Your folks didn't notice a thing as I wandered around the place last night before coming up to your room."

"While you really don't strike me as a mean kind of person and I never imagined the doll form of you being one, is it possible for you to hurt other people?"

"I suppose that in theory, under certain circumstances I could but unless your life is in immediate danger, I don't believe any violence will be necessary. Go eat now Joanie. I'll be looking around your house a little bit and then I'll join you."

The bacon was already right there in my plate waiting for me in my designated spot. I reluctantly sat at the little wooden dining table. I'd been told at school that having blue walls in your kitchen made you eat less but I'd lost my appetite no matter which color the wall tiles were.

"Good morning my dear," my mom greeted me as I sat down.

"Good morning," I muttered trying not to sound too pessimistic so I wouldn't irritate Mike.

"Did you have a good night? You appear to be well rested."

"Yes, thank you."

That was a lie of course. My evening had been absolutely terrible before Adler showed up and his presence had consumed my existence and turned a bad situation into a tolerable one. The cuts on my arm were completely gone and nobody ever had to know I'd put them there! I touched my arm again because it was still so much for me to take in after the kind of night I had just lived through but the skin was nice and soft.

Before I could get lost in contemplation again Mike cranked up the radio to listen to his beloved news program that appeared to be stuck on repeat day after day. I grabbed the bacon and quickly brought it up to my mouth, took a big bite and attempted to swallow it immediately in the hopes that I could get it over with quickly and wouldn't have to taste it in the process but that backfired.

I should've known better, but I did it anyway. The bacon got stuck and I began to choke on it so I quickly got up and ran outside through the back door onto the little porch and spit everything out on the ground. I noticed that Adler walked right through the closed door a few moments later and sat down next to me on the little bench back there. His colors were even brighter and more spectacular in the sunlight. His medals shined too and I was reminded that he wanted some civilian clothes from the thrift store sometime.

"Can't you just creep into any store or even somebody's closet and steal whatever you want because you're invisible?" I grumbled as I was still trying to get the bacon that remained stuck in my teeth. "It might be kind of funny to see them find a Wehrmacht uniform instead of whatever you took."

"The problem is that doing that isn't nearly as fun as putting on a fashion show at the thrift store!" Adler exclaimed with a hint of sarcasm in his voice.

"Yeah, a fashion show that only I will see."

"It's still better than looting someone's closet!"

He always knew how to make me smile. He was adamant that he couldn't read my thoughts but I was equally adamant that he could see right through my soul.

"How old are you?" I asked out of curiosity after a moment of silence.

"Thirty-six," he replied blankly.

"Like Stauffenberg," I responded as I looked up at him in awe.

"Like Stauffenberg," he confirmed, knowing how much I admired Claus von Stauffenberg.

I smiled at him and the two of us went back into the house. I knew that if I stayed outside too long I would get in trouble. As I sat back down on the chair Adler followed me and walked right through Aaron before standing behind me. As he did so my step-brother caught a chill that lasted a fraction of a second. He brushed it off as nothing but I grinned. It was incredible. Adler was flesh and bones to me but something like a ghost to everybody else. It was like our own dirty little secret. The rest of my food was cold but I force-fed it to myself anyway, letting out a grunt at some point. Of course my step-father heard it and that made him angry.

"That's what happens when you eat like a pig!" Mike grumbled angrily. "Oink, oink Joanie!"

I bowed my head in shame. They all finished their food before I did and left the table to continue their daily morning routine so I got up too and motioned for Adler to take my spot and finish my food. He did so happily and devoured it like he hadn't eaten in a thousand years.

The cold taste didn't bother him and the food itself had no nutritional value to someone who wasn't actually *human* anymore, but it was nonetheless something enjoyable for him. In some way we were both on the same level. We both enjoyed the small pleasures of life like tasting food, except bacon of course. It wasn't even healthy for you, Mike's stupid news program had even said so, but it seemed like he had selective hearing.

After Adler was finished eating the food we both went to sit in the living room for a little bit. I sat on the small leather sofa that only smelled like Mike's beer and stared blankly out the window at the townhouses on the other side of the street for a while. The *living* room was too small for much *life* but everything fit. I missed my former living room with the bay window and elegant ceiling lights. The current living room was Mike's man cave more than anything else.

The walls were a dark cherry red and the entire room was dimly lit which made it look like a warlock's lair from one of those children's books. It was the darkest room in the house. There was color everywhere, however it was devoid of any vibrance.

There were no picture frames on the walls like in my old house with my old family. I loved seeing the large framed photos of our trips to various parts of the country and the smiles on our faces. The pictures created a beautiful contrast with the otherwise undecorated room. It wasn't blank though, it was timeless and beautiful. Or at least it had been, it wasn't anymore.

All of that was gone. My family was gone, my house was gone, the meaning of my life was basically gone. What was the point of trying to move forward when these things were all out of your control and you couldn't get them back no matter what you did?

"Tell me what just stabbed you in the heart this very moment," Adler spoke very gently as he obviously felt my emotions.

"I was dwelling over everything I lost in my life recently," I muttered with a sigh, "and I was on the verge of imagining a future for myself."

"You're having adjustment issues Joanie, and you can't hold that against yourself because you've been through a lot in a very short time and these feelings are completely normal, I promise."

"I know, that's what people always say. That, or that I'm weak and entitled like Mike says. I'm so tired of this boring and meaningless existence of mine. Aren't you by now?"

"No, not at all. I like things just the way they are between the two of us."

"Me too."

I looked at Adler and smiled at him. Maybe he didn't have all the answers but Adler had much clarity and insight, not to mention wisdom. I didn't have any of those things and that was part of the reason things were so hard to deal with. I was only stuck existing in limbo seeing no way out.

"Stop doing that," Adler commanded as I began dwelling over my life all over again.

"Sorry man," I giggled slightly at being caught in the act, "I'm still not used to my thoughts no longer being private anymore."

"Only your emotions Joanie, whatever is going on inside that head of yours is forever a mystery to me."

"I'm still not used to my emotions being public record. I don't even have to cry for you to wipe away tears that haven't even come out of my eyes yet."

"Perks of being a keeper! Now let's go outside, it's a beautiful day out there."

Indeed it was a beautiful late August day in Bluepond. The sun was high in the sky and was shining brightly against everything it touched, but especially my keeper. Adler and I decided to go to town so we got up and walked out the front door into the warmth of the outdoor atmosphere.

Adler technically walked right through the wall just to amuse me and of course I laughed at that. A wind of change blew through my hair as Adler gave me the taste to rediscover life. I knew it was just a side effect of his presence and not something that came from within me but nonetheless it made me feel good about myself.

"Did you hear the advertisement on the radio for the theme park down by the boardwalk earlier?" Adler spoke in an upbeat voice, "That might help you with those feelings of wanting to enjoy life again, plus I'd love to see the ocean."

"It's so awkward that I can't feel anything without you feeling it too," I laughed at how Adler once again was on top of everything before I even realized it, "What if I have a crush on someone or fall in love with a boy? Won't that be very strange for you?"

"I'll feel the burning love in your heart but that doesn't necessarily mean that *I* will like him."

We both looked at each other and giggled. I admired him, my

keeper. Sure, maybe I didn't know much about him, but he was still my keeper and he was still helping me out. I had created him out of goodness and that same goodness was at the centre of his core. That was all that mattered to me.

"Now you're inflating my ego with your constant admiration," Adler spoke after a few moments of silence.

"You're amazing," I replied, "you really are."

"I'm pretty pain Joanie, just a man, a soldier, a person with a heart, nothing special."

"Now you're starting to sound like me. Nothing special."

"There's nothing wrong with being *normal* Joanie. Society might look down on you if you're not a cut above the rest but I'm telling you that you don't need to be extraordinary to be a good person, to be valuable to someone and to be wonderful to be around."

"That's easy to say but so much harder to believe."

"I know Joanie, but it's true. Tell me my own story Joanie, but more than that, listen to it and believe it."

"You were a lieutenant in the Wehrmacht during the war but as time went on and things got worst you discovered the atrocities being done by Hitler's regime and that disturbed you greatly so you decided to join the German Resistance and save people."

"And?"

"And you were just an average man, an average soldier of the time."

"Exactly."

I thought about that in a silent contemplative moment of my own. Adler was right. He was right about everything. I still swore that I'd amount to absolutely nothing every single day and that belief was reinforced by people putting me down in life and not having much of a support system. With Adler it seemed like I'd have all the support I could ever need but erasing everything that happened was much easier said than done too. I would have to rise above everything that happened but that's also where the problem was.

I didn't have the inner strength to do it. I was still too battered and bruised from the previous fights that I had lost. My problem was that I dwelled on things that I couldn't change and I was made aware of that but I couldn't stop! I couldn't help myself!

"Pain might seem like it's limitless at times but I promise you that it's not how the story ends." Adler continued. "And I know that healing is so hard to come by because it seems like you always have to do it all over again."

"Now you're diving off the deep end," I tried to lighten the mood as Adler was heading into a direction delicate for me.

The two of us ran the rest of the short distance to the bus stop because we could see the next bus coming down the road and we didn't want to miss it. We made it just in time for it to stop and let us on board. I paid for my ride but Adler didn't have to. Perks of being invisible. The two of us sat at the very back of the bus away from everybody else. Rush hour had passed but there were still many people crowded near the doors of the city bus.The busses travelled not only all over the city, but to several smaller outlying municipalities as well.

The scenery in the suburbs was compelling. The ocean, the boardwalk, the large bridges, rural areas and farming communities. It would be a beautiful ride and we'd see a little bit of everything before getting off at the fairgrounds.

"Is it weird that I'm the only person who can see you?" I asked Adler yet another question once we were sitting comfortably and the bus departed.

"Is it weird that you're the only person who can see me?" Adler flipped the question around right back at me.

"No, actually I think it's awesome that you're all mine. I've never really had anyone all to myself before."

"You say that with such longing and sadness in your voice."

"Well, now that I don't have my family anymore it's really only you."

"You sound like you've lost a lot of friends in your short life."

"Lost some, maybe, but never having any sounds more like it."

Adler looked at me with compassion in his eyes but didn't say anything further. It was true though, I'd never had many friends at any point in my life. It had always really been just me, my mom, my dad and my goldfish. Neither one of my parents came from big families either and the few relatives we did have lived far away and weren't exactly involved in our lives.

That was never something that bothered me or either of them, up until they got divorced and my life as I knew it was turned upside down. My dad had left my mom for another woman that he'd apparently been having an affair with for almost a decade and started a new family with her, completely disregarding me. It was as though I'd disappeared, as though I became invisible to him like Adler was invisible to the world.

I desperately missed him, his big brown eyes and his old-fashioned facial hair that belonged to a different era. He was tall and looked like a lumberjack but he had actually worked an office job at a fancy travel agency. I missed our fishing trips and the times he took me up to the country and we went hiking through the forest and the mountains.

The last time we'd gone for a trip just the two of us was two summers ago. We'd gone the mountains of Vermont to see the spectacular autumn foliage. Sure, we had plenty of that in rural Nova Scotia too but the New England experience was something else entirely. We'd been to Maine the summer before that as a family, but Vermont had definitely been my favorite of them all.

"Stop," Adler spoke softly as he put his hand over mine and all of my negative feelings disappeared within a moment of me beginning to dwell over my former life.

"I'm sorry," I muttered, half-smiling at how well Adler's powers worked.

"We're a team Joanie, we'll figure this stuff out together."

"By the way, I have a random question for you again. Are there any circumstances that you know of where could be visible to others?"

"To be honest Joanie, I don't really know. I guess we'll have to find that out won't we?"

Nobody on the bus had noticed Adler but a group of people came to sit next to us in the back and one person sat right over Adler in the seat. The young man caught a chill but nothing more.

He only caught a second one when he got up and left. I looked out the window as we passed through the most beautiful rural regions of Bluepond before crossing into Snowmaple.

The fields seem to stretch on forever underneath that clear blue sky. The barbed wire cattle fences lined the road as far as the eye could see. The scenery was so serene, almost like it was a different world beyond that fence. A world away from the chaos and pain. A world so close but seemingly unattainable. But the same could be said about Adler. He wasn't from this world, yet here he was. Why couldn't the rest of my life be the same way?

"Take your own advice Joanie," he said with a smirk on his face, further convincing me that he could indeed read my thoughts.

"You're lying when you say that you can't read my mind," I retorted, still not accustomed to having my innermost feelings intruded upon.

"No, I'm not. I don't know what your thoughts were about, but I did feel that breath of hope after the contemplation. Whatever gave you that hope in life, take it, go for it, don't ignore it. That's what I meant by telling you to take your own advice. Listen to your own heart. It's that same heart that created me."

"I did pour a lot of goodness into you, I just can't seem to connect with that inner goodness in other areas of my life aside from when I'm in my room creating little guys like you from broken and unwanted parts."

"Yep."

What was he trying to tell me? I knew that he was leading me onto something but I was still missing the point. Keepers were manifestations that came out of ones innermost soul, certainly that's where I would also find the answers to my own questions if only I weren't so confused about everything.

"You can make beautiful things with old and neglected doll parts," Adler spoke softly after a moment of silence as we both looked outside, "and I am confident that the broken and painful parts of your life can be recycled into something great."

"I want to believe in you so much Adler," I replied with a sigh, "but it's much easier said than done. I mean, how can anything great come out of losing your family? My mother used to be my best friend and now she disregards me most of the time. Sometimes she's affectionate and caring and sometimes she's the exact opposite and I have no clue what I do that's so wrong because she's never treated me like this before we moved in with Mike."

"It's not you Joanie, I can promise you that. These might not be things that you understand because you are still very young and you don't have the insight of someone that's outside looking in, *but you are not the problem.* The abusive relationship your mother is trapped in is what's the problem."

"But Mike never hit my mom, he's never ever laid a hand on her."

Adler's comment about the abusive relationship only confused me further. I wasn't blind, I saw all of those posters about battered women's shelters around the city showing women with black eyes and cuts on their arms. The problem was that my mom wasn't one of those women. Sure, Mike could get a little rowdy and belligerent when he was drunk but his insults and grumblings never put black and blue marks on anyone except himself that one time he took a tumble down the basement stairs thinking he was stepping outside instead.

"Abuse isn't always physical," Adler continued, "in fact the majority of the abuse isn't physical at all."

"I don't understand," I replied, waiting for Adler to explain.

"Tell me, even if Mike never actually uses his hands, does he make threats of any kind? Does he call you or your mother names or tell you that you're crazy? Is he constantly criticizing or destroying things? Does he limit or keep tabs on where you or your mom can go, talk to or do? Does he apologize and promise to change even though the same pattern repeats itself periodically?"

"Okay, slow down please, that's too much to absorb all at once."

"Joanie, if you've answered yes to any of those questions then you are living in a domestic violence situation."

"Well, Mike doesn't really seem to care about me or anything I do as long as I don't break the rules but he's always all over my mom's business."

"Control and isolation are forms of abuse in a domestic partnership. They may not leave any physical scars, but they leave very deep emotional and psychological ones. I know that you've suffered them at his hands."

Adler was right about everything. I hadn't previously understood any of that and had always erroneously believed that domestic violence meant taking a hit or leaving a mark. I swallowed hard as I thought about it and all of the mean things Mike ever said came back flooding into my brain. *You're stupid! You're not a child anymore so stop behaving like one! You're good for nothing. You'll never amount to anything in life!* Thankfully Adler's energy quickly blocked me from feeling more pain from the intrusive memories and those were only a few of the things that he'd said to me over time. He'd said way worst to my mother, and Aaron wasn't exempt from any of that either.

"Many people often don't realize that they are in an abusive situation and just from observing your mother for a couple of hours convinced me that she's one of those people."

"But how can she not know? I mean, she's a fully grown adult who had an excellent relationship with my dad. How can she even compare what she had with my dad with what she has with Mike?"

"That's something else that afflicts victims of domestic abuse Joanie, it's the cycle of abuse. In the beginning everything is wonderful and looks so promising, especially to someone in a very vulnerable situation like your mother. Her life as she knew it was shattered too and when Mike showed up like a knight in shining armor she fell into the trap."

"Yeah, Mike did seem like a good guy in the beginning. I mean, I was never happy about her being with someone other than my dad but I never thought he would be the jerk he is now."

"Neither did your mother. He promised to fix her broken heart, give her a nice home after she let go of the house and provide for her anything that she needed to put her life back in order. And then abusers force or encourage the victim's dependency by making them believe that they are incapable of surviving or living a good life without them."

"You are describing Mike word for word."

"And there's more, there's way more, but do you see now what I'm trying to tell you? You are not the problem despite what Mike might tell you directly or indirectly. He insults, criticizes and blames the victim because he is an *abuser*, not because the victim did anything wrong."

"You have amazing insights Adler."

"Pull out your smart phone and read up on the topic while we ride through the industrial wasteland."

I did as he said and got my outdated phone out of my pocket and waited for it to connect to the internet. Adler's invisible fingers worked well on my touch screen as he typed a link into the web browser. I had to wait another few moments for the page to completely load but as soon as it did I saw behaviors exhibited by Mike right off the bat.

*Using actions, statements or gestures that attack the victim's self-esteem and self-worth with the intention to humiliate. Using any form of coercion or manipulation which is disempowering to the victim.* Mike controlled everything. He really made my mother believe that she wouldn't make it out there as a single mother without someone else after he marriage had collapsed. I supposed that after being told the same thing over and over again a person came to believe it. I knew I did.

The section on financial abuse also rang a bell. Although my mom still held a job, it was Mike who controlled what she could do with the money. The small allowance that Aaron and I got came out of my mother's paycheck too, and if we wanted something like new clothes we had to buy it ourselves.

The more I thought about it and the more I learned about domestic violence the more it was apparent that it's what we were all living in our house. The article made a point that it wasn't just adults who could be victims, but teenagers and children too. It also said that women weren't the only victims and men weren't always the perpetrators.

Society never spoke about any of those things. Nobody had ever told me about that before. What the article didn't say was why people chose to abuse or why the victims often decided to stay. For the moment that would have to wait because the bus had finally arrived at the boardwalk where Adler and I planned to get off and visit the theme park.

It was a perfect day for that. The salty breeze cleared my airways as soon as I stepped off the bus. There were many attractions of many kinds lined up on the board walk as well as kiosks and food trucks, souvenirs, games, photo booths and more. Too bad Adler was invisible because I would've loved to take my picture with him and keep it forever. The ferris wheel was really the main reason why I came so the other things would have to wait after the ride but first and foremost I wanted a funnel cake.

"Have you ever had a funnel cake before?" I asked Adler.

"No, in fact I have not," he replied in a neutral tone of voice, "we didn't exactly have access to those on the battlefield. Don't forget that I want to get out of this uniform after we're done here too!"

"I haven't forgotten about your request, in fact there's actually a great flea market that carries a lot of nice men's clothes for big and tall dudes on the way back home."

"That sounds like a plan to me!"

# FOUR

From up at the top of the ferris wheel I could see everything in the city of Bluepond. The theme park by the boardwalk gave you a spectacular view of the skyline. In the distance towards the south you could see the city of Garamond-on-the-Lake as well. Adler sat in front of me in the pod as we looked out through the windows seeing civilization on one side and the endless ocean stretching out on the other.

The sun was shining bright with nothing but a few clouds in sight. It was a truly beautiful day on the coast. For a moment it seemed like everything in the world was perfect. I forgot about everything that was wrong in life and admired the beauty of what I was seeing in front of me.

"How long does a dosage of energy last?" I asked Adler as I turned away from looking at the ocean to look at him instead.

"Indefinitely," he replied still looking at the ocean, "as long as you keep it going really."

"I hope you don't mind me keeping you hostage!" I said as a grinned at him.

"Of course not!" Adler replied with a big smile that stretched from ear to ear, "And you see, it's not so hard to sustain the energy field needed to keep my around. The love you feel for me ultimately does it all by itself and the love I feel for you does the same."

I turned to look back at the city as our pod went around the wheel and back down for the second time. The funny thing was that I had only bought one ticket for the ride. At the end of the day there were many perks to being invisible.

Certainly my life could've been easier at times if I could appear and disappear at will, or better yet, make others appear and disappear whenever I felt like it. I let out a little chuckle and returned to looking at the ocean which was still just as spectacular every single time.

"Where are you from?" I asked after a moment of quiet contemplation on my behalf.

"I was born in Vienna, Austria," Adler replied with a smile on his face as he reminisced about Europe, "but I grew up in Berlin where my father had a prominent job as a journalist. I moved there when I was seven and loved Berlin my entire life."

"I've always wanted to visit Europe and see what life is really like there. All the different cultures and languages are so enchanting."

"They are now indeed, but in the aftermath of the Great War the entire continent was a disaster and of course we all know how the Second World War went. Countries ripped each other to shreds all over again but hopefully the world has learned its lesson by now."

My prayer was indeed that it had. The world may not have been at war anymore but my soul was still caught behind enemy lines. I needed to gather my courage and keep on fighting, I knew that, but of course that was much easier said than done.

"Tell me Adler, who were you during your life?" I asked as my emotions began running high again, "Tell me. There is so much more to you than the enlightened amazing invisible keeper you are now."

A soft smile appeared on the side of his mouth as he turned to look at me for a brief moment as our pod started going back up the ferris wheel. It stopped a couple of times along the way to let off some people and let new ones on.

"I've always been proud of my country and I wanted it to be able to stand on its own two feet now that we were moving on from the Great War because I'm telling you Joanie, things were terrible during the Great Depression. I can't even begin to tell you. Joining the military was something I thought I could do precisely to support my country, but it wasn't long before I had a change of heart. My conscience came to haunt me."

"But the Wehrmacht was just the regular army, I mean, take Stauffenberg for example. He wasn't a Nazi, he only did his military job for many years before the plot to assassinate Hitler."

"And I agree with that on the surface, but some Wehrmacht officers are also guilty of committing war crimes and that was simply something I couldn't do. I couldn't use force to invade and destroy countries. Maybe I was blind but when I joined the military I thought I'd defend my own country, not rip to shreds another one."

"I understand."

"I've also always been apolitical, and maybe even a little politically naive, so when I learned of Hitler's true plan, especially when it came to the extermination of the Jewish people, I knew I had to do something. It was never hidden that Hitler had grand ideas, borderline delusions I could say, and that he hated Jews but I never actually believed that it would've gotten to the point it did."

"Believe me, I understand that too."

Adler and I stopped speaking and looked at each other for a brief moment as our pod reached the top of the ferris wheel and stopped there momentarily. Adler and I both felt like pawns in a much larger game of chess that we had next to no say in. I knew that it should've been comforting that he understood me and could relate to my feelings because he'd experienced something similar in one way or another, but hearing his story had the exact opposite effect.

"So, what did you do?" I asked after a moment of silence.

"I think you know that already," he said with a smirk on the side of his face, "you created me, remember?"

"Yes, but you've sort of taken on a life of your own. Please tell me the rest of the story!"

"So, I decided to shift my military career back into journalism by becoming editor of a newspaper run by the government. I basically had unlimited access to a printing press and supplies and since I was already close to the other men who worked there, my activities weren't closely monitored. I decided to make fake identity and travel documents for the Jews I could find in the area. From there they could either decide to live as Aryans or go to a country of safety."

"That's amazing! So what happened next? How many people did you save?"

"I guess you'll need a second ticket for me to tell you the rest of the story."

Our ferris wheel ride had come to an end as our pod stopped at the bottom and the doors opened. I thanked the operator for the ride as I got out and immediately went to the back of the line. Thankfully it wasn't very long so it was only a few moments before the two of us were able to get on again but that was still too much waiting for me. I wanted to hear the rest of Adler's amazing story. The last couple of things he'd said had really uplifted my mood and made me be in awe of him even more, not like I wasn't completely enchanted by his existence alone.

"One day when I went up to the supply room on the second floor, do you know what I found?" Adler continued his story.

"What?!" I asked anxiously.

"One of my coworkers was also making fake documents. He seemed horrified when I walked in there but then I showed him some of the documents I'd made and at that point we had a mutual unspoken understanding."

"So what happened for you to stop? I remember you telling me that you died in combat."

"Yes, because we got caught by the Gestapo."

"Oh..."

"As it turns out, plenty of guys in there were stealing stationery and had been for years! Once the authorities got wind of the long list of missing supplies they conducted an investigation and we ended up getting caught. Obviously my actions made me become faced with a severe penalty, but I was offered to be sent to fight on the Easter Front in exchange for making this go away quietly."

"And you accepted."

"Yes. I didn't know what I could do to continue helping people on the Eastern Front but I knew that I couldn't do anything if I was stuck in a jail cell, or dead."

"So what happened on the Eastern Front?"

"I didn't last long. I made it merely a week in the unbelievable cold with our inadequate clothing and the hunger with our inadequate supplies. Then I got wounded several times and ended up in a trench."

"I'm so sorry."

"I don't actually know exactly how many people were saved or escaped in totality, but I helped save a few hundred I suppose. The whole process of finding these people and making them fake documents and then convincing them that I wasn't setting them up was much more complicated that it sounds."

I extended my hand to the other side of the pod and placed it on top of his. My throat tightened as I swallowed hard. That was the reward for being a good person. While I hadn't lived through the most disastrous conflict of all times, I could certainly relate to that aspect of it. All I wanted to do was be a good person in life but all I got was the exact opposite. Indeed Adler was the perfect person to be my keeper.

The second ferris wheel pod seemed to go much faster than the first one because before we knew it we had went around for the second time and were about to go up for the third and final time. I didn't want it to have to end again because Adler and I were having such a deep and heartfelt conversation.

"The lesson from this story is that you alone may not be able to change the world, but you can certainly make it a better place," Adler continued, "you can contribute to the problem or you can contribute to the solution."

I nodded my head in agreement. I agreed with what he was saying but I didn't have a clue regarding how I was actually supposed to do any of that.

"And don't be ashamed to ask for help. You know Joanie, the worst thing you can do for yourself is deny yourself the help that you need when you need it. Swallow your pride and ask for a hand. You don't have to go through all that you're facing alone. Had it not been for my comrades I'm not sure I would've had the courage to do what I did."

"I think I've got all the hands I'm ever going to need."

We both smiled at each other as we shook hands over our own unspoken agreement. Our ride was going to be over again soon and that was bittersweet, but I was definitely happy about the experience because it had definitely uplifted my mood and my outlook on life.

"Before this ride ends I just want to say one last thing Joanie," Adler went on, "I might not be able to hear your thoughts despite what you might believe, and that can definitely be frustrating for me at times because your emotions only tell me what you're feeling and not why, but you need to know one thing. Don't ever be afraid or ashamed to open up about your true feelings and thoughts around me. It's not good to keep them bottled up inside and I am your safe place to land. I understand that sometimes it seems easier to just push them aside and not deal with them but you must also understand that it's by bringing them out into the open that you can conquer them."

I took his advice to heart, I knew that he was right. What still frightened me, though, was the unknown. What did the future have in store for me? Would it be something good or would it be something bad? How would I react to it? How would I cope with it? Maybe my new life in Bluepond would turn out for the better down the line or maybe it would be a disaster of epic proportions. The latter seemed to be most likely scenario.

"What's making you anxious?" Adler asked me with a concerned tone of voice.

"The future," I muttered, "in general I don't adapt well to a change of circumstances and I certainly haven't this time around."

"Let me guess, school is a big trigger for you."

"Yeah, that's part of it. Well, when my parents first got separated and then divorced I wasn't exactly my usual self. I got into a bunch of trouble and mischief at school that landed me and some other people in hot water. I know that it's a different school with plenty of different people but there's no doubt going to be some familiar faces there and I know that the word will spread quickly and everyone will end up holding my past against me."

"You also have no idea how many other people just like you will be there, or how many will be looking for a good friend."

"I know but I just can't help but having so much anxiety!"

"Anxiety no more!"

And with those words an overwhelming feeling of peace and serenity came sweeping over me. Absolutely all of my anxiety immediately vanished just like it had never came. Our pod arrived at the bottom of the ferris wheel and the doors opened for us to get out once again. Adler and I decided to grab some more junk food and walk over to a vacant bench overlooking the ocean to eat it quietly away from most of the other people.

I probably looked like a pig bringing all of that food myself since nobody else knew that most of it was for an invisible lieutenant who had a sweet tooth. Adler walked through a bunch of people, giving them chills as he passed through them which was quite comedic to see because it was such a warm day and those people couldn't understand why they caught a frigid chill out of nowhere!

I sat down on the bench and began digging into my food by myself while Adler was still having fun playing around with the abilities that came with being invisible. I loved his fun side. Really, he behaved more like a teenager most of the time but I supposed that all people were young at heart. It was just society that looked down on what they would call childish behavior.

Adler walked through people, levitated and floated around, and even walked on water! As he walked back towards me on land he walked in front of a woman walking her dog and the giant poodle began completely freaking out. It barked and jumped up and down and ran all over the place nearly choking itself on its leash. Whether or not it could actually see Adler or not, it knew that something was there. Adler shot a worried glance at me, completely shocked that the dog was aware of his existence. Suddenly the fun was over and Adler walked back to the bench and sat down next to me.

"I guess it's not just you after all," Adler muttered in a blank voice devoid of any emotion.

When Adler was away from the dog, it returned to behaving normally but it was obviously still shaken by whatever it had experienced. Neither one of us could fully understand what exactly had just happened because as far as we'd both been concerned, I had been the only person who could see Adler. Something had obviously changed. Something was different. Giving ourselves headaches over the details would have to wait though, because we both wanted to enjoy the rest of the afternoon taking more rides and eating more junk food.

After we'd taken a ride on every attraction at least once we decided to go to downtown Bluepond and stop by a little ice cream shop called Giorgio's Gelato. I used to go there with another girl in the past but after the onset of my behavioral issues following the separation of my parents her mother forced her to cut all ties with me because apparently I was a bad influence.

I wasn't someone who was suffering, I was just a bad person. I remembered the legendary ice cream floats Giorgio's Gelato sold, but the place wasn't limited to only ice cream. They had all sorts of interesting treats but the locally famous ice cream was the only thing I'd ever wanted each time I'd walked in there.

"Save me some from your bowl?" Adler asked as we walked into the shop. "I could die for some ice cream right now."

"You can't die," I retorted, "but you can have plenty of ice cream."

At the counter Adler pointed out what he wanted and I ordered that for him. I then went into the bathroom and handed Adler his caramel mocha sundae with a cherry on top. He dug in immediately and the most delighted expression swept over his handsome face.

"Sorry about the women's bathroom," I giggled, "but it would have been a lot weirder to give a bowl of treats to my invisible friend when we are so close to so many other people, and there's no way I was going into the men's bathroom."

"It's completely fine Joanie," Adler replied with one last mouthful of ice cream, "thank you so much for this."

"It's my pleasure. And let me guess, keepers don't really have to use the bathroom either?"

"Nope, no going to the bathroom, no need to take a shower either because I can never get dirty."

Adler then handed me the half-eaten ice cream and I walked back out of the bathroom and went to sit at a picnic table on the sidewalk outside since the place was getting incredibly crowded. I took the spoon in my hand and dug into the ice cream myself.

Keepers had no saliva or germs so I didn't have any second thoughts about reusing the same spoon, but that's definitely not something I would've done with a regular person. The sundae was delicious! I finished it quickly and could've had another one but I ordered myself some poutine instead. I looked over at Adler to see if he wanted some but he shook his head in disgust.

"Sorry but Canadian food is not my cup of tea," he said politely, not wanting to insult my taste in food.

"It's alright, I understand," I giggled as I dug into my poutine.

After I finished my food Adler and I got on the bus again and made it to the flea market on the other side of town. It was inside an old decommissioned sports centre and had the most items I'd ever seen at one time. Everything you could imagine could be unearthed in that maze of treasures. I especially loved going there to buy doll parts, and in fact some of the parts I'd used for Adler came from there.

Going back there was bittersweet, bitter because of what ended up of my most special doll but sweet for the exact same reason. I never could've believed what had actually ended up of my most special doll.

The aisles were tightly crammed inside the flea market with

wooden racks stacked up on top of one another everywhere you looked. I let Adler pick out clothing from the men's section while I browsed around the toy section. I didn't really feel like digging around through the many, *many* toy bins in the dimly lit arena so I gave up after finding only two pairs of boots for my little soldiers.

I quickly passed by the equally large books section in case I could find an encyclopedia on world history with lots of pictures and maps but all I got was a book about the Titanic, which was another one of my favorite topics of study. For the size of the place and the amount of stuff in there, the flea market was surprisingly always very quiet with very few people shopping inside.

Once I returned to where Adler was he showed me some of the clothes he'd picked out for himself. He had a nice vintage-looking brown dress suit in excellent condition that I encouraged him to try on in the fitting room, not than an invisible man needed a fitting room to begin with but I knew that it made him feel normal and human.

Once he emerged from the fitting room Adler looked very handsome in coffee-colored suit with a matching vest and tie over a white shirt underneath. I found him a charcoal grey wool trench coat on a nearby rack and handed it to him to complete his outfit considering that the fall was approaching fast. Of course a keeper wouldn't get cold because they were immune to temperature, but it still made both of us feel better.

"You look like an old-school university professor," I told Adler as he spun around and showed me his new thrifty outfit.

"I look like a civilian of my time," he responded with a smile on his face.

"You look very handsome!"

"Thank you!"

"Please keep your Wehrmacht uniform though, just in case war breaks out in my house I'll want a real soldier on my side."

Adler cocked his head to the side and looked at me sympathetically.

"You are mature beyond your years Joanie."

I didn't respond to the comment. He wasn't the first person to tell me that, whatever it was supposed to mean. Adler changed back into his military uniform for the moment so I could pay for his new clothes. Technically he could've walked out with them on and nobody would've known because his invisible energy field did something strange to visible objects because his visible suit became invisible when he was wearing it.

That is of course, invisible to other people, not invisible *on* him thankfully! His complete new outfit including the matching brown leather shoes cost me twenty dollars and after it was paid we decided to head back home after having been outside for the entire afternoon. I would've loved to have bought a second outfit for Adler but I couldn't spend all of my money at once.

Back at the house I arrived before everybody else did and took the opportunity to lay down on the couch and watch TV a little bit. There was another mass shooting on the news so I changed the channel to watch a cartoon instead.

Adler faithfully sat beside me in the lazy chair next to the sofa and looked around the room. He looked like he was deep in contemplation, probably puzzling over what he had discovered about his new existence earlier during the day. The house was rarely so quiet that it was almost eerie. My mother and Mike were still at work for about an other hour and nobody would see Aaron until late at night, if at all until the next morning.

"I'm still trying to wrap my mind around what happened today with that woman's dog at the boardwalk," Adler spoke softly, "I swore without a single doubt in my mind that you were the only person who could see me Joanie. Of course that's said in the past tense now."

"So far it still does seem like I'm the only person who can see you Lieutenant," I replied as I turned over to look at him, "that dog was not a person."

Adler chuckled slightly, he knew I was right but I knew he was right too.

"But that dog knew," Adler went on, "it knew that I was there and my presence scared the hell out of it."

"Do you know anything about chemistry or quantum

mechanics?" I asked, thinking back to a book I'd read about atoms and atomic energy.

"Yes I do, I love science quite a lot actually."

"Then you should know a thing or two about quantum energy. You know how electrons need to absorb a certain amount of quantum energy in order to move up a level so to speak?"

"Yeah, up an electronic shell that orbits around the nucleus."

"Maybe that's what happened to you."

"So, somewhere along the way my being would have absorbed some energy and hence my invisibility would have upgraded to being visible to animals now."

"Sure, if you want to think of it that way."

"That sounds plausible actually, but the only question is how? What triggered this change? I haven't felt or noticed anything different."

"Do you think atoms notice when they begin to vibrate at a higher level?"

"I don't know. I've never really thought of atomic matter as something capable of having feelings."

Adler was paying extremely close attention to what I was telling him. Finally I had someone I could talk to! It was even more special considering that we could have deep conversations. I loved to read thrifty books about all sorts of things, such as science even though I didn't understand most of it but I rarely got to share that with anyone and that definitely covered me in a shroud of longing and loneliness. Well, as long as Adler was around that would no longer be something I needed to worry about.

"We're all nothing but a bunch of atoms, yet we feel things. We have emotions and thoughts. The possibilities are endless." I continued.

"I wish I had an answer to all of these mysteries but if there's one thing I'm absolutely sure of it's that it's okay to not have all the answers. However, I believe that some of them will come in due time."

"I say that you and I should simply do our best getting to where we are going, and whatever happens is going to happen. I understand now that I need to walk towards the things that I want and not just away from the things that I don't."

"That's excellent reasoning Joanie, I'm very proud of you for your insight despite that you've convinced yourself that you don't have any."

Adler and I smiled at each other, we had mutual silent understanding at that point. I looked at him in awe again and suddenly remembered that I hadn't given him the new clothes I'd bought!

"Oh dear, I'm so sorry," I apologized as I got up in a jiffy and handed him the bag of clothes from the thrift store that I'd dumped next to the front door.

Adler decided to change into them immediately and gave me his uniform so I could put it in storage in my room. I debated with myself over whether or not I should order myself a small pizza and skip dinner but decided against it because I didn't want to spend too much money just in case I needed something in the future. I'd just suck it up and deal with another dinner. End of story.

So I decided to take a bath to wash off the sweat from being out in the sun and by the water and grabbed some pink and white striped pajamas. When I came out of the bathroom my mom was home and already cooking dinner for Mike who would arrive shortly.

She looked tired. Her hazel eyes were sunken into her head and there were big bags underneath them. Her brown hair was tied up in a high ponytail, the kind that Mike liked. My mom was still in her work clothes, she hadn't changed out of them since she'd arrived home.

She hadn't even noticed me coming down the stairs either. On the other hand I had noticed that Adler had descended through the floor into the kitchen instead of using the stairs like he usually did even though it wasn't necessary. I figured that he was just having fun. After all, being a keeper did have its quirky benefits. It's not like I didn't think it was comedic to see the things Adler did like levitating and walking on water.

"Oh, hey there Joanie," my mother exclaimed as she turned around, "I hadn't even noticed that you were home!"

She actually looked happy to see me. I was confused because I didn't understand why sometimes she rejoiced at the sight of me and other times she disregarded me completely. Then I thought back to what Adler had said about domestic violence and figured that abuse was probably the culprit. Maybe she was just as confused as I was. Adler and I would need to have a more in-depth conversation about that.

"How was your day honey?"

"It was good mom."

"I'm very happy to hear that! What did you do?"

"I went to the boardwalk and then to the flea market."

"All by yourself?"

"No, actually a friend came with me."

Our conversation was interrupted by Mike barging through the door. His short dark hair was soaked in rain and his boots were covered in mud. His dark menacing eyes in the middle of his square head had no place to land as he ripped off his jacket and dropped it on a small bench near the door. My mother greeted him and he walked over to kiss her as she was making food.

He said nothing to me, he sat at the kitchen table and I joined him shortly after. My mom served him mushroom soup and sat down with us as the three of us ate peacefully and quietly. It was strange really, very strange, almost like a calm before the storm. Part of me couldn't help but wonder if it had something to do with Adler's new energy despite that I couldn't feel any difference either.

"I'll be waiting for you in your room," my beloved keeper spoke softly as he disappeared right before my eyes.

# FIVE

Adler was right there sitting in the chair in my room just like he said he would be. I jumped into bed immediately since it was getting late and I was absolutely exhausted and invited Adler to sit on the edge of my bed next to me. I wanted to talk to him before going to sleep. I put my hand in his as I rubbed my eyes with the other one.

"I'm so confused," I muttered.

"That's completely understandable Joanie," he responded softly, "and that's actually part of the cycle of abuse. Using statements of behaviors that create insecurity and confusion like saying one thing and doing another is a classic one for abusers."

"But what about my mom? She's basically doing the same thing now."

"She's just as confused as you are Joanie, and I promise that she's not doing it to intentionally hurt you. She's just a pawn in Mike's sick game of chess and this is just a tactic he uses to prevent people from ganging up on him. That scares him actually."

"Seriously?"

"Abuse is a vicious cycle Joanie, a sick cycle of manipulation. Now things are quiet, things seem fine, Mike has such a grip on your mother that she's convinced that things will be fine but it's just a matter of time before things start to tense up again."

"But why do people stay? I mean, my mom isn't a stupid person."

Adler let out a loud sigh. I knew it was a complicated topic that had no easy answers. Adler thought in silence for a moment before answering.

"People stay in abusive relationships for various reasons and we can't generalize all of them because every situation is different, but your mom thinks that she can fix Mike. She blames herself for the split with your father and erroneously thinks that by fixing him she'll somehow fix her own broken heart. She's also struggling financially and although Mike withholds most of the money, making ends meet isn't something she has to worry about. He also has her convinced that she'll never make it on her own but Aaron is also a big part of why she's still staying."

Aaron? I definitely wouldn't have thought of him being a reason because the two of them had a relationship that was nearly non-existent. My mom had always been a kind-hearted person but Aaron was basically a completely independent person. He didn't need her to stand up for him.

"Aaron, really?" I asked, surprised.

"Aside from you and your mom he really doesn't have anybody else," Adler replied in his usual gentle voice, "I know it sounds weird to you because the two of you don't have a relationship but he has the potential for being a great ally."

I didn't respond. I'd never really thought about Aaron that way but now that Adler said it, it really sank into my head that although I'd had a great family before the divorce, all Aaron ever had was Mike. Aaron's mother had died when he was three and it didn't seem like he'd ever had an easy life.

I rolled over in my bed and buried my face in the pillow. I still had so many issues to work through and I knew there would be a lot of hard work ahead of me but I firmly believed that the end result would be worth it when the time came and with Adler's help and guidance I wouldn't be on my own. I would never have to be again!

Certainly I wasn't in an ideal place and I knew there was even more hell coming my way in the next couple of weeks as I was going to start school again in a strange establishment filled with people who didn't like me because I had previously screwed things up for myself. Adler's divine energy soothed me immediately as soon as intrusive thoughts came into my mind and I realized just how tired I really was.

"Please stay with me tonight," I whispered to Adler.

"Of course," he responded with a smile, "just allow me to sit in your chair and read your books while you sleep."

"Sure, you can do whatever you want. There's room for two if you want to sleep even though I know you don't need to."

"I'll stay until you fall asleep and then I want to read that book about quantum mechanics under the night table."

"Thank you."

"Now go to sleep my dear."

I took a deep relaxing breath and pulled the covers over me. Not only was my body exhausted, but my mind was as well. Too many things were swirling around in it and even though Adler could soothe my emotions and my stress, he couldn't fuel me with energy. I closed my eyes and listened to Adler's unnecessary shallow breathing for a while until sleep consumed me.

For another night I fell into a deep dreamless sleep with no disturbances. No nightmares, no waking up in a cold sweat because you're falling off a cliff and you're about to hit the ground, and most of all there were no external disturbances to wake me up in the middle of the night.

The only thing that woke me up in the morning was the obnoxious nuclear-catastrophe-imminent sound of my alarm clock. I reached out and turned it off and as I was debating whether or not I should go back to sleep I happened to glance over towards the chair that Adler was supposed to be sitting in and noticed that he wasn't there. I sat up in my bed and looked around the entire room and realized that he wasn't anywhere to be found.

"Adler?" I called out as I looked around the room one more

time.

*Nothing.*

"Crap!" I muttered to myself as anxiety came flooding over me, "The energy flow must've ran out while I was sleeping and Adler returned to non-existence!"

And so I took a deep breath and connected with the agape deep inside of me. Soon, with a little effort on my part, I immersed myself in the love and serenity and just a few moments later I felt Adler's hand on mine. I turned my head and looked over and sure enough, he was right there with me. In that moment of excitement I got too distracted by his presence and let the energy field come crashing down, making a puzzled look come over Adler's otherwise serene face.

"Keep it going," Adler urged me, "don't try anything grand, just focus on the love."

I did exactly as he told me and in less than a minute our energy fields merged and we both reached a stable energy level that was easily sustainable.

"My energy ran out while you were sleeping," Adler admitted in an almost embarrassed tone of voice, "and I didn't wan't want to wake you up to tell you that I'd be returning to a state of non-existence for a while until you summoned me back."

"You should have!" I grumbled as I brushed my hair out of my face and got ready to get out of bed, "I was kind of wondering what happened to you when you weren't here this morning but then I thought back to what you had told me about feeding off energy that won't last forever."

"I knew you'd bring me back. I also know that if you focus on the agape every day like you did this morning, your mind will be trained to sustain it by itself so you'll never have to wake up without me."

"You're so full of yourself! But what exactly happens when you run out of energy?"

"I leave this dimension and there is absolutely nothing until you bring me back. The last time I saw the clock before my energy went out it was just before two this morning and now it's seven and it's exactly as though I simply closed my eyes and opened them again yet here we are several hours later."

"That's incredible! At least you don't have to suffer or anything like that."

I couldn't help but think back to when Mike destroyed my doll. Adler's energy blocked out the feelings from the intrusive memory but I couldn't help but remember how painful that was for me and how painful it would've been if my doll of Adler could actually feel anything.

"And I always want you around," I went on, "I've never gotten along so well with another person before. You're simply absolutely perfect."

"I'm just a keeper," he retorted without emotion.

"Yes, a keeper. You're a keeper!"

"You're cute, but now you need to get up and get ready for the day."

Basically as soon as he said that my alarm clock rang again and I had to reach out to turn it off a second time. I got off at the edge of my bed and began digging around for some clothes. Adler voluntarily disappeared from the room as I got dressed, putting on some faded blue jeans, a black and white striped shirt and a lightweight grey sweater over it.

Once I was done I called Adler back and the two of us went downstairs for breakfast. My mom was already making *bacon* and eggs. Her cooking did indeed smell delicious but what would it take for people to understand that I didn't want any of that darn bacon?!

I sat down in silence at the table and waited for my food to be served. I looked at Aaron contemplating if we could really ever be friends. He was three years older than me but appeared to me much of a loner like me. He often went out to hang out with a friend or two since they weren't allowed inside the house but he was far from being Mr. Popular. My mother served the food and I began eating my eggs as Mike's radio show came on. I didn't pay attention and instead kept staring at the two strips of bacon on my plate.

"Can I have that?" Adler asked as he looked at the bacon strips too, "It won't affect me to eat it."

I couldn't speak to him in front of everybody else so I took a strip of bacon and brought it close to my mouth like I was about to eat it but instead swung it over my shoulder and threw it on the floor behind the chair. Nobody had noticed a thing. *Mission accomplished!*

I was surprised that Mike hadn't heard on his beloved radio show that eating pork was terrible for you! Science had proven that, and both Jews and Muslims had somehow known that for thousands of years before as well! I contemplated that for a moment as I repeated the same process with the second piece of bacon.

My family had never been religious but I was definitely curious about spirituality after hearing stories of people having their lives completely changed once they'd found God but I had no idea how to to that or where to even look for God to begin with. Did Adler know? I glanced over a him quickly and found him enjoying the bacon. Of course it had absolutely no health effect on him. He could technically eat the furniture and nothing would happen.

"Thank you," Adler muttered with a mouthful of floor food, "it's good, it doesn't taste like the floor."

I had to refrain from laughing, but part of me felt guilty for having to feed him some floor food after all the kindness he had shown me and the hope he had brought back into my life. And he felt that guilt too, because he immediately made it disappear.

"Don't feel guilty," Adler continued, "the floor was a nice move. You're good and you're quick. But most of all, you're kind enough to actually feed me even though I don't need to eat at all."

I knew that eating could be such a great thing despite it being so simple. Eating and drinking was necessary to stay alive — for humans anyway — but it could still be such a blessing at the same time. As I thought about the joys of food I became hungry for ice cream. And potato chips. And chocolate chip cookies. And a whole lot of other things. I finished my breakfast and left the room so I could talk to Adler.

"You know that I'll feed you anything you want," I whispered to Adler, "absolutely anything you want, even non-edible objects, whenever you want."

That made me kind of curious to know what certain substances tasted like. I'd only ever put shampoo in my mouth when I was younger to see if it tasted as good as it smelled and I had certainly learned it the hard way that shampoo was nasty! On top of all the things I was already hungry for I also thought about eating birthday cake.

I would be turning fourteen soon enough but I wasn't hungry for a cake a month into the future, I was hungry for cake *now*. Oh, and pizza. I wanted a pizza more than all of the other things combined! I decided that I would wait until everybody left and I would order myself a big pizza with my leftover money after all. I couldn't help myself anymore.

"Please, no mushrooms on that pizza alright?" Adler pleaded as I dialed my favorite pizzeria's number on my cellphone.

I giggled at his request because there was no way in the world that anyone could ever make me eat something with mushrooms on it! Thankfully Mike didn't like mushrooms either because those nasty things were worst than bacon! Adler and I were so much alike it's like it was meant to be. I ordered a large vegetarian deluxe pizza and had it delivered to the house. The half hour it took to get it seemed like an eternity with my stomach grumbling like that but Adler kept me from going completely crazy.

Once I heard the doorbell ring I quickly ran down the stairs and pounced on the doorknob but I found an unpleasant surprise waiting for me on the other side. I opened the door and was handed the pizza by Alana Overton, an older girl I used to go to school with that I didn't like very much.

"Oh Joanie, it's you! I guess we'll see each other in school." Alana muttered half-heartedly as she handed me the box and left after I handed her the money.

I would have loved to tell her to shove the pizza right up her butt but I wanted to eat it too much for that. As I brought it into the kitchen and opened up the divine-smelling box I saw that the pizza was covered in *anchovies*. So much for a *vegetarian* pizza. I knew that it was a taunt from people who knew who I was and who didn't like me.

Although I didn't hate anchovies they definitely left a bad taste in my mouth in such situations. The excitement over the pizza had been all for absolutely nothing because I felt more deflated than anything. It was safe to say that my time at Bluepond District High School wouldn't be an easy one. I honestly didn't know how I was going to survive.

"At school people used to call me fish face or say that I looked like canned anchovies," I admitted to Adler with sadness and shame in my voice, "and it still makes me feel really self-conscious."

Adler's energy blocked out all the negative feelings and honestly made me feel better than I had before but my keeper still couldn't get these things out of my brain. Adler looked at me with compassion but didn't say anything. I was certain that he had a plan in mind and could look beyond the things I couldn't get passed but for the moment he wasn't sharing his ideas with me.

Even though I fully trusted him I did wish that he would've at least said something to reassure me because the mess going on inside my head was too big for me to start sorting through all by myself and just the thought of school made me want to be sick. I knew that at some point I'd have to tell Adler to put his Wehrmacht uniform back on because war was about to start.

The two of us ate our pizza which ended up being delicious despite that it wasn't what I ordered and I ultimately ended up being very happy with what I'd eaten. I didn't regret it despite everything. By the time we were done half the pizza was gone and I knew that if I put it in the fridge the other half would vanish before the day was over too so I brought it up to my room and shoved it in the closet and covered it with clothes so nobody would find it.

I'd just eat it later when I got hungry. Cold pizza was actually pretty good, albeit not nearly as good as fresh pizza. Pizza got nasty when it was put in the microwave because it turned rubber-like and that ruined everything. As for the clothes that would end up smelling like anchovies, well they sold deodorizer for that at the dollar store.

"We have yet another whole day to waste," I told Adler, "what do you want to do?"

It was another beautiful day in Bluepond so Adler and I decided to make the most of it before my days would be spent miserably confined to a classroom, hence I thought it would be a good idea to bring him back downtown and show him around some more. The two of us rode around on the city buses for most of the day, stopping at various places as I showed Adler around and reminisced about good times spent in those places back when taking a trip to the city was a big thing.

Redmont wasn't very far away but the dynamic was definitely different when you lived in a place instead of only going on a day trip there. It was incredibly uplifting and I was able to easily connect with the agape inside of me and sustain an energy field that had grown considerably larger.

"You see," Adler told me on the bus ride home after a long outing, "when you take up this positive attitude the energy becomes much easier to sustain. But most of all, your entire outlook on life is better."

"Sometimes I have to remind myself that things are going to be okay," I muttered mostly to myself, "because I don't have all the answers."

"Nobody does Joanie, but we can enlighten each other by sharing the things we do know. Keepers may not have a supreme understanding of everything, but we do have much clarity and insight."

"Too bad most people let the flame go out instead of passing on the torch. Honestly, most people I know are really stupid."

"Well, we are not most people aren't we? If there's one thing I've learned from my life and also from being here it's that if you can make a positive difference in the life of even just one person, it was all worth it."

Was it really? Would being a positive influence in someone's life, sometime in a future that wasn't even guaranteed, balance out the scale after having my family and my entire life be ripped to shreds?

"It's a symptom of life," Adler whispered softly to me.

"What?" I asked in surprise.

It seemed like he had been able to see right through my soul and read my thoughts, *again*.

"Pain. It comes with the territory."

"Oh. For a moment there I swore you had gotten inside my head! I've often heard people say that suffering is an optional state of being but I never understood how exactly you stop suffering when you're practically not in control of anything in your life."

"In life I've learned to keep an eye on the end result you're aiming for but to dedicate all the time you have to *now* because *now* is the only time you have and once *now* is over, it's gone forever."

"So I take it you're telling me to stop dwelling on things I cannot change and focus on the things I can do right now."

"Exactly. Nothing will change overnight, but you can do small things to make your life better now, and eventually all of these little things will have amounted to something much greater."

That was so much easier said than done. It seemed like it was going to take me a million years just to amount to something big. My efforts were merely like a drop of water in an endless ocean.

"It feels like all the rivers that go back to the sea yet the sea is never full."

"If you think that you are too small to make a difference, just try going to sleep with a mosquito in the room. If you're looking for someone to change your life look in the mirror Joanie."

I smiled at Adler. Looking at him wasn't necessary to feel better, his presence already did that all on it's own but I still loved admiring my creation. I knew that he was right. I often didn't realize it, but I was more powerful than I gave myself credit for.

Mike's strategy of making us all feel like we were powerless and not in control was really working. I reminded myself to connect with the agape deep inside of me to make sure the energy field was complete so Adler wouldn't go back to a state of non-existence because I desperately needed him around if I was ever going to get through anything.

At the end of our wonderfully pleasant outing and bus rides all over the city, Adler and I arrived home just a little after my mom and Mike had arrived from work. I knew that I'd be in trouble for not having gotten home before supper was served but I believed my outing was worth it. Maybe Adler was right about that part, maybe things could be balanced out in one way or another eventually.

I didn't know how, but I had to believe. I had to believe that there was something more. I knew that Adler wouldn't let me *not* believe, so I pledged to stop overthinking and worrying too much. Although I couldn't feel anything in my heart with Adler's keeper abilities, everything was still dwelling inside my mind.

As I walked up the street and into the driveway of the little house I noticed that Aaron was just a few steps ahead of me. I was surprised to see him coming home so early! I selfishly kept my distance behind him so he would absorb most of Mike's rage once he walked through the door. He largely seemed unaffected by it, unlike me. I knew that was bad but it was easier for me that way.

Maybe I could just slip in behind him and disappear upstairs to my room to eat the pizza I'd left in my closet earlier that day since I knew very well that the punishment for not coming back home on time was not getting any supper. I still could've made myself something but considering my non-existent cooking skills, it was probably better that I didn't.

"Where were the two of you all day?!" Mike grumbled as soon as I stepped into the door.

"I don't know what Aaron was doing," I grumbled back, "we weren't together. I went around town riding the bus."

That wasn't a good enough answer for Mike because he kept

yelling profanity at both Aaron and I like we were accomplices in some type of conspiracy against him. Of course those claims were completely unfounded but there was no telling Mike otherwise.

"It's not like you care what we do all day Mike!" I snapped back at his verbal assaults, standing up for myself for the very first time. "As long as we're not in your way and we come home on time to do our chores it's none of your business what the two of us do the rest of the day!"

Nobody had been expecting me to snap back. My mother sat dumbfounded at the table eating her tomato soup and Mike was momentarily frozen on the spot and I ended up realizing a little too late that my outburst was only making the situation worst. Aaron saw that coming from a mile away so he bolted for the basement and a few moments later I heard his bedroom door slam shut.

Mike grabbed his bowl of soup and violently threw it on the wall perpendicular to me. For a moment I cringed and braced for impact despite that Mike hadn't actually been aiming for me. The bowl broke into a million pieces and the hot soup splashed everywhere but nothing hit me. I was seriously afraid of being physically hit so I too bolted for the stairs quickly and made it up to my room. I slammed the door shut and pushed a piece of furniture in front of it before I leaped into my bed and began crying. Adler appeared next to me a few moments later and put his arm over me to comfort me.

"Nothing's going to happen to you," he whispered in my ear, "I won't let it."

"No matter what I do I only make a bigger mess of my own life!" I grumbled through my tears.

"Never dwell over anything that happened Joanie. It cannot be changed, undone or forgotten, so take it as a lesson learned and move on."

"I know you're right but it's easier said than done. Lesson definitely learned that challenging Mike's authority only aggravates everything."

I was overheating up in my room so I got up and opened the window to let in the cool evening breeze because my mind was running wild and I was feeling it physically. I stuck my head out of my bedroom window to look passed the nearby valley. I could only see some gas station lights down the highway and a few vehicles going by, going *away* from Bluepond in the other direction. How I wanted to be in one of those cars!

I then let myself flop on my bed for a second time but there was no way I could relax. I was feeling exactly the way I had been when I'd first encountered Adler; sick, confused, angry, depressed, and wanting to pass out and puke and die all at the same time. The only difference between the two situations was that at the present moment I couldn't feel any emotion in my heart, Adler absorbed everything which was definitely a weight lifted off my shoulders but it didn't change much else.

Once I calmed down I took the pizza out of my closet and had a piece since I didn't have any supper. Adler didn't eat, he sat on my bed and flipped through the pages of a history book. I thought back to what he said about Aaron being a possible ally of mine and wondered if he had anything to eat down in the basement.

I still had a considerable amount of pizza inside the box so I waited until the coast was clear downstairs, grabbed two slices and headed down to the basement. I'd never been down there before. Aaron never let anyone into his dungeon and I knew that he'd probably be angry to find me in there but I would never find out if we could be friends if I didn't try, right?

I slowly opened the wooden basement door so it wouldn't creak and tiptoed down the narrow concrete steps. The basement was unfinished and looked like something that came right out of a horror movie. It was very creepy and dimly lit so I couldn't see much of where I was going. Once I reached the bottom I made my way around the furnace room on the cold unfinished concrete floor up until I reached Aaron's room.

His room was finished but the door was off its hinges and hanging awkwardly in the door frame. I peered inside the room and saw a typical unorganized teenager's room that wasn't too different than mine except that posters of heavy metal bands and action movies covered the walls from top to bottom.

"Aaron," I whispered, "I have some pizza for you."

He'd been playing on his laptop facing the wall and was surprised to find someone else in his personal space but once I slid my hand through the crack of his door and handed him the pizza he seemed to rejoice.

"Thank you," he muttered but didn't invite me inside.

I didn't blame him because I probably wouldn't have invited him inside my own personal space either but I hoped that my gesture opened the door to us at least being on good terms irrespective of whether or not we ended up having much of a relationship.

I then left the dark and cold basement and ended up knocking over something that I didn't see before reaching the stairs. I didn't hear anything break but I still didn't want to make anyone angry nonetheless so I quickly ran back up to my room where Adler was still looking at the book. The house was very quiet.

"I'm very proud of you," Adler spoke softly as I went to sit next to him, "I knew that you'd eventually realize that your life wasn't completely doomed, and that was one step in the right direction."

"I know that you're right deep inside my heart," I replied, "but it's still so hard for me to believe in myself."

He put his arm around my shoulder and gave it a reassuring squeeze. The worst part was still yet to come.

# SIX

The horrific sound of my alarm clock awoke me from a deep slumber with a jolt of fear. Thankfully, my incredible keeper was there to wash away the anxiety before it even touched me. I wished that his amazing supernatural powers could also extend to erasing the weight of everything inside my mind and not just block the feelings inside my heart.

I knew that he wanted so much to be able to read my thoughts but having our emotions be connected like they were already gave him a pretty good idea of what was at the back of my mind. Whatever keepers were, they sure knew how to go about their miraculous business.

"Joanie," Adler's voice was the first thing I heard after he made my alarm stop, "you have to get dressed and I have to bring you to school."

*School.*

"You can't tell me that you don't want to go," he went on when I didn't move, "you have no anxiety and no pain of any kind. Many adventures lie ahead for the day."

"Maybe you can make my emotions all nice and peachy," I finally grumbled after a few moments of silence, "but you can't make me interested."

"Sorry."

"But I suppose you could still try to make things interesting..."

"I'll do my best, but first you have to get up."

"I'm trying my best."

"Try harder!"

I giggled for a few moments before I *finally* managed to pull myself out of my bed. It took a considerable effort on my part but I knew that I was damned if I did and damned if I didn't so I might as well just get it over with.

"Maybe there will be some cute guys at school!" Adler tried to encourage me.

"I'm not interested," I muttered as I rubbed my tired eyes and dug around for clothes.

"Cute girls maybe?"

"Even less interested!"

"C'mon Joanie! I'll be there!"

Adler and I smiled at each other for a brief moment before I pulled his Wehrmacht uniform out of the closet and handed it to him.

"Please wear this today," I told him in a serious tone of voice as I handed him his clothes.

He tilted his head to the side and wore a look on his face asking me if I was really serious and he could bet everything that I was! I was going to need a soldier in class if I was going to survive my first day of school. Adler went into another room to change into his clothes while I also got dressed for my very first day of high school. I did not dress to impress. I put on a plain raspberry long-sleeve shirt and some black jeans. My outfit was just the way I liked it. Plain. Simple. Carefree.

"Okay, you can come back now," I told Adler, "I'm decent."

Adler reappeared in the room wearing his military uniform and admired my attire as I looked at myself in the mirror of my room.

"You're beautiful," he complimented me in his usual sweet voice.

"Thank you," I whispered as I looked at myself in the mirror one more time, "but you're the one who's the handsome one Lieutenant Adler."

"I wouldn't wear this for anyone else."

"You know, I think I might want to cut my hair or at least get a different hairstyle."

"Change isn't always bad you know."

"I'm beginning to see that now, mostly thanks to you. I don't really want things to go back to what they were before, but I definitely want them to be different than this."

"Well, Joanie, we're just getting started! Oh, and before I forget I have a little gift for you."

Adler then handed me a doll of Tom Cruise playing Claus von Stauffenberg in the movie *Valkyrie*. I had neglected my action figure hobby since Adler had literally come to life and that doll absolutely and totally made my day! Stauffenberg had always been my favorite, but only second to Adler.

"You stole this!" I exclaimed after my initial surprise and excitement died down.

"Joanie, I'm invisible," Adler retorted in a serious tone of voice, "I couldn't have paid for it anyway."

"And you made *me* pay for your civilian clothes at the thrift store a few weeks ago!"

"It was in the middle of the night when I got Stauffenberg from the consignment store! Nobody could've paid anyway!"

I burst out laughing but somewhat felt bad because I didn't believe that stealing was right. Nonetheless I was very happy about the doll, I couldn't have been happier in fact!

"So, do you know how I can resurrect Stauffenberg by any chance?" I asked Adler. "If I'm gonna have a keeper I might as well have two!"

"It doesn't work that way," Adler replied as he put his hand over his face and laughed at the same time.

I put Stauffenberg safely in my schoolbag and went downstairs for breakfast. As soon as I stepped into the kitchen the talk of school immediately smacked me in the face. The thing was that I *wanted* to be in a mediocre mood about school. I wanted to be bitter about it because frankly there wasn't anything about school that didn't leave a bitter taste in my mouth, but Adler wasn't about to let me be bitter or morose.

"Indulge in the energy Joanie," he reminded me sternly, "don't try to fight it. I'm a military officer and these are orders."

Sometimes I had to be reminded that Adler needed my energy in order to exist. Energy could not be created nor destroyed, but Adler was caught somewhere between two different material states. Although nobody could quite explain his existence, I wanted him to exist so I happily gave him the energy he required in order to do so.

"Feels better huh?" Adler spoke with a sweet smile on his face.

Everything at the table was quiet with Mike listening to his radio show and drinking his coffee as he always did but the atmosphere was surprisingly light in the room. There was no tension in the room but I wasn't able to read the feelings of anyone at the table. My mom looked more tired than usual with her hair visibly dirty, something that was highly unlike her. Aaron and Mike were there usual selves so I sat down and waited for my food to come to me. I got plate with bacon again of course.

"You can eat it," Adler said from behind me, "it's turkey bacon this time."

Since I'd come down a little late for breakfast Mike's radio show ended while I was eating my turkey bacon which was surprisingly very good and a lot healthier for a person. I wanted to leave some food for Adler but it was so good that I didn't want to leave anything in my plate! I supposed that it wouldn't hurt his feelings if I ate it all just one time.

"You've been awfully quiet these days Joanie," Mike muttered with food still in his mouth, "you usually like to talk after the program ends."

"I have a lot on my mind," I responded in a mousy voice not wanting to say something wrong and make him angry.

"Are you excited to start high school?"

"Yes and no, I'm really more nervous than anything right now."

Of course that was a lie. I was not excited and I couldn't feel anything at all. I still had plenty of thoughts to sort out even though I had no more foul emotions to get me down. It was hard for me to fathom that keepers came from within us because God couldn't have matched me with a better person. Adler was just the person I needed even though I had no idea what I was needing. I ate the rest of my breakfast slowly, chewing and savoring every bite just so I wouldn't have to talk to anybody because I definitely wasn't in the mood.

"I know that this is a lot for you," my mother added in a gentle voice, "it's nerve-wracking for everyone to walk into high school for the first time, but you'll be okay."

"Yeah mom," I muttered, "this is just a lot for me, like you said, that's all."

Getting on the school bus meant getting out of the house but it also meant getting to school. I took Stauffenberg out of my bag and held him tightly in my hands as I sat in the front of the bus with Adler during a trip that was much too short. I couldn't feel any anxiety with his energy blocking it but I still wanted to delay my arrival to school as much as possible just so I could enjoy being in limbo away from both school and the house for a few more moments.

Too soon the bus came to a half in front of the high school and Adler dragged me out of the vehicle by the arm. I felt like a small child walking into school for the first time as I latched on to Adler with one hand and carried my doll in the other as we walked towards the large brown brick building.

The big building with three floors and a flat roof intimidated me but it didn't intimidate Adler. He truly was a fearless soldier as he walked ahead of me passed the parking lot on the west side of the building and in through the main entrance to the guidance counsellor's office where we first had to zigzag through an incredibly packed lobby.

There were so many students of all ages and all backgrounds lingering outside the office like lost souls looking to find their purpose in a world that valued nothing but power and material wealth. There was no valuing hard work, integrity or dedication. I was nothing more than a grain of sand on a beach amidst a sea of faces.

"I know that right now you feel small," Adler commented almost like my emotions gave away my every thought, "but you are bigger than all of this."

"Says the dude who is invisible," I retorted dryly.

"If you think you're too small to matter or have an impact, just think about trying to go to sleep when there's a mosquito in the room. Don't forget that one."

"Adler, you're amazing and I love you so much, but there's nothing you can do or say that will make me like school."

I looked around cautiously to see if I could find somebody that I knew, but only somebody that I didn't have negative feelings towards. However, I didn't see any familiar faces. The place was mostly packed with lost freshmen just like me trying to find their way around or somebody that looked semi-trustworthy to help them.

I somewhat knew my way around the school already since my elementary school had brought us over for an activity day one time in a futile attempt to make the transition to high school smoother but the thought of crowded hallways still made me want to be sick.

Despite all the people in there, school was one of the loneliest places on the planet. Following the huge fallout after Byron Overton's party over a year ago I got shunned a lot because apparently it had been underage brats like me who had ruined the whole gathering. His arrogant tramp of a sister Alana had invited me to her brother's high school party under the pretext that we were friends but it hadn't exactly gone according to plan.

Although I'd ended up leaving before the whole ordeal went down, the fact that I was there and that I now attended the same school as Alana Overton and others who were involved in one way or another didn't lessen my involved in their eyes. Thankfully Byron Overton had graduated a while back so that was one less person to worry about, not that it changed a whole lot, however.

"Keep the faith Joanie," Adler whispered to me as my emotions began shifting slightly, "we're a team."

Adler grinned as he walked through people and they caught a chill as he did so. I sat back and observed the show but had to be careful not to laugh so I wouldn't land myself in unnecessary trouble. Some woman's dog on the boardwalk had obviously seen my keeper or felt his presence and that freaked it out big time so it really made me wonder at times if Adler was really only visible to me. Was I really the only person who could hear his gentle voice? Touch his soft hair? Feel his miraculous presence?

"In between all these people I have a hard time believing that you exist only in my world," I muttered in a low voice so nobody else would hear me, "you're presence is powerful on so many levels."

"When I walked from that muddy field by the water all the way to your house that night we met," Adler replied as though he seemed to be thinking hard about something, "I walked around a little bit before making my way there and nobody saw me. Cars drove right through me and nothing happened!"

"But the dog in the park saw you! And I *see* you! And these people *feel* you when you pass through them!"

"I truly don't know how to explain Joanie, keepers don't have a godlike understanding of anything, we're just like humans with merely a little more insight."

"The bottom line is that I need you around and I love being in your presence. Regardless of who sees or doesn't see you, I want you around no matter what."

Adler and I looked deep into each other's eyes for a moment as I contemplated his mysterious existence before the reality of being back in school came looming over my head again. I felt no stress, no agony of any kind, in fact I felt nothing but calmness but there was a catch.

Even though I couldn't feel those negative emotions they were still there in my mind and I did feel the weight of their psychological impact. I didn't like school, I never had, and I had lost hope a long time ago that anything good was going to come out of school. Just as my train of thought was wandering down a dark path my name was called.

"Let's go get your paperwork," Adler commented as he signaled me to follow him to the guidance counsellor's office after I didn't move from the bench.

I reluctantly followed him into the office where Mr. Jackson greeted me like he would greet an old friend. He still looked exactly as he always had with his John Lennon eyeglasses, his bald head, his nose too large for his round face and his big brown eyes. He had so many certificates hanging on the walls of his office that it looked like he could've been a doctor but for some reason he ended up turning into a guidance counsellor at some boring old high school in some boring old city.

No famous people had ever come our of Bluepond, we didn't have our own Nirvana or international hero. When people had to pick between Bluepond and Halifax, they picked Halifax. There were so many opportunities there that they didn't have in my boring old city.

"It's good to see you again Joanie," Mr. Jackson spoke as he dug through a pile of papers on his desk and handed me one, "here is your schedule for this semester, you have one week to switch classes and make adjustments if you don't like this."

Mr. Jackson and my dad had been great friends for the longest time and our family often had him over for supper and other events so seeing him was sort've awkward. Once upon a time those were cherished memories of mine but they since become rather painful and I didn't want to think about them so I quickly grabbed the paper from his hand and looked at it.

English. Science. History. Math. Sounded like a boring semester but on the bright side, an easy one. I told Mr. Jackson that I was fine with my classes and quickly bolted out of the office. The secretary handed me a lock for my locker along with the combination on a sticky note before Adler and I walked up endless flights of stairs all the way up to the third floor.

The bare light grey walls were depressing. The black and white floor tiles were dirty and the top floor was mostly vacant of students as there were very little lockers up there. Three science labs were up on the top floor as well as a massive storage room with an industrial supply of dusty old books that nobody wanted.

The student newspaper was written up there but the newspaper club was a pretty skimpy one. Nobody was actually interested in reading, and much less in writing, the paper. At the end of the hallways of bright red lockers there was a vacant room with two couches and even a fridge as well as multiple desks given to students to study quietly as the student lounge was a zoo and the library was constantly crowded.

Things had always been that way as far as I was concerned and with constantly growing class sizes, the extra space was needed. There were many elementary schools all over Bluepond but only four high schools in total for a city of such size. No wonder the building was huge, and I went to the smallest of all the high schools too. As I walked down the hallway I spotted my locker so I walked over and opened it. It hadn't been used in a while because it was dusty in there!

Ironically enough, somebody had written profanity in black ink on the inside of the bright red door. I grinned slightly to myself and deposited my jean jacket as well as my bag in the locker before sitting Stauffenberg up on the shelf and putting the lock on it and then walking back down to the second floor for my first class.

Even on my way there, having to pass through what seemed like clouds of students, I didn't see anybody that I knew. I knew that this was going to change however, because all of my classes were mandatory to complete in order to graduate so I wasn't going to be able to get away from anyone.

"See anybody you know yet?" Adler asked me as he looked around the sea of people going in and out of classrooms trying to find their way.

"Not yet," I muttered in a low voice as I walked into English class, "but that's about to change."

And yup, that did change. I saw a bunch of people whom I had gone to elementary school with and others that I used to hang out with. I hadn't seen them in an eternity, or so it seemed to me. I wasn't sure if that made me feel better or worst though. My emotions were too blank to come to any conclusion either way. Way at the back of the class I saw a girl that used to attend a school I'd briefly attended in Redmont several years ago.

I didn't really know her as that time in my life had been so brief and I had never actually spoken to the girl either. I didn't even remember her name! In some way seeing her there at the back of the room made me feel less alone amidst a bunch of faces despite that I had known most of them for years so all in all, finding a piece of the past again was better than I'd anticipated.

"You seem to have found someone Joanie," Adler commented as he felt the energy change, "go see them!"

I sighed, composed myself and gathered my strength, and walked towards the no name girl sitting at the back of the room. I was almost there when I chickened out and went to sit by myself at the other end of the room. Adler sighed loudly, totally disappointed in me, but I knew that he also understood the fact that I was still weak and not quite ready for such a big step just yet.

I sat down on the cheap metal folding chair and Adler sat next to me in a vacant seat. He took my hand into his and gave it a reassuring squeeze to remind me that we were a team and that everything was going to be alright. Seeing him in his military uniform comforted me knowing that I had a soldier on my side.

Throughout the class I tried desperately to focus but it wasn't exactly working. It wasn't because I was anxious or afraid or depressed or out of place or any other foul emotion. I wasn't interested in being in school. End of story. I didn't want to be there. Nothing and nobody could make me enjoy something that I had always disliked. I didn't like the classroom environment of everyone yoked together like dolls being built in a factory somewhere in China, except that these dolls weren't like Stauffenberg or my Adler.

The school didn't understand that the students didn't all learn the same way, and some of them didn't want to learn at all. Sure, I wasn't the smartest kid around nor was I in the gifted kids program, but it was frustrating for me to sit there and pretend that everything was alright and just go with the flow. A flow that I should mention was going down the drain of a toilet.

The graduation rates at Bluepond High were exceptionally low compared to the national average and it wasn't hard for me to see why. For some reason nobody was interested in getting somewhere. Even some teachers didn't care, they just showed up in the same classrooms we did every day to get paid. I wasn't completely innocent in that whole thing either though. I had thrown aside my studies and my future in the past to party with the high school seniors just so I could be part of the popular crowd at my elementary school.

Everybody thought that being all grown up was awesome and badass but that hadn't sat too well with my parents who were in the process of getting divorced at the time. Was it any wonder that I was frustrated coming back to the people that had made me go off the rails in the first place? And then there were a bunch of people who seemed to believe that my problems weren't real, but they were real to *me*.

"How are you doing?" Adler asked me after the bell rang at the end of the class as the students swarmed the hallways.

"Not adapting so well," I admitted shamefully, but that came as no surprise, "I know it's not terrible to have different opinions or perceptions about certain things and to stand out of the mainstream crowd sometimes but nobody seems to understand that I am not adapting well to this and I cannot cope with everything that's happening at once! They all dismiss me as the *oh it's just a phase* or *it'll all work out for the better* crap and they don't understand that I'm suffering *now*. It just frustrates me so much because they don't know how bad it hurts!"

Everything was painful. I looked up at Adler, wondering silently to myself what I'd do without him. He put his arm around my shoulders reassuringly for a moment to give me the courage to make my way to my second class. This time around I was going to sit in front of the class because science had never really been an easy topic for me even if I loved it greatly.

I didn't want to fail a class during my very first semester of high school either, that only would've added to the shame and the frustration. Even under the cheap artificial lights of the hallway Adler's eyes sparkled like only a keeper's eyes could. Before entering my next class I closed my eyes and took a deep breath and connected with the energy inside of me.

I couldn't quite sustain the energy field and it came crashing down around me but Adler was replenished on energy as I fed him some every chance I got. It became easier and easier to do each time I did it and as he had told me in the past, there would come a time where I wouldn't even need to focus on connecting to the energy, it would come to sustain itself. The seat I wanted in the classroom was available so I sat right down in the mostly empty classroom as I was actually early for my last class before lunchtime. My stomach was running on empty already and as a student walked by with a chocolate bar in hand I couldn't help but notice Adler's eyes staring down the candy, obviously his tastebuds were also getting desperate.

Since I felt bad that he stole the Stauffenberg doll I gave him a few coins and told him that there was a vending machine at the end of the hallway. Adler thanked me and went on his way to get some snacks. I didn't understand how invisible Wehrmacht officers could eat visible chocolate bars but as long as Adler enjoyed it that was the only thing that mattered. Adler was gone a while, most of the class actually, but when he came back he looked delighted. I smiled when I saw him walk right through the closed classroom door with a big smile on his face, showing off a perfect set of pristine white teeth.

He sat down next to me again and waited out the remainder of the class in silence. Not much had been going on in class during the time that he had been roaming the halls. On the first day it was the usual introduction crap and very little work but that was going to be short lived, that I knew.

The bell rang so Adler and I raced down to the cafeteria to get some food before my favorite food, pizza rolls on Italian bread, was completely sold out. I didn't know if the pizza rolls would be as good as those from my favorite Italian restaurant but they definitely seemed more appealing than lasagna, chili, poutine or mundane sandwiches. The high school cafeteria was a nice break from packed lunches in elementary school but I knew that I wouldn't be able to eat there everyday since it was bound to get pricey after a while.

"Sorry for bailing out on you dear," Adler apologized in his usual soft voice, "I saw things in the halls that I wanted to investigate further."

"That's okay," I assured him, "I understand your curiosity considering that I'm the one who constantly probes you with questions and you've never asked me a thing."

"That's not what it was about Joanie, I wanted to experiment with something after we talked about only you being able to see me. I walked around aimlessly just eating my chocolate and minding my own business you know, but I *swear* that one kid saw my shadow on the wall."

"What happened?"

"He was coming down an adjacent hallway minding his own business like I was but then he stopped abruptly. I walked over to see what was going on and when he saw my shadow he became apprehensive for some unknown reason. He must've thought I was somebody else, but I know that he saw me!"

"What did he do when you approached him? Did he feel something? Did you notice something particularly about him?"

"I walked right up to him but nothing happened further, except that I had fun giving him a chill, but he didn't see me in my actual form the way you do. I can only feel your emotions and not other people's but it was obvious that whoever that kid was in the hallway, he was afraid of whatever he thought was coming down the other hallway."

"That's incredible. I honestly don't know what to say, this is beyond my comprehension!"

"Mine too Joanie, but for now we need to get you some food."

Down in the cafeteria on the first floor it was crazy. Swarms of students filled up the place, but thankfully not everybody in the building had lunch at the same time. Otherwise there wouldn't even be enough room inside the cafeteria itself for everybody. After a while of waiting in line I finally got my pizza roll and bought a second one for Adler although he hadn't asked me for one along with two sodas and two packs of cookies.

I shoved all the food into my tray and went to sit outside in a little grassy area with picnic tables and benches behind the school. It was the only quiet place on the lot. I needed some time away from all the commotion in order to take a deep breath and collect my thoughts. Adler and I sat side by side at a picnic table in quiet solitude as I handed him his food.

"Thank you so much for this," Adler spoke with food in his mouth, "I could start eating and never stop."

"It's not a problem," I retorted before taking a big bite of my own pizza roll, "but how can you be invisible and eat visible food?"

"Well, if I remember the laws of physics correctly, atoms can exist in two places at one time so that would mean that I can exist in both the physical and non-physical world at the same time. It's kind of a crazy metaphysical concept but in this form I can transcend time and space. If I've transcended non-existence there is no reason why I shouldn't be able to eat human food."

"You're right, but I'm still trying to understand what happened with the other kid in the hallway."

"That was beyond my comprehension too! But the more I analyze it, the more it seems to relate to the laws of matter and energy. With enough energy, I should materialize to more than just you, but why exactly I am this way around you, I don't know. I guess that one lies within the secrets of keepers that I have yet to discover."

"On that note I suppose that my science class should be an interesting one!"

"Physics is great but don't ignore philosophy. You can create a million equations to explain the way things interact but science can't always explain *why* things are a certain way."

"You're so smart and witty it's almost contagious! I want to listen to everything you have to say and hang on to your every word!"

"Perks of being a keeper! I may not have all the answers but this still has its benefits."

I chomped down on the pizza roll like the world was going to end if I didn't swallow it because it was so good! Well, I barely tasted it actually, but I'd tasted enough to know that I loved it! Just seeing it and smelling it had been enough for me, but eating it was beyond heavenly. Unlike me, Adler savored every bite of it and let it go down slowly to not miss a single second of enjoyment.

"Can I ask you a keeper question?" I muttered with my mouth full.

"Sure," Adler responded enthusiastically, "I'll do my best to answer it!"

"Let's say that you wanted to go back to Europe for whatever reason, could you go by yourself in your current form or would you have to be accompanied by me?"

"Theoretically, I could go by myself. The catch is, however, that the farther away I am from you the harder it is to sustain the energy. It also takes much more to keep the flow going as it has to travel so far and to tell you the truth, I would probably fall back into non-existence long before I ever reached Germany."

"I've always wanted to go to Berlin and I thought that maybe I'd have my chance living vicariously through you, but I understand what you mean. So much energy would be lost in transit somewhere over the ocean for you to be able to fully manifest yourself."

"Exactly. The metaphysical world of keepers still has its limits. On top of that I'm *your* keeper, meaning that I'm here to be with you. There is a reason why I keep being drawn back to you and not just wander of wherever I please because believe me there are a lot of places I'd like to go and people I'd like to see."

"I guess we could explain the reasons why we keep being drawn to each other with the laws of attraction even though your existence defies almost every, if not all, physical laws."

Adler and I enjoyed each other's company for the short amount of time we had before the bell rang indicating that we'd have to go back to class and sit through another long and boring introduction.

IF YOU THINK THAT YOU ARE TOO *TO MAKE A DIFFERENCE IN SOMEONE'S LIFE just try going to sleep WITH A *mosquito* IN THE ROOM*

# SEVEN

The bell rang and I had to go back to class but that didn't interrupt the serenity or the incredible overwhelming feeling of peace that I carried around with me. Adler had always made me feel incredible with his keeper powers but it had never really been quite like the moments we shared sitting at the picnic table. The energy had definitely gone up to a higher level of vibration. The atoms had absorbed some quantum and they were happy about it because the feeling of serenity was unlike anything else I'd ever felt. What I felt was pure bliss! It was almost otherworldly just to put it mildly.

Honestly, there wasn't much that you actually did feel, it was mostly what you *didn't* feel that made all the difference. I was an anxious and nervous wreck, there was no doubt about that, but what nobody seemed to take into consideration was that I also had many unresolved feelings. If there was peace in how a keeper made you feel there was nothing else. And there was only peace. Adler and I walked up to the third floor for my third class of the day and the two of us sat in a secluded spot in the back as the place soon filled up.

"There's the girl from Redmont!" Adler pointed out as she walked into the classroom.

Sure enough it was her. She was short with a few extra pounds and short light brown hair. Her round dark brown eyes complimented the shape of her face even though her unruly hair fell over most of it. She wore a fitted baseball shirt and some baggy jeans. Her style was similar to mine. Not a big deal, shirt and jeans kind of thing.

As she walked into the classroom she looked around the room to find a spot to sit and much to my pleasure she came to sit at a vacant desk right next to mine. Sometimes I couldn't help but wonder if Adler could manipulate certain sets of circumstances in a particular way without knowing it or being aware it was happening.

"Hi there," the girl greeted me as she sat down next to me, "I hope that you don't mind me sitting here, you're the only face I recognize from Redmont."

"I don't mind at all," I replied trying to sound as friendly as I could, "you're one of the very few people I've recognized here too."

"I'm Rosanna Hampton, in case you don't remember, but everybody calls me Rosie or Rose."

"It's nice to meet you for a second time! I'm Joanie Bowen, in case you don't remember either."

"It's good to meet you again too!"

Adler smiled at me as he sat in a vacant chair in front of my desk. He'd moved spots so I could scoot over and let Rosanna get closer. Sometimes I had to remind myself to make an effort towards the things I wanted and not just away from the ones I didn't. I wanted Rosanna to be my friend so I'd have to make a move at some point. I also had to remind myself that it was useless to dwell over my life if I didn't do my part to make it better.

"Well look at that," a kid that I knew named Dylan exclaimed, "fish face is here too!"

Just as I had anticipated. My welcome to my first day of high school wasn't a very warm one. I felt part of the energy field around me begin to fall as the words cut me deep but Adler gave me one of those looks prompting me to connect with the agape inside of me and keep the energy flow going because it was only going to make me feel better in the long run. That was exactly what I did and almost immediately the inner peace was restored.

"Sorry that I didn't sit with you this morning," I apologized to Rosanna, "I've been in a somewhat foul mood today but it's better now."

"That's fine," Rosanna spoke in a mousy voice, "I wanted to go say hi at lunch but I saw that you were sitting with some dude dressed like a soldier and I didn't want to intrude on whatever that was about."

In that moment I felt like the whole world was falling out from under me. Rosanna had seen Adler! A look of shock and pure horror swept over Adler's face as he heard those words too. Rosanna was completely unaware that Adler was sitting merely an arm's length away from her but that didn't undo the fact that she had actually seen him earlier!

"Are you okay?" Rosanna asked after a few moments of silence

She obviously wasn't oblivious to the look on my face and I didn't know what kind of lie I would tell her to get out of the situation. I couldn't say that he wasn't real, because he had obviously been real to her.

"Uh, yeah," I muttered as I struggled to compose myself, "it's just, uh, supposed to be a secret."

"Oh! I'm sorry, I won't tell anybody."

"It's okay Rosie, don't worry about it. It's just, uh, it's just my, uh, parents, you know."

That was lame but I couldn't come up with anything better on the spot. I was so shocked, I'd never imagined that somebody else could see my keeper! What would I do if he became visible to everyone? What kind of explication would I provide then?

"I've had a boyfriend that my parents didn't approve of before, Joanie. Your secret is safe with me."

That did not make me feel any better. Adler was *not* my boyfriend, he was my *keeper*. I did not think of Adler in *that* way. That would have been so weird and vile, not to mention that someone my age dating someone his age was illegal, and him being invisible didn't change a thing. I didn't know how to respond to the comment so I didn't respond at all. Hopefully Rosanna would just forget about Adler and never see him again because I wouldn't have known what to tell her otherwise.

I took a humongous deep breath and exhaled slowly as I let all the anxiety cool off. I knew that Adler was currently feeling the same wave of intensity but unlike me, he was available to perennially keep himself perfectly composed. As much as I had the urge to run into another room and discuss endless philosophy with Adler, I had to remain calm and do my best to focus in class until we could have some time to ourselves to reflect on the events of the day.

"She actually saw me!" Adler's soft voice seemed exasperated.

Dylan walked over to the desk in front of mine after having had a short chat with another student and flopped down on the chair Adler was sitting on. Immediately he caught a gigantic chill and the hair on his arms and the back of his neck stayed raised until Adler decided to get up and move aside. Dylan had obviously felt something out of the ordinary because his eyes were wild with some powerful unspoken emotion.

"I'd love to kick you right out of your chair you little brat!" Adler shouted angrily at him.

It was the first time that I'd seen a glimpse of anger in Adler. Sure, I knew that he had plenty of emotions of his own and he wasn't immune to the situations around him simply because he was a keeper but he had never shown any sort of aggression towards another person.

Adler's anger towards Dylan after having called me a name was so *human* despite that the rest of his emotions had been expressed with a much higher degree of clarity than regular emotions. Fellow humans didn't have the same degree of clarity that keepers did but I came to see that despite everything, Adler was really just as human as I was.

"I reckon that you've been successfully reformed since we've last seen you because you're not part of the party scene anymore," Dylan taunted me as he slouched over my desk, "how's the pizza in Redmont compared to the one here by the way?"

In that moment Adler violently slapped his hand down on my desk, giving Dylan a huge electric shock. Even though I had my hands and arms on my desk too, I hadn't felt the jolt of electricity that had been accompanied by a loud popping sound. Dylan moaned in pain as he held the hand that had sustained the shock and all I could do was look on in pure shock and horror as everything happening around me was way beyond my comprehension.

Adler continued tormenting Dylan by slapping him upside the head and poking him. Although Dylan didn't feel the actual slap, he later complained of a headache and random aches and pains. The teacher ordered him to go see the nurse on the main floor if he was in so much distress as the rest of the class looked on laughing. I giggled under my breath too. He had totally deserved that!

"I guess you'll have to start calling me an electric eel huh?" Adler giggled as he retook his seat in front of me as class was about to begin.

I smiled at him and although I couldn't speak to my invisible friend in the middle of class, I focused on the agape within me and let him know that I loved and appreciated him and that I was thankful for what he had done for me in a moment of vulnerability where I didn't have the strength to fight back. I admired his military uniform and was grateful that I had a soldier on my side.

"Take a step forward, and don't be afraid of what it might cost you. It might cost you something or you might be rewarded," Adler spoke gently as though he could read my thoughts again, "but do not let what happened in the past cripple you. I know, believe me I know, how hard it is to move on from something but what is worth the prize at the end of the line is always worth the struggle and the fight. Take it from a soldier."

I knew that I wouldn't be able to depend on Adler forever and at some point I'd have to stand up for myself, but that of course was much easier said than done. For the moment I knew I was in good hands so I wouldn't waste too much energy thinking about things that only made me anxious. If I couldn't fight I'd somehow have to resist. Adler could teach me all about that, he'd been part of the German Resistance and he was a hero. He was *my* hero.

The school day came to an end without incident and I returned home taking more time than necessary. Surprisingly my mother was already there and looked exasperated as well. She didn't even notice me coming in as she was busy cleaning the kitchen. I didn't really know what to say because I had an idea that the reason she was home so early wasn't a very good one. I approached slowly not to startled her and deposited my bag by the door before taking my shoes off on the fuzzy grey carpet.

"Hi mom," I muttered, not really wanting to deal with the situation.

"Oh, hi there Joanie," she said as she turned around to look at me, "you're home early."

"So are you."

"Yes... well, I got laid off from work today. Things are going to be tight financially for a while before I get to find another job."

"So that means that we're completely at Mike's mercy? Mom we have to get away from him!"

"Sweetie it's not that easy, and I know that you don't understand, but we can't just get up and leave and everything will be alright. You know that I'm here to talk if you need somebody to lean on though. I know that in the past things have been tense between us but I am wanting and willing to repair our relationship."

"I want that too, but you can't expect me to just forget about everything after so much has happened."

My throat tightened. There was so much I wanted to say in that moment but I didn't know where to begin, or if the words would even come out. Could I really squeeze everything into a single paragraph? My parents broke up, my dad left me, our house disappeared, Mike showed up and kept me constantly walking on eggshells, among other things. Why wouldn't my mother leave Mike? What was stopping her? Did she really love the guy? Did she believe that I would believe such a thing?

"Please Joanie, give me a little time to get back on my feet and to put something together and I promise you that this situation will change. I know that we have to get out of here but we can't just run away without anything and expect everything to be fixed. Where will we go? What will be do? I know that exposing you to this isn't healthy but I'm not convinced that right now the outside will have anything better to offer us. Let me put a plan in place Joanie, please."

I didn't have much of a choice. There wasn't much I could do on my own, and I didn't want to simply run and leave my mom behind. Where would I go anyway? I shot a glance at Adler who had a blank face. I figured that I'd just have to put my faith in my mother that she would come up with something to keep the situation under wraps and exit it without causing further harm. We'd have to move towards the things we wanted and not just away from the things we didn't.

"You should prepare what you want to bring with you in the case that you must leave quickly," Adler spoke softly, "and trust your mother. It's difficult and daunting to leave and a person must have a plan to ensure a safe exit because the separation is often the most dangerous time in these kinds of situations."

I knew deep inside that this wasn't a situation in which to act hastily or irresponsibly because one wrong move could have devastating consequences. There was no easy way or right away to go about any of that stuff and all I could do was trust that my mother would do the right thing.

"I'll fix things," my mother spoke almost like she was trying to convince herself more than she was trying to convince me, "I promise."

"All I can say is that you can't undo things or take them back," I muttered, "so take it as a lesson to do something positive in the future. At least that's what Adler constantly tells me."

"Who's Adler?"

"Oh, he's a guy I met recently."

I bit my bottom lip. I had slipped up and let my keeper be public knowledge. I was going to have to find a way to get out of it sooner or later because now two people knew about Adler. My mother would never believe me if I actually told her that I had such a thing called a *keeper*, also known as an invisible hero soldier part of the German Resistance during the Second World War who reminded me of Claus von Stauffenberg. Not a single chance.

"That's wonderful Joanie! I'm so happy that you've made yourself a new friend!" My mother seemed to be genuinely happy for me. "What is he like? Where did you meet him?"

"Adler is very intelligent," I muttered as I scrambled to make up something plausible to say about my ghostly friend, "and, uh, I met him on the bus."

"Oh dear Joanie," Adler giggled, "that was pretty bad."

"And he likes history, just like me. He reminds me a lot of my Adler doll..." I continued.

"If you only knew," Adler muttered, trying not to burst out laughing.

Feeling severely deflated mentally but not being able to feel it emotionally I grabbed my schoolbag and went up to my room. Wanting to talk to my mother hadn't really gone the way I'd expected and after the day I had at school I wanted to be alone with Adler for a while. I wanted to talk to him, but more than that I wanted to listen to him.

His stories were always very interesting and inspirational. Once up in my room I flopped down on my bed and stared at the blank ceiling. I thankfully didn't get any homework on the first day so I basically had a free pass for the rest of the day since I didn't have any chores to do.

"What do you want for your upcoming fourteenth birthday?" Adler asked as he browsed through my books.

"I don't want you to steal anything please," I replied in an emotionless voice.

"You know that I couldn't pay for it even if I tried!"

"I know, but seriously, I don't need anything. Just stick around please, because you are the one I need."

"You also know that as long as you don't make me disappear there's not much I can do."

I giggled because he said it with a joking taunt in his voice. He knew that I wouldn't make him disappeared but he also knew to stay on my good side because I *could* make him disappear.

"Please talk to me about the good times in your human life," I tried to lighten the mood.

Adler told me many stories of growing up in the 1920s and the 1930s and I attentively listened to him for the rest of the evening. I skipped dinner because I didn't want to interrupt him telling his stories. With Adler around time flew by extremely fast no matter what the situation.

Before I knew it my birthday had flown by, my mom had taken Rosanna and I to an ice cream shop and I'd gotten a few pieces of thrifty clothes and other items as gifts. My favorites were my camouflage cargo pants and a new khaki schoolbag. I'd had a good day and life had been quiet and peaceful for a while. The holidays also flew by and and it was unbelievable how soon the first week of the new semester arrived at Bluepond District High School.

Rosanna and I had ended up spending a lot of time together at school as we were really the only two students from Redmont who shared several classes together during the second semester. I'd successfully survived the first one, and Adler hadn't even whispered all the answers to me on the exams. He'd keep me from having a complete meltdown as a result of my constant anxiety, but the rest I'd done it all on my own!

I learned that Rosanna had recently moved to Bluepond after always having lived in small towns and she wasn't adapting too well to such a big city. As far as I knew Rosanna hadn't seen Adler again and there was no evidence that anybody else had seen him either since that one time at the beginning of the school year.

Adler never had to zap Dylan again with jolts of electricity of wicked proportions as Dylan never bothered me again. A lot of people asked a lot of questions as to what exactly had happened at my desk that particular afternoon that it all went down but nobody had a good answer. Even Adler hadn't exactly comprehended what had happened. He had gotten angry as he was sensitive to injustice towards others and that was what had resulted from it. That was as close as any one of us could get to a half-decent answer, and it wasn't much of an answer at all.

When I lost focus and became anxious and disoriented, which I'll admit was more often than I would've liked, Adler was always right there to make sure that I didn't get caught up in corrupt ideologies and went completely off the rails for a second time.

He was with me in my every moment and that greatly helped me in immersing myself in agape and keeping the energy flow going so both of our energy fields could merge together and create some amazing things. Thus far the second semester of school was moving along as well as could be expected and I was very happy that things were thawing out but I had no reason to complain because the winter had been unusually mild.

"Sometimes I feel guilty making friends," I told Adler in a low voice as we both sat on my bed one morning, "because then I don't get to spend as much time with you as I'd like."

Adler patted me on the back without saying a word and gave me one of those compassionate glances like he always did during my moments of doubt.

"In the history of keepers, or at least what I know of them," Adler retorted softly as he looked straight into my eyes, "I'm the luckiest one because none of them have had the privilege to spend every moment of every day with somebody so amazing."

"You're getting ahead of yourself," I whispered as I giggled, "you're the amazing one."

"Seriously Joanie, I don't think that regular people have their keepers around *all* the time like this. You're intelligent, talented and interesting. You're a million times better than non-existence."

"Are you saying that I'm not a regular person? But I'm serious too Adler, I wouldn't be in this place if you didn't keep me walking in a straight line around the clock like this. I'm the lucky one!"

"You do realize that it's by you keeping our parallel energy fields flowing smoothly that I am doing this for you, right? We're a team, this goes both ways."

"We're a team and that's why I feel guilty to put you aside to hang out with other people or pursue other hobbies and that kind of stuff. You are the most amazing creature I have ever encountered. I want you there to be part of everything in my life."

"I am, and will always be. I want you to make other friends and to enjoy your human life Joanie. I'm still gonna be here afterwards."

"You know Adler, I've been thinking and realistically, if Rosanna saw you once it would be erroneous to believe that she'll never see you again. Heck, maybe she'll get to experience you the way I do."

"I agree with you, I have no reason to believe that it wouldn't be possible, but I'm quite certain that Rosanna thinks it's strange to see a soldier of the Second World War just like on TV."

"You can wear whatever civilian clothes that you want as long as I'm not at school, you know that! But at school I need Lieutenant Adler."

"Well, I suppose that if we want to find out if Rosanna will be able to see me again we should head to school!"

I still didn't like school, in fact I still *hated* school, but Adler always made it so much better. Soon after our conversation breakfast was being served so I went down and the morning routine proceeded as it usually did. I saved Adler some of that infamous bacon by shoving it in the pocket of my jeans underneath the table.

The single slice of bacon greased up that pocket for the rest of the day but at least Adler had the chance to enjoy a little piece of humanity that he otherwise wouldn't have access to. Seeing him enjoy the bacon was even more enjoyable than me actually eating the other food on my plate. *Side effects of being a keeper.* Since it was still so early in the day I decided to walk a few blocks to school and then take public transit the rest of the way instead of the usual school bus.

That way I would have a better opportunity to spend quality time with Adler doing nothing other than immersing ourselves in agape. It was hard for me to do that in the classroom because I had to devote most of my energy to focusing on the subject matter being taught and at home there was no telling what would happen.

It seemed like my mother no longer wanted to terminate things with Mike because I was under the impression that they'd worked through some of their problems as things were going smoothly and that bag I had packed was still hidden in my closet even months afterwards. I'd also told my mother about my idea and she'd even done the same thing.

I was definitely disappointed about that but those feelings had been pushed on the back burner with more important matters at hand, like successfully finishing my second semester which was harder than the first one. Adler was quite helpful in giving me tips and hints on various subjects but he insisted that I gave it my best anyway.

"The weather is so mild and beautiful today, do you want to head outside for a bagel and cookies during morning break?" I asked Adler as my first class of the day was coming to an end.

"Sure," Adler spoke softly as usual, "let's see if I'm going to appear to somebody and scare the life out of them again."

I wanted to laugh but I knew I needed to keep my cool during class so people wouldn't think that I was nuts or something because I seemingly talked to myself and laughed by myself when nothing was funny. They knew nothing about my keeper and despite my curiosity about his existence and abilities, I wanted to keep it that way.

"Too bad I didn't come into this world with a million dollars," Adler muttered to himself, "I feel guilty making you spend actual money for somebody who is invisible."

*You're real to me,* I wrote on a piece of paper and handed it to him before the bell rang. Adler took it and put it inside the pocket of his uniform to keep it as a memento, and probably to remind himself that he was actually real from time to time too.

After the bell rang swarms of students flooded the hallways but Adler and I got some cheap dry bagels from the vending machine and then went outside to the student meeting area, another little grassy area away from from the secluded area where Adler and I had previously eaten our lunch several months prior when he had appeared to Rosanna.

The place was filled with students but for once that was what I wanted. Both Adler and I wanted to know if somebody, anybody, was going to see or feel something. I knew that Adler wasn't a scary dude but I could imagine that seeing a Wehrmacht officer in the flesh could scare a teenager. Most students went across the street to smoke as it was illegal to smoke on school property but a few of them still dared to light cigarettes and stand by the side of the building to smoke them anyway. The punishments weren't a deterrent. Alana Overton was one of them.

She was standing there leaning against the building with her long shiny trampy hair blowing all over the place as a gentle breeze roamed through the trees on the other side of the fence. She thought that she was so much better than everybody else because she was good looking but wasn't that typical, even stereotypical, of someone who's never had to work a day in their life to earn the world?

All the guys might've liked her but her head was up in outer space and anybody who had a head on their shoulders knew that. Her brother Kevin had been much more intelligent and actually could've had something going for him if he hadn't been such a jerk with everyone who approached him.

All of the burnouts who thought they were cooler than everybody else leaning on the brick wall seemed to be oblivious to Adler and I standing a few feet away but when they saw Rosanna coming from the opposite direction they immediately began verbally attacking her. They hurled insults at her, said she was fat and ugly among other things, and it was obvious that it was ripping her heart to shreds. Like me, she had next to no self-esteem and she couldn't fight back.

"You need to defend Rosanna!" Adler commanded like he was giving a military order.

Defend Rosanna? Seriously? Me out of all people?! I was a complete nobody that was defenseless myself! I was just Joanie Bowen, the girl everybody knew from a group of underage kids who had crashed Kevin Overton's party and got it broken up by the police. But Rosanna was my friend and Adler was the voice of reason. I began doubting myself though, and doubt was toxic to the transfer to agape keeping Adler visible to me. Although I couldn't feel the emotional stress and anxiety that the current situation brought, a million and one things were swirling around my head and I felt the walls closing in on me. I wasn't brave enough to do that.

"Did you ever consider what would've happened to those people if I hadn't done something to help them during the Holocaust?" Adler spoke slowly with a voice filled with pain.

In that moment everything in the universe stopped turning, *literally*, and a giant hologram appeared on the wall of the school. I saw trainloads upon trainloads of people arriving into a concentration camp and being unloaded. I knew that they would be going to their deaths and for the first time it really sank in *deep* what Adler had actually done by saving even just a few them by getting them to countries of safety.

I looked in horror at the images in the hologram but also in awe at Adler's ability to project such a thing. I didn't know he could do that and by the look on his face he didn't know he could either. That was all it took to convince me to act. I fully understood the importance of standing up for those who couldn't defend themselves and I knew I had to gather the strength from somewhere to stomp over there and defend my friend's honor.

# EIGHT

In the past I had never really associated school and the Holocaust, but if I was convinced of one thing it was that no selfless act, no matter how small and no matter what the cost, went to waste somewhere in the order of the universe. It only took one push for a person to fall off the edge and one hand to pull them back. The hologram disappeared as soon as it had arrived and the world started spinning at high speed around me all over again.

"Hey! Stop that right now!" I shouted at the group harassing my friend, "Leave Rosanna alone!"

"What the hell do you want?" One of them snapped back, "Why the hell would you want to mingle with a loser like her?"

Rosanna was the shy and mousy type of person that was defenseless against merciless predators like those burnout kids and I definitely wasn't the brave type to put my foot down during times like those but I knew that Adler wouldn't let me *not* put my foot down for my friend.

"You shut your mouth and mind your own business! Leave Rosanna alone and get a hold of yourself!" I shouted angrily at the group of idiots.

Rosanna had walked away from all the commotion and quietly retreated to a bench near the doors to enter the south hallway while I was having a screaming match with a bunch of kids that I didn't even know. Me hurling insults didn't go over too well with Alana, whom, after just a few moments came racing towards me about to tackle me to the ground. She was much stronger than I was so I knew that I didn't stand a chance, and running wasn't an option either.

I looked over at Adler in pure fear just to catch one last glimpse of his beautiful face before feeling the pain. He gazed back at me reassuringly like nothing was about to happen and me getting my butt kicked wasn't imminent but I made the choice to keep the faith that forces greater than me were going to intervene because I really had nothing else to hold on to.

Right when I turned my head to look back at Alana and duck to avoid a blow to the head, Adler tackled Alana and sent her flying up against the brick wall. The school had been multiple feet away from where Adler and I had been standing, there was no way that a human could have pushed up another person like that, not even a strong military man!

Alana not only went flying a couple of feet away to a brick wall, but she also had went flying a couple of feet into the air! Only a supernatural force could have dealt such a blow and by the looks on the faces of the few people who had witnessed that, they clearly had no other explanation either.

After Alana hit the brick wall, and hit it hard, following Adler's forceful push her limp body came crashing down to the ground. For a moment I couldn't breathe, the oxygen had left me completely as I didn't know what Adler had done to her, but she then began to move and cry out in pain. After an incident like that, there was no way that she didn't have a few broken bones somewhere.

Following Adler's move a bunch of other students gathered around the scene and looked on with a mixture of awe and horror on their faces as faculty members came to Alana's rescue and started asking questions as to what had just happened. Everybody knew that a small fourteen-year-old girl like me could not have possibly pushed a much bigger girl like Alana Overton four feet into the air and onto a brick wall several more feet away!

Even I myself could not believe my own eyes! Yet everybody had seen it. I had seen it, Rosanna had seen it, the burnout junkies had seen it, but most of all Alana had *felt* it. There was no saying that it didn't happen a certain way when almost a dozen people had witnessed the event.  One problem that was much bigger than what had actually happened however, was finding a way to explain it and talk myself out of it.

I had no good answer to give as to how I could have pulled off a such a thing, because I hadn't done it to begin with. In that moment I did all I think of doing, and that was to look over at Adler and hope that he could come up with something plausible. Unfortunately he looked just as shocked as the rest of us did.

He totally hadn't expected things to go like that either and he clearly had no good explanation for what had happened any more than any one else did. Adler seemed to be very shocked and saddened by his own actions because he ended up letting himself slide to the ground without saying a word.

The ambulance ended up being called as Alana Overton had suffered a concussion, a whiplash, a broken ankle and a fractured wrist. If you asked me it was a small price to pay because Adler easily could have killed her with force of that magnitude. I knew that he had never wanted to hurt her, that he had only wanted to protect me by putting himself in between the two of us, but nobody could have anticipated the results of such an action.

Adler had always been largely unaware of his keeper powers hence he didn't know what could result of them and it was obvious that he felt incredibly guilty but in my heart I was still grateful to him for what he had done for me. The feelings of affection and gratitude I had for Adler were definitely more powerful than any of the negative feelings of guilt and anger at himself that he might have had following the incident and I knew he felt that because our emotions were connected.

On the other hand though, none of that solved the problem of finding a plausible explanation to the event once everyone on the scene was interrogated by the school personnel. At last I decided to not stress over what I was going to say too much because no explanation would've been plausible anyway.

"It was a ghost!" One high student rambled on in a fearful voice, "It was nothing other than a ghost! Fish face threw herself down on the ground and then Pixie just went flying over my head against the wall!"

"That's exactly what I saw too!" Another one added equally terrorized, "It was the ghost of a big Nazi! Everybody be careful!"

"I was never a member of the Nazi Party!" Adler grumbled at the comment that had only added insult to injury, "Being a German doesn't make me a bad guy!"

Once it was my turn to be asked questions I simply replied that I had ducked, which I had actually done, to avoid being potentially knocked out and that when I had gotten back up from my fetal position on the ground, Alana Overton was lying facedown on the pavement and I had no idea how she had gotten there.

That was also partially true, because quite frankly I hadn't seen that much from my vantage point and I definitely didn't know that something like that was going to happen. Even if I had decided to say it was Adler's doing, who would even believe something like that? School staff did what they had to do and I went to a different area to collect my thoughts.

"What the hell was that?!" Rosanna asked me in disbelief once she joined me in a more secluded spot of the property, "You can't tell me that you don't have some idea of what happened! I saw it with my own eyes!"

Once again all I could think of doing was looking over at Adler and praying that he'd give me a hint as to what I should say or what I should do. All he did was nod slightly, giving me the okay to tell Rosanna about the secret that I had kept to myself for a long time.

"My keeper did that," I admitted, not entirely sure of how she was going to react.

She was either going to believe me or laugh at me, but she

couldn't deny that something greater than all of us had been at work.

"Your keeper?" Rosanna asked mostly confused, but not necessarily not believing me.

"Yes," I replied trying to gauge her reaction, "my keeper."

"We've all heard the ancient legend but I never actually thought it was real."

"Neither did I, until my keeper came to me one horrible night, and he's been with me ever since. You know, he's that soldier dude you saw me sitting with a while back."

"That's incredible! Good for you Joanie, you and your keeper seem to have a very special bond."

"We do, he's flesh and bones with a heartbeat to me."

"I've heard of ghosts and guardian angels but they aren't like *that.*"

*That* obviously meant *Adler* because Rosanna looked straight into his eyes. There was no doubt in my mind that she could see him. Adler gently smiled at her as she looked up at him in awe, completely mystified and intrigued by his existence. Rosanna extended her arm out to Adler to touch him to make sure that he was real and in response he extended his arm towards her too and the two briefly held hands. Rosanna caught an enormous chill as she touched Adler's skin but it was short lived. Unlike other people that had caught chills, Rosanna's didn't last very long. She was touching Adler the same way I could without negative side effects.

"Don't worry," Adler spoke in an overjoyed tone of voice, "the chills will stop happening completely once your energy field gets synchronized with mine."

We were all in awe. The agape being exchanged between the three of us was so powerful that you could almost see it radiate all around us. The feeling within our circle was nothing short of pure absolute bliss. Rosanna reached out her hand to touch Adler's hand again just to remind herself that he was real and in response he pulled her closer to him and pressed her ear against his chest so she could listen to his heartbeat.

"You're actually just like a real person!" Rosanna couldn't believe what she was experiencing, "I've always been a believer in spirits greater than humans but I could never have imagined this!"

"Most of us don't Rosanna," Adler spoke softly as he smiled at Rosanna.

"But how can this be?"

"I have no solid answer, but I have a few theories."

"Tell me please."

"Energy cannot be created nor destroyed and since the soul is immaterial, it does not disappear like the physical body does. Atoms can exist in two different places at one time, be it the physical and non-physical worlds simultaneously. That means that I can both be here and not be here at once, sort've like being both dead and alive."

"Wow, that sounds a lot like Schrödinger's cat."

"It does. That's as best as I've come to be able to explain my existence after the endless hours or racking my brain and trying to make sense of everything."

"So I take it that the mysteries of life and existence aren't known to you."

"Nope, only what I've been able to observe here and the things that I've learned from my time as a soldier in a parallel universe, you know they are scientifically possible and they interact with each other!"

The parallel universe theory definitely filled in some of the blanks when it came to understanding Adler's existence. The theory of keepers suggested that I had completely created him from my own innermost soul yet he was so human in his own way with his own story. He's taken on a life of his own, and the idea that keepers were somehow related to an alternate reality definitely made things make more sense. He could exist in two different places at once, so he easily could've been a soldier in one universe while an alternate version of himself was a keeper in my world.

"I might not have believed this if I hadn't seen it with my own eyes," Rosanna admitted in awe, "but now I believe in this more than ever. The proof is right in front of my face."

"That's often the way it happens," Adler retorted in a neutral voice, "your eyes are opened only after something blows up in your face."

"So when I saw you sitting with Joanie at the picnic table you weren't some creepy old man she had as a boyfriend, you were her keeper all along."

"That's right!"

"I'm sorry that I even thought about something like that to begin with. That's so vile and disgusting and I sincerely apologize."

"That's alright Rosanna, with all the sexual predators out there I can't blame anyone for thinking the worst."

Adler didn't have a bad bone in him but I understood what he and Rosanna were talking about. All in all, I could always make Adler disappear if I became displeased with him but I didn't think that was going to happen anytime soon.

"I have another question," Rosanna went on, "why do I see you now and I've seen you once before but was completely oblivious to you the rest of the time?"

"My take on that is that the energy I feed off of in order to exist isn't constant, and the higher its degree of vibration is, the more materialized I become for a lack of a better way to put it."

"I can understand that, and it makes sense too. Well, now at least I'm glad I'm able to see you and interact with you. You're definitely majestic and amazing!"

"Thank you, and me too. Just earlier Joanie was going on and on about how she feels guilty that she doesn't spend all her time with me during the day but I reckon that won't be a problem anymore, at least not as long as I'm visible to you."

"Considering how you've just saved her from a fist fight and maybe something worst, I'd definitely want you around all the time too! And I reckon that you're probably the one who zapped that idiot Dylan in class too?"

"Yup, that was also me. I never meant to hurt anybody since I've come here, but I also acknowledge that by being Joanie's keeper I have a duty to protect her. I'm very sensitive to injustice and I cannot simply sit back and do nothing.”

“That’s perfectly understandable, uh, whatever your name is.”

“I’m Adler, and I know you’re Rose. I bet it’s kind of creepy knowing that I’ve heard every word you’ve ever told Joanie but it wasn’t done out of malice.”

“I know. It’s going to take some time getting used to this but it’s for the better I’m sure. Can you hear my thoughts?”

“Nope. I can’t hear anybody’s thoughts, not even Joanie’s. I can, however, feel her every emotion. I have no emotional feelings of my own but I can still feel the weight of things mentally.”

Rosanna listened attentively to what Adler had to say and she hung on to his every word just like I did. When she looked at him she was just as mystified and in awe the same way I’d always been too. As far as either one of us were concerned, Rose didn’t have a keeper, or at least she hadn’t met him or her yet. Maybe the innermost depths of her soul hadn’t created that keeper yet, I had no idea how exactly that all worked. I had no idea how my soul had even made Adler, that is *keeper* Adler, because I’d never even heard of such a thing as a keeper before mine showed up.

During my last class of the day I went to the computer room to “do some research” for a project but in reality I looked up online information about keepers. Dozens of websites said dozens of different things but all of them said that keepers don’t always manifest themselves in the form of a person and often don’t manifest themselves at all.

A bunch of websites said that keepers were the “proof” that our loved ones were still around in some way even if they were dead, without supplying actual *proof* of anything but keepers were never believed to be departed souls to begin with. One particular website did mention the parallel universes theory that Adler had also talked about but that stuff was too complicated for me to understand.

The webpage seemed to imply that somehow once a person’s soul opened the door to a keeper who manifests itself as a person it’s possible for two parallel universes to interact and things to warp and cross over in some way. I didn’t really understand but it did seem plausible considering what I had observed and experienced. Or maybe I was just dead just like Adler and he was around to help me realize that and come to terms with it. What I did know out of all the ideas that had been put inside my head was the fact that I was getting ahead of myself.

After the school day ended Rosanna and I, accompanied by Adler of course, decided to go down to the boardwalk and hang around the park for a while and do nothing other than enjoy life and reflect upon it since it was such a beautiful and mild day. The three of us bought only two tickets for the ferris wheel and as only two people could sit on the benches of the pod at once, Adler had to sit on the floor next to our feet but he didn't seem to mind.

If he had wanted he could have easily levitated and floated next to the pod while we went around the wheel but he enjoyed being human as much as he could way too much to start doing things like floating around in the air or walking on water or some other weird things that nobody could understand because his existence straddled the line of the metaphysical world and ours didn't.

Sometimes mysteries were frustrating but honestly, the mystery behind Adler's existence was what made it so beautiful. Mysteries weren't meant to be solved, but they were meant to be pondered and reflected upon. The answers were really only interpretations and they wouldn't be so intriguing, and much less infinite, if we had all the answers. If Adler's existence had been fully revealed to me, I never would have been able to experience all of those intimate moments with him doing nothing but contemplating life and appreciating the present moment.

"I remember the last time Joanie and I sat in a pod like this, except that I wasn't on the floor," Adler spoke softly with a hint of humor in his voice as we reached the top of the wheel, "we had a deep conversation about life and my existence."

"I remember that day so vividly," I replied deep in thought, "I remember every moment we've spent together so vividly."

I really did. I reached out and took Adler's hand into mine and squeezed it tightly. I was eternally grateful to have him in my life because the more time we spent together the more I came to see how much he had helped me right from the start, and not to mention all the times that he'd saved my butt!

"How many people know that you have a keeper so far?" Rosanna asked me as our pod went back down the ferris wheel.

"So far, just the three of us," I muttered, "but I have the impression that it won't be like this for very long."

"The people who witnessed that incident at school will wonder what happened for the rest of their lives."

"And good luck trying to tell them that my *keeper* did that, they'd just make even more fun of me than they already do. More than that though, I wouldn't want to force Adler to turn into some violent maniac zapping people with jolts of electricity every time they displeased me or hassled me."

"I can't say that I'd mind a few idiots being zapped from time to time. It might keep them in line."

The three of us burst out laughing at once. There were indeed more than a few people who deserved a couple of shocks without being thrown three feet in the air onto a brick wall.

"You know," Adler spoke softly after a moment of silence, "I feel very guilty for hurting Alana."

"Don't," Rosanna protested boldly, "you would feel so much guiltier if you had let Alana hurt Joanie."

"You're right Rosie, thanks for reminding me of that."

"Everybody needs a friendly reminder from time to time Adler, even keepers."

A beautiful smile appeared on Adler's face. He knew that Rosie was right. As our pod went around the ferris wheel another time I couldn't help but let my fingers pass through Adler's amazing keeper hair glowing in the sunlight. His mysterious atomic existence had probably gone up another level of vibration because he hadn't been *that* vibrant in the past.

"You both seem to be adapting to life in Bluepond quite well," Adler commented after a brief moment of silence, "and Joanie you're undoing all that hard work I put into my hair this morning!"

"We have each other," Rosanna added in a gentle tone of voice.

"And we have you," I added, "my apologies about your hair."

After the ferris wheel ride was over we all hung out for an hour or two by the boardwalk together, Rosanna and I said goodbye to each other and we each went our separate ways. I hopped onto public transit and only paid for one person despite that two came along and stopped by a fast food restaurant before walking the rest of the short way home. By the time I got there and everything was said and done it was just passed seven.

Before I could hang out with my friends or be granted my own free time I had to have all of my homework done on top of my household chores and anything else that might have been required of me. I knew that all of those things were to teach me how to handle responsibilities and to prepare me for the next stage of life but they all definitely felt like drab considering that my dad had never made me do anything like that before my family was ripped to shreds. At our old place all I had been required to do was clean up after myself and wash my own clothes. I didn't have to clean up after everybody else. That was plain annoying.

"I know that it's probably impolite of me to ask this of you," I told Adler as the two of us sat on my bed to unwind, "but could you do my homework and my chores while I call my aunt Kendra?"

I gave my school assignments to Adler who happily read them over and wrote a beautiful report that I simply needed to copy in my own handwriting while I spoke for just under two hours with my aunt Kendra. After all I didn't feel too bad about giving Adler my school assignments because I knew that it gave him a little sense of being human, and he liked that probably more than he should have.

"Tell me about some of your keeper philosophy about life please."

"Absolutely, but are you sure it's not going to make you fall asleep?"

I giggled lightly and Adler joined in with a couple of afterlife jokes before we returned to being serious. I listened attentively to his otherworldly wisdom as he spoke in his usual calm and soothing voice.

"Okay, so since I've been here I've come to realize that it's okay to not have all the answers," Adler was obviously deep in thought as he spoke, "you'll be given all the information you need to move forward when the time is right. Healing comes in due time, but it's what you do with that time that matters most. It's erroneous to compare your life to others, it's like apples and oranges. Joanie, you know all of this stuff already. Are you still awake?"

"Of course I'm still awake Adler," I replied giggling, "I could listen to you for hours, even if you only repeat stuff that I already know."

"No one is in charge of your life except you," Adler went on, still pensive, "and all of the problems in the world don't fall on your shoulders. You're not responsible for all the pain in the world, or even in your own life."

"You sound like my aunt Kendra again. She used to tell me that if you took away something constructive and positive from a situation then it was all worth it." I replied, equally deep in thought. "She also said that just because something has ended doesn't mean that it never should have been. It's easier to say than to believe though."

"My keeper clarity tells me that it is absolutely true, but you should go to sleep now Joanie if you don't want your doomsday alarm clock to wake up in the morning."

I knew that Adler was right, he was always right, but I didn't want to sleep. I wanted to hear more of his philosophy, even if deep down inside I knew all of it already.

"I'm not ready to go to sleep right now," I protested, "I want to hear more of what you have to say first!"

"Alright dear," he replied softly, "but I promise you that it's nothing that you haven't already heard before!"

"Reminders never hurt."

"Okay, here's something else for you. What's worth the prize at the end of the line is always worth the fight, and even if you don't reach your goal, you lived, you loved, you grew and you moved forward."

"Right now you sound *exactly* like my aunt Kendra, are you

sure you can't read her thoughts?"

"I promise that I can't hear her thoughts, but I am convinced that her and I are cut from the same cloth. Why don't you enlighten me with some of her philosophy now?"

"She religiously believes that even a single loving touch, a smile, or a kind word has the power to completely turn a life around."

"Keep going, I'm listening!"

"Never give up on something you really want and believe in yourself because it's easier to persevere than to regret."

"Remember that every flower must grow through dirt and every diamond was once just some big ugly chunk of rock."

"My aunt Kendra also religiously told me that direction is so much more important than speed because a heck of a lot of people are going nowhere fast."

Adler smiled at me softly, I knew he wanted me to take my own advice and I knew he was right. For some reason it was always easy to give others advice but on the other hand it was difficult to be on the receiving end of that same advice.

"I'm not keeping you as a hostage here for you to do all the work. We're a team, and I need to put into it what I want out of it too," I said out loud, mostly as a reminder to myself, "my aunt *also* told me that the takers may eat better but the givers sleep better. I honestly wish my aunt could meet you."

"If we keep up this energy flow and live according to the principles we've set for ourselves tonight, there is no reason why she shouldn't be able to see me at some point. If she believes in her heart that I exist, then I'll exist to her too."

"It's like your soul is immaterial but we can make it material by believing."

"That sounds about right. Faith is a decision you make to believe in things unseen, and in life you've gotta have faith."

"I'm looking forward to discovering what the future holds as long as you're by my side Adler. Thanks for fixing my life."

"I didn't fix anything Joanie, and there's still so much that's still ahead of us. And I didn't make you do anything either. You made the choices you did all on your own, so be proud of yourself Joanie, this is all on you! You should go to sleep now, there will be plenty more wisdom in the morning. I'll be right here when you wake up."

# NINE

Over time Rosanna and Adler became quite close even though I was the one doing nearly all the work to sustain the energy field. That was really the only downside. The energy field needed in order for Adler to exist was static and could never be consistent. The amount of energy flowing in and out of me at any given moment on any given day was never the same and because of that Rosanna couldn't always see Adler or feel his presence the same way I did.

She could give it her best shot to put in as much energy of her own as she could but Adler still wasn't her keeper, he was mine. Subsequently, when my level of agape was too low Adler was only visible to me. He was *my* partner after all. There was no being seen by Rosanna, giving electric shocks to morons in class or throwing people up against buildings in such a situation.

My only excuse for not giving the agape my all at all times was that I also had to focus on reality and not always the mysterious metaphysical world that Adler was part of. I still kept enough focus to have him with me at all times but I unfortunately couldn't always put other people's needs ahead of my own so Rosanna had to pass up on interacting with my keeper from time to time but she understood that, though I knew that she often longed for a keeper of her own.

One particular mild spring day however, the beautiful fantasy that Adler and I had created for ourselves came crashing down around us. It was a record high of 15°C in Bluepond and Adler and I were peacefully sitting by ourselves in the backyard, soaking up the sunshine and the often short-lived dry weather of a coastal climate.

The meteorologists on TV who predicted the weather like they were the ones in control of it kept on saying that the seasonal temperature would be colder than usual, so 15°C was absolutely perfect weather for my personal taste. The early afternoon sun was shinning brightly over my skin when my mom came barging out of the doors and onto the deck where Adler and I were both relaxing. Whatever was wrong, my mom looked pretty upset about it.

"Joanie, I just got the phone off the phone with Rosanna's mom," she tried to sound as calm as possible even though she was obviously distraught, "and what she told me concerned me greatly."

Was something wrong with Rosanna? Adler and I shot a quick look at each other hoping that whatever was going on, it wasn't something absolutely terrible. Rosanna was my best friend and I cared about her deeply, and whatever my mother was talking about now concerned me too.

"Rosanna's mother Rebecca is concerned about, well," my mom struggled to find the right words to express herself, "what she referred to as an imaginary boyfriend that you and Rosanna share."

*Excuse me, what?!* Adler and I shot a second glance at each other with both eyebrows raised in shock and confusion. I didn't know how to react and even less what to say in response to what I had just been told. How did Rosanna's mom come to the conclusion that we had an imaginary boyfriend? Adler had never been my boyfriend to begin with! That was was weird and gross and wrong!

"What?" I asked after a brief moment of silence.

"The way Rebecca explained it to me is that she found out about her daughter's infatuation with this so-called imaginary boy when she heard Rosanna speaking to you over the phone," my mom replied in a concerned tone of voice, "not that she was spying, she just happened to overhear a few minutes of conversation between the two of you and she confronted Rosanna about it."

"And?"

"And Rosanna told her everything. She told her all about this mutual obsession with this imaginary friend of yours and Joanie, I'm concerned about you."

"Why? What does Rosanna's so-called imaginary friends have to do with me?"

"Because her mother was adamant in telling me that you're the one who has gotten Rosanna consumed with this idea. She said that Rosanna herself told her that she went along with this game of yours so she could make you feel better because you were having a hard time coping with life here."

I knew even less what to say or how to react to that. Why would Rosanna lie like that? She had seen Adler, touched him even! She couldn't say that it was all just a game and that it wasn't real, that Adler wasn't real!

"Adler is real mom," I protested, "he's my keeper!"

It was only after the words came out of my mouth that I realized I shouldn't have said them. At the same time it felt wrong of me to deny Adler's existence when he meant so much to me. I glanced over at him but I couldn't decipher the look on his face.

"Honey, I support you having friends and connecting with your inner spirituality," my mom went on trying to be as gentle as possible with me, "but Joanie, this Adler person isn't real."

"Yes he is!" I protested.

"Joanie," Adler spoke softly to me, "let it go."

*Absolutely not!*

"Mom, listen to me," I continued, "in just a moment Adler's soul is going to pass through your body and when it does you'll feel a chill.”

As I spoke those words Adler walked right through my mother and just as I had told her, she caught a chill. She didn’t know how to react or what to say about that. The look on her face indicated pure shock but she still refused to believe that Adler was real.

“Joanie, this is delusional,” she went on in a confused tone of voice, “none of this is real.”

“Alright, well, whatever,” I muttered angrily just to shut her up, “none of this is real.”

“Honey, tomorrow I’ll make some phone calls to get you the appropriate services you need. I promise you that everything is going to be okay.”

“Oh my goodness! Mom!”

“Joanie, please listen to me. I know that in the past you weren’t able to cope with the divorce and your father and I have neglected to see your point of view and now with all the recent life changes you might be confused, but honey these delusions are not the answer.”

“Look mom, right now I really don’t give a damn that you have regrets about the way things turned out! I am not going to therapy! I don’t need to talk to a stranger about my problems, I need my family!”

“Yes, you’re going to therapy Joanie, I’m not giving you a choice! I’m not a professional when it comes to mental health but I acknowledge my part in this and I’ll do everything in my power to make sure that your wellbeing is a priority.”

“You’re a liar! When has my wellbeing been your priority since you’ve been with Mike? Do you not see that he abuses you, and all of us for that matter? Yet you keep running back to him every single time! I still have the emergency bag in my closet that you made me pack *months* ago and guess what? Your promise that things would be different was just another lie because you went running right back into Mike’s arms! *You* are the one who needs therapy!”

Both my mother and I were surprised by my outburst. I had never been the type to be confrontational, I’d always been the girl who cried all by herself in her room. Adler had a blank expression on his face, but no matter what happened I knew that he would make it okay somehow.

"Every parent makes mistakes Joanie," my mother's voice was cracking as she tried to remain calm, "I made a mistake! I've made many and now I'm trying to make up for them!"

"And how is that exactly? By always picking an abusive man over me or sending me to therapy when you know absolutely *nothing* about me or my feelings?!"

"I'm sorry for what happened in the past, and I know that this has hurt you a lot, but you need professional help to get through these dark times!"

Before my mother and I could engage in a full-fledged screaming match, Adler tapped on my shoulder and gave me one of those looks telling me to quit it. As much as I wanted to scream at her and get in her face about all the pain she had caused me, I knew that it wouldn't actually help anything.

"Don't prolong something that's already over," Adler whispered to me in his usual tender voice.

I took Adler's wise words to heart and shut my mouth, but I also subsequently got up and stormed upstairs into my room. Passing by the kitchen to reach the stairwell I noticed Aaron sitting at the table, absolutely speechless as he had obviously heard the commotion and yelling outside for a few brief moments. He had always been aloof and distant, you rarely ever saw him except for breakfast, but I didn't even acknowledge his existence as I ran up the stairs and loudly slammed my bedroom door behind me.

I hadn't even let Adler pass through the doorway but considering he could walk right through walls, it wasn't a problem for him. I flopped down on my bed and rolled over onto my back to look at the ceiling and calm myself down before I took things too far, something I usually had a bad habit of doing.

"Joanie, agape," Adler muttered in an urgent tone of voice, "right now!"

For a moment I had to really focus more than anything on feeding Adler's energy flow and momentarily putting aside my own emotions that were overwhelming me. I knew that it was crucial to keep Adler with me because ultimately he was the one who was going to make me feel better about the whole situation. I took a deep breath and found the agape deep inside of me and did my best to connect to it and sustain it. The energy field kept on crashing every time I tried to raise it up to a higher level but Adler had enough energy to nullify my negative emotions and replace them with an inner calmness and serenity nonetheless.

After several tries I was able to completely indulge in the blissful agape and was subsequently able to sustain the energy field at a comfortable level for both Adler and I. During the dozen minutes it took to get the agape just right nobody had come upstairs barging into my room whatsoever, but I could hear some commotion downstairs. I couldn't hear too well, but it was either my mother arguing with Aaron or Mike had come back from his outing and he'd been told about my imaginary boyfriend and the long list of inflammatory comments that had been said.

"I haven't felt this kind of pain in a long time," Adler whispered in an exasperated tone of voice, "not since I first found out about the Final Solution."

"I'm sorry if I upset you by bringing back bad memories from the war," I whispered softly to him, "but I feel better now that I let that out."

"Don't you worry Joanie, you've done me no harm. It simply hurts me to see you in so much pain, to *feel* that kind of pain coming from you."

"I should just take that bag out of my closet and leave once and for all because nobody here is interested in remedying the situation. Just you and me against the world, it can't be worst that this existence."

"Joanie, you're fourteen years old! You are in no situation to make it on your own!"

"I swear that my parents hate me sometimes. My father walked away and never gave me a second thought and my mother would much rather hold an abuser in her arms than her only child!"

Adler did not speak. All he did was hold me in his arms and

wipe away my tears because he knew that there was absolutely nothing he could say to alter my feelings, but his amazing keeper powers did put me in a state of bliss once I was able to properly sustain the energy field. My mind and body relaxed but the relief was only superficial. The thoughts and the trouble still lingered even though I couldn't feel their effects anymore.

"I can promise you that your parents don't hate you Joanie," Adler spoke softly once he determined that the coast was clear.

"It certainly feels that way sometimes," I muttered emotionlessly.

"I hear you my dear, and they've absolutely done you wrong, but they don't hate you."

"I don't hate them either even though sometimes I swear it would be easier if I did! People are quick to dismiss me as just a hormonal and dramatic teenager but I honestly don't know how to process both of my parents turning their backs on me the way they did at the time I need them the most. My mother suffocates me and sabotages me constantly and then she turns around and tells me that *I* have a problem."

Sure, my life had plenty of problems. I had difficulty at school sometimes, I had a huge problem with Mike and his abuse, I was unhappy with living in Bluepond and I'd just lost the one and only friend I'd made. None of those things made me crazy, neither one of them warranted to be dropped off at a therapist's office and only welcomed back home when *I* had been fixed. I was not the problem!

"How do they expect me to spread my wings when they oppress me?" I pondered out loud to Adler, "My father made himself a new family that I'm not a part of and my mother wants to hear absolutely nothing of what I have to say. Aaron is basically just an unapproachable ghost in the shadows and you are a real ghost of some sort. I feel like I don't even know my own people and truthfully I don't think I know myself."

I sighed loudly and let my head flop over Adler's shoulder. It rested uncomfortably against the edge of his shoulder board for a few moments. Despite that I'd bought him some civilian clothes I much preferred seeing him in his military uniform. It comforted me to see him dressed as a Wehrmacht officer — one who saved vulnerable people — because I definitely felt like the world around me was a battlefield. At least the world *inside* of me was a battlefield. I closed my eyes and zoned out. I felt absolutely no pain and no anger inside of Adler's aura.

"What were your parents like Adler?" I asked after another moment of silent contemplation.

"They were the absolute best parents I could have ever asked for," my keeper's voice was tender as he reminisced about his parents, "I can't imagine what it must have been like for them when I didn't return from the war. They survived the destruction left behind by the Great War, and then a few decades later I died in another war. I hope there's never another war like that."

Adler's voice was cracking up towards the end of the sentence and it was as though he was about to cry. I put my arm around his shoulder in return to comfort him the same way he had done to me when I was upset earlier.

"I'm sorry," I whispered to him, "I know I probably shouldn't have asked something like that. I know that the war has left you with many lingering scars."

"It's fine, you're forgiven," Adler reassured me, "it's important that things like this are discussed. A society will not overcome its problems if nobody talks about them."

"You know that I'll always listen to you no matter what you want to say. We're a team, we're in this together."

"Joanie, in all honesty, I'm not sure that this feeling of serenity is always such a good thing. Nobody can move forward if they don't leave their comfort zones, and it's when we become too comfortable that the biggest problems arise."

Our conversation was interrupted by my mother barging into my room and making the door slam behind her. I sighed loudly because I knew too well that another speech about how I was just a problem child who needed therapy was coming. My mother sat on the edge of my bed next to me and by the look on her face I knew that impending doom was coming sooner than I expected.

"Joanie," my mom spoke softly, trying to gauge my reaction but I cut her off.

"I'm not interested in any more of your crap," I muttered angrily, "you and Mike and Aaron can just shove it because I'm done!"

"Joanie watch your language! You need help and I'll make sure that you get the appropriate services to deal with this phase that you're going through."

"Phase? You think that this is just a phase?"

"Joanie, calm down and stop this nonsense. You need some professional help and your father and I have made arrangements to get you some."

"Oh don't bring my father into this. He's not around anymore, he has no say in this!"

"Joanie, we are trying to help you. You need a break from what you've been going through and your father and I both think it would be in your best interest if you went and lived with him for a while."

"What?"

How in the world did they think that I would be okay with something like that? How did my mother think that shipping me off to a man who had basically become a complete stranger would solve anything? How did my father think that giving me a room in his big house would somehow make up for everything that had happened? Adler squeezed my hand into his but his kind gesture did not reassure me the way that I'd hoped it would.

"You will be going to live with your father for a little while, until things are better," my mother replied in a more authoritarian tone of voice, "and you'll be leaving imminently so pack your bags."

"Looks like you'll finally fulfill your promise to make me use that rescue bag in my closet," I grumbled sarcastically.

Adler put his hand on my shoulder, signaling me to cut it out because I had no further say in the matter. As angry as I was, and as angry as I wanted to be, there was nothing I could do and I knew that. I got the impression that both my father and Mike also knew about my apparent delusions. It would just be a matter of time before more people knew about my so-called insanity because Rosanna would probably be forced to go to therapy too, and eventually I would be the laughingstock of the entire country.

My mother left without saying anything more but she left a coldness that lingered in the atmosphere. I suspected that it had probably been Mike who'd convinced her of the cleaver idea that their lives would be better if I wasn't around. That honestly didn't surprise me, I was only surprised that he hadn't convinced her of that sooner.

"You might not understand this Adler," I began in a shaky voice, "but I want to be with you, in another world, in another life, far away from the drama of humanity. Far away from conflict and wars in some parallel universe where there is nothing but peace and tranquility. I don't want to live anymore."

"No, I understand you completely," Adler's voice was softer than usual, "but believe me when I tell you that you don't want to go down that road. Being stuck somewhere between life and death in some weird, restricted and overly complicated state of being is nothing to wish for. The best days of your life haven't happened yet, so don't punish yourself or deprive yourself of something wonderful that hasn't had the chance to come your way yet."

"Nothing good ever comes my way, not anymore. I've lived my good life once upon a time but that's over now."

"You don't know that."

"Then please convince me otherwise. I'm right here. I have plenty of time to listen."

"Remember our talk about your aunt Kendra's philosophy of life? I think that this is the moment where you need to really hang on to that and have faith."

"It's much easier said that done to have faith. I don't feel like I have anything to believe in."

"Maybe that's your cue to search your soul and find something to believe in."

I let my head rest on Adler's shoulder again and smiled as I looked up at him in admiration. He always knew how to go about making me feel better. I did not want to go live with my father because I'd only be walking into another house full of strangers but maybe a change of scenery wouldn't be the worst thing. I knew that remedying a situation wasn't always possible no matter how much people wanted to, and that sometimes walking away was the best option. Starting anew elsewhere was sometimes the only option.

I did not know if I would be dealt a good hand or a bad one but I had no say in the matter so I could only hold on to Adler's hand and trust that he would find a way no matter what. He had found a way to help all of those Jews during the Holocaust, certainly he would find a way to help me too.

"Do you believe in God?" I asked Adler.

"Of course I do," he replied as though I'd been supposed to know that, "do you?"

"I don't know honestly. I've never really asked myself that question before."

"I encourage you to contemplate it, it's not something that will hurt you in any way."

"But I don't know where to start Adler."

"How about you start by talking directly to God? All faiths teach that God is almighty and if you believe that's true then certainly God is mighty enough to answer you."

"And how do I know what God's reply to my question is supposed to be?"

"That's something that is between you and God, there's no right or wrong answer. God works in mysterious ways so open up your heart to that conversation and follow it. God will bring you where you need to be in due time."

"Thanks for the words of wisdom, *again*."

"You know that I'll give you my two cents as long as I'm around. I don't know if I'm immortal somewhere in a parallel universe because I've already died here in this world, but until whatever comes next happens, I'm right here with you."

"Maybe the Many Worlds Theory is true after all. I don't know, all of this is beyond me. I'm not sure how to reconcile everything that's happening at once."

"I don't think we're supposed to have all the answers Joanie. Even if we did, you're not asking the right person because I'm just a soldier, not a scientist! There's no fun in knowing everything either!"

The two of us let the energy from inside us overflow everywhere to the point that it could almost be seen radiating all over the room. That energy never got old, it felt just as good each and every time. It was no different with Adler's wisdom. It didn't matter how many times he would repeat something, his words were just as breathtaking the tenth time as they were the first time.

After our little pep talk my keeper helped me pack up my few belongings, but in truth he did most of the work while I loafed around asking him a bunch of questions about existence and just about any other topic that entered my brain.

# TEN

Downstairs Mike and my mother had tidied up the house and made it look pretty in anticipation of my father's arrival later in the evening. I knew that I should have thought that it was beautiful but in reality I was disgusted. It was nothing more than another superficial ploy to make everything look good and to cover up the evil hiding beneath. The more time went on the more I could see right through everything.

Adler's guidance and wisdom had really opened my eyes to the true nature of the situation and although he couldn't make me feel less helpless and like a pawn in a giant game of chess, he did make me see the silver lining in everything. I wanted to do more than just see the silver lining in something though, I wanted to resist. I wanted to make a tangible difference in some way, though I did not really know what that would be yet.

I sat on my luggage by the door in the kitchen and waited for my father to arrive. I didn't know if he was going to bring his new wife or his new family but I didn't really want to see them. I wasn't up for another lecture or anything of the sort. In fact I didn't want to talk to anybody. I'd make an exception for Adler, however.

He was the only person that I needed and in truth the only one that I *wanted* by that point. I had no reaction when my father's blue SUV pulled up into the driveway. I hadn't seen that vehicle in a long time, an eternity it felt like to me, but I had no urge to get up and go running towards it. I felt nothing. No emotions. No thoughts of my own. Some strange acceptance of the situation swept over me. I didn't know if that was Adler's doing or not, but I knew that things were probably better that way.

My father got out of his SUV and walked towards the door with something in his hands. I couldn't see what it was from where I was sitting but once my mother and Mike let him in I saw that it was a box of my favorite chocolates. He handed it to me and opened his arms to give me a hug but I didn't move an inch.

The look on his face indicated anger and disappointment but it didn't faze me. Going outside and taking a long drive in bad weather was the last thing I wanted to do but I knew that I didn't have a choice. Adler signaled me to get up and get moving as he looked outside, like he could somehow foresee the future, or at least *feel* something that I couldn't.

"It looks pretty bad out there," Adler commented to himself as he looked outside the living room window.

My father looked nothing like himself. He'd gotten much thinner, leaner, shaved his beard that he'd had for as long as I remembered and traded in his jeans for some expensive dress pants. He looked much older too, the lines in his face had doubled since the last time I'd seen him. The only thing that remained the same were his grey-blue eyes but sadly I no longer knew the man whom they belonged to. Even thinking of him as my father seemed strange. The man that had walked through that door was not my dad.

"Come on Joanie, let's take a little drive before going back home," my father proposed in a soft voice, "we can talk and I'll listen to whatever you have to say."

After a brief moment of futilely wanting to delay the inevitable I finally accepted my dad's offer. I put on my jean jacket that I'd left on the back of a chair when I came down and draped it over my shoulders before grabbing some of my luggage and putting it in the SUV. Both of my parents and Mike helped put my few bags in the vehicle before attempting to give me a hug but I refused their advances. They were just for show anyway, and I was tired of the circus.

The grim clouds reflected my mood in that moment. The weather out there had definitely gone from a record high to the calm right before a wicked storm. The angry clouds only got darker and as they moved over Bluepond they completely obstructed the remaining sunlight. The weather did what it pleased and in the Maritimes those rainstorms were often merciless.

Before getting into the SUV my mother called all of us back inside for a few moments as she went down into the basement to get my winter gear that had been stored away and that everyone had forgotten about until that last minute. At that point I knew that I'd be gone for a couple of months, maybe even an entire school year.

My father looked outside the window from a distance for a few moments as he walked by and I swore that he saw Adler's reflection in the window. He stopped abruptly in his tracks and by the look on his face I knew that he had seen something, or *someone*, that wasn't supposed to be there but he didn't say a word about it. I figured that he didn't say a word about what he saw because he didn't know what he saw. Maybe he thought that he was becoming just as crazy as I was!

"What did you see outside?" I asked my father after a few moments of silence.

"I thought that a guy in an old military uniform was standing in the front yard," my dad was caught off-guard by the question but it confirmed what I thought, "but it turns out that there wasn't. It might've been just a peeping Tom passing by looking to see something, I've heard about several such incidents on the news."

"What did he look like?"

"Nothing. He didn't look like anything because he wasn't there."

My father knew that I was onto him and I could tell by his tone of voice that he was getting anxious. He knew deep down inside that he'd seen Adler even if he didn't want to admit it to himself.

The peeping Tom from the news excuse wasn't going to work on me.

"Well, obviously you saw *somebody*. You've just admitted to it!"

"You're trying to trick me into telling you that I saw your friend Adler, aren't you Joanie?"

"Did you?"

"I'll tell you the truth darling, I don't know what I saw."

"But you saw *something*."

"Yes."

My mother came back up with my winter gear and interrupted our conversation. Despite the kind of winters we had in the Maritimes, nobody I knew took out their winter gear prior to that first major snow storm. My father grabbed the bag, took out his car keys from his pocket and the two of us went outside one more time. I got into the front seat of the SUV and Adler sat right behind me. When we pulled out of the driveway it started drizzling slightly but it soon started to get a lot worst. The downpour increased by the second it seemed as we went driving down towards the boondocks of Bluepond.

I glanced over at Adler who was sitting quietly in the backseat. He didn't speak a word about whether or not my dad had seen him but we all knew that he had. Just for a fraction of a second Adler had materialized enough for my father to see his reflection in the window. He didn't want to admit it to himself that what he had seen was indeed real but he couldn't deny it either and it was apparent that he was struggling with a moral dilemma as we drove further into the darkness.

Although Adler could soothe my emotions, he couldn't alter my thoughts and I had a huge lump in my throat about the whole thing. I'd never wanted to go to begin with, but the longer I sat in that front seat the more uneasy I became.

"Don't let me go," I whispered to Adler as I reached for his hand that he'd laid gently on my shoulder.

The rain was pouring out there and the sky was as dark as night even though it was still early in the evening. It rained so much that it was blinding to us as we drove, nobody saying a word to each other. So much for our little chat, he wasn't interested in opening his mind to Adler's existence.

After a few minutes of very poor visibility my dad mentioned that he wanted to turn around and bring me back home for the evening and attempt the drive a second time in the morning, but that too was going to be tricky because we could barely see the road in front of us and every now and then out of nowhere a set of headlights passed by at high speed.

My father was apprehensive about stopping on the side of the highway and decided to wait until he could make a proper U-turn somewhere that wasn't in the middle of the road instead. He kept his calm but it was obvious that he was stressed out, and maybe even afraid, and I could relate because I shared the same sentiment inside even though Adler prevented me from *feeling* them normally. I might not have been able to emotionally feel the fear, or anything for that matter, but I was still very much aware of the tension in the atmosphere around me.

Out of nowhere the vehicle started to swerve and my dad struggled to regain control. I squeezed Adler's hand to comfort myself but deep down inside I doubted what he could do to help us in a situation beyond anyone's control. He couldn't control the weather. The weather wasn't like life, it couldn't wait and you couldn't make it change course.

The SUV went from one side of the road to the other and back for a few moments before it became apparent to me that my dad wouldn't be able to recover. The best possible outcome was landing upside down in a ditch somewhere along a lonely road on the outskirts of town but as I looked at the road ahead I knew that we probably wouldn't be so lucky.

A lump formed in my throat as I thought that maybe it would be my last car ride. Maybe in the afterlife I could be a keeper like Adler, and heck it might be fun to give a couple of electric shocks to those who do wrong from time to time. Maybe the next person who had Adler as a keeper could also have me as a ride along, if things worked that way. It was still hard for me to fathom how *my* soul had somehow created someone like Adler.

There was no way he had come from an innermost part of me, he was from another world and there was no telling me otherwise. Maybe in the next life, even in a parallel universe maybe, I would find all of the answers to his mysterious existence. I swallowed hard as I saw a white dot in the distance on the road ahead and as it got closer I quickly realized that it was a set of headlights headed straight in our direction.

The tractor trailer in front of us was swerving too and struggling to stay on the road. I could clearly see the truck headed straight for us in a head-on collision despite the rain. Or maybe I imagined what the truck looked like. Maybe it was all a side effect of knowing what was about to happen to you and some sort of end of life vision right before you got killed in a freak accident.

Maybe I was just about to be granted my wish of leaving the world I was in and joining Adler in that transition phase between life and death. I glanced behind me to look at Adler one last time in the backseat but he wasn't there. I hadn't even noticed that his hand was no longer on my shoulder, and that I was just making a tight fist.

I screamed his name and begged for him to be there with me in my last moments but nothing happened. My father was pleading with me to remain calm but there was no such thing as remaining calm when you were about to die and you were painfully aware of it.

In those last few moments everything seemed to be in slow motion and as the truck was inching closer and closer I saw a mysterious glowing figure standing in the middle of the road between our vehicle and the transport truck. My father yelled as he swerved not to hit the person who was standing in the middle of the road but that's when I saw that it was Adler.

He was the fully human person who was standing in the middle of the highway and my father clearly saw him too. Adler calmly walked in front of the truck and stretched out his arms in front of it, seemingly to push it in the other direction and away from our SUV. But how could he? He was invisible! He could walk right through walls and people so the truck was going to go right through him too.

I closed my eyes and held on tightly to the edge of my seat, and then everything went black. All I remembered was something cold surrounding me completely. I didn't feel anything else other than cold. It was almost like a dream-like state. There was no pain and honestly not any sort of reality either. There wasn't even fear or confusion. There wasn't anything at all.

Bright lights were all around me and I could hear faint voices in the background, possibly coming from another room. I focused more on what was surrounding me and I could hear a constant, steady beeping sound. A beeping sound like on those annoying hospital machines. The thought didn't sink in immediately, but then I realized that I was in the hospital and I was hooked up to those machines!

The beeping sound then increased drastically as I began hyperventilating. Doctors quickly rushed over to me and gave me some sort of sedative. I woke up a short time later and I could feel something on my head, like a hand. I opened my eyes to the bright lights again and as they slowly adjusted the entire hospital room became clear around me.

Adler was sitting on the left side of my bed and gently caressed my forehead. His gentle touch was soothing me and calming me as well as keeping my blood pressure down. I examined him from head to toe to make sure that he was okay and in one piece after the accident and it brought me great joy and relief to see that he didn't have a scratch. His perfect hair hadn't moved a millimeter, his uniform didn't have a single speck of dirt on it and his glasses were still intact. There was absolutely nothing different about him.

Everything was still the way I remembered it about him. He had on the same uniform he was wearing before we left my house and that same eternal peaceful look on his face. He was just like he had always been. He had the same serene effects on me, as he always had. Our energy fields merged again and everything went back to the way it had always been between us. In that moment it also occurred to me that he had saved my life. Adler's actions had saved my life after all.

"Everything is fine darling," he whispered to me in that soothing gentle voice, "you're going to make a full recovery and so will your dad. The other driver is going to be fine too. And yes, I'm okay if that's what you're worried about."

I smiled at him and he gave me a reassuring kiss on the forehead. He stayed seated on the edge of my bed until I became fully awake and aware of my surroundings as well as my condition. I didn't have any serious injuries except a broken arm, but I was pretty banged up. Adler then walked around my room as he talked to me and eventually turned on the TV.

The six o'clock news had just come on and I tuned in since Adler seemed to want me to watch them. The first thing they showed on the large TV screen in my hospital room was an awful car wreck with a white silhouette in the form of a man standing next to it. There were no details or features on the silhouette, but it was obviously an outline of Adler. The wreckage was something to see.

Both the vehicles had been completely destroyed and pieces of wreckage were scattered all over the road and the ditch, there was *nothing* left. The female news anchor spoke in an overly dramatic tone of voice, seemingly not believing her eyes and she recounted the details of the devastating crash.

"Here's an update on yesterday's devastating car accident just outside of Bluepond. A small SUV collided head on with a freight truck heading in the opposite direction. First responders on the scene said that the crash was due to poor visibility during yesterday's rainstorm that also created record flooding in many parts of the province." she said, "In this photo you can clearly see what's left of the wreckage in the middle of the highway along with a mysterious white silhouette seemingly looking over the crash site. Everyone survived."

That was unbelievable! I couldn't believe what I was seeing! How was it possible that we had all survived a crash like that?!

Both vehicles were totaled! Your average person probably wouldn't have known that the debris scattered all over the road was once a vehicle if the news anchor hadn't said so! I looked over at Adler who had since returned to my side. I looked deep into his sparkling eyes with such admiration and gratitude. He kissed my forehead again like you'd do to a small child to comfort them as tears escape from my eyes when the full scope of the situation began to sink in.

Adler had saved my life! I sat up on the bed and reached for him. He too seemed to be overwhelmed with emotion as he took me into a tight embrace and took a series of deep breaths even though he technically didn't need to *breathe*. His touch calmed me down and relaxed my stiff, aching muscles. Once Adler touched my body all the pain dissipated, never to return again.

"You saved my life," I whispered to him through my tears.

"For the millions I couldn't save," he retorted with pain in his voice.

I squeezed him tighter. I knew that he struggled with guilt for not being able to save more people during the war, but he was still a hero to all the people he had rescued. He resisted an evil regime, he did not have to bear the shame that the others did. He was pure gold to me and to a lot of people.

"Can you die?" I asked him, still not completely believing what had happened.

"I'm already dead," he replied chuckling through his emotions, "I don't think I can die again."

"Are you hurt though?"

"No sweetheart, I didn't feel a thing. Don't worry about me, it's *my* job to worry about *you* my dear."

A sweet smile appeared on his lips as he said those words. It was another perfect moment until a doctor and some nurses walked in to check up on me. They all smiled broadly when they saw that I was awake and sitting up in bed. They told me that I had only been out less than twenty-four hours, which was quite something considering that I had also suffered a severe concussion as a result of being ejected from the vehicle.

"Wow! Look at you!" Dr. Jericho exclaimed enthusiastically, "You've just survived one wicked crash! You are *very* lucky to be alive. I'd even go as far as saying that it's a miracle that you weren't shredded to pieces in that wreckage. You've got a broken arm and a concussion, a long list of cuts and bruises but that's all, but you should also expect to be sore and stiff for a while."

As long as I had Adler by my side I knew that I wouldn't have to worry about a thing. I held his hand and looked at him with such gratitude filling my eyes. The doctor was telling me that my dad had suffered six broken ribs and one broken wrist as well as a concussion like me.

The driver of the other vehicle only had minor injuries but he was scratched and bruised up too. Now that I was awake and in stable condition my mother and Mike were allowed to come and see me in the regular hospital rooms instead of the ICU. My dad's face was bruised and scarred and he had stitches on the side of his neck but he was all in one piece and so was I.

My face looked pretty much like my dad's but I was simply thankful to be *alive* after such a horrific crash. As much as I would have liked to have been with Adler for eternity, or whichever other time span, in another world to get away from my own out of control life sometimes I was more thankful than ever to still be human and to still be alive and in one piece.

It was odd how life had a way of using bad experiences to teach us something valuable even though we couldn't always comprehend it and that only made me more curious about Adler and God too. I was beginning to realize that there were forces greater than me pulling the strings somewhere in the cosmos.

When my mother saw me she started crying and hugged me tightly like there was no tomorrow. She tried her best to not squeeze me *too* tightly as I was injured even though I was under the effect of a pretty great painkiller called Adler, not to mention the load of drugs the hospital had injected me with.

I didn't have the chance to say much because my mother and Mike kept on rambling on and on about how grateful they were that I was still around. I knew that my mother was sincere as she spoke because despite everything, I knew that deep down inside I was her world and she loved me unconditionally. Mike, on the other hand, didn't love himself so I could not really expect him to love me.

The doctor ordered my dad and I to get plenty of sleep and quiet time in those crucial first stages of recovery and they decided to keep both of us under observation overnight as a precaution before sending us home in the morning if they deemed us fit to resume our regular lives.

Even though I had plenty of time to relax and to think while I was alone in my hospital room that evening, I could recall very little of the actual crash. I remembered clearly what had happened *before* but not during or after. I figured that I could just ask my dad, Adler or even the other driver to help me fill in the blanks if they remembered anything themselves.

"Can you heal my arm?" I asked Adler as I fiddled with the bulky white cast on it.

"Absolutely," Adler spoke softly like he always did as he took my arm into his hands.

"Why don't you just heal me automatically?"

"That wouldn't be nice of me to do something without asking permission or against your will, even if it was something good like healing your broken bones."

"You're a real gentleman you know, a true gem from the past. Now I'm just wondering what I'm going to tell my folks and the doctors when they see that my arm isn't broken anymore."

"Tell them whatever you want Joanie, they won't be able to tell you that your arm is still broken once they see this no matter what you say."

Adler kissed a scratch on the same hand while he was at it and it dissipated just like it had never came. I figured that he'd been doing the same thing when he'd kissed my forehead a couple of times. My face was still in bad condition, but I definitely looked better than I should have after surviving a crash like that.

"Leave me semi-injured okay?" I grinned at him as he worked his magic, "At least for a couple of days."

"No problem," he said with a smile, "there isn't a single thing under the moon that I wouldn't do for you."

"Everything is perfect when I'm around you. You are absolute perfection!"

"This, whatever *this* is, has its perks I'm not going to deny that, but I wouldn't recommend it to anyone."

"Do you think that you came back as a keeper before making it to the realm of the afterlife because you had some unfinished business in your human life? Like saving more lives?"

"You know, it's not impossible, but then again I haven't figured everything out yet."

"Well, if it gives you any peace of mind, I don't regret that things have ended up the way they did for the two of us because you've had the biggest positive impact on my life. I can't even begin to describe it."

"I'm grateful for the chances and the opportunities you've given me Joanie, I've gotta say that you have helped me a great deal too because I still have much unfinished emotional business from the war that I carry with me to this day. But right now you should sleep because even though you don't feel it right now, your body is running on empty."

"I know, but sleeping is rather useless when I could be spending more time with you."

"You are well aware that I'll be right here when you wake up."

In the morning I was faced with the impossible task of explaining how come my arm was no longer broken. As I had woken up very early from another very peaceful sleep I sat up in my bed and fiddled around with the cast, contemplating what I should do about it. Should I cut it up and show the world that my arm had healed perfectly? Or should I tell the doctor to take an x-ray so he could find out for himself that my arm wasn't broken?

"Get me some scissors," I commanded Adler.

He actually found some in a cabinet by the door of the room so he didn't have to look around the place and swipe a pair of scissors which would eventually have lead to another dilemma of trying to explain how I got a pair of scissors without even leaving my room or having any visitors.

Adler handed me the green pair of scissors and I started cutting up my cast as best as I could with them. It wasn't as easy as I had originally thought it would be and I hadn't gotten far when a nurse came into the room and took the scissors away from me.

"What in the world do you think you're doing?!" she asked, shocked by my behavior.

"My arm isn't broken," I protested, "take an x-ray and see for yourself!"

After a few minutes or arguing, she finally called the doctor to come and check me out. I skipped the part about having a keeper and him having the ability to heal me and basically begged him to take an x-ray to see for himself. The doctor ended up agreeing to book me another x-ray in a few minutes once that department opened for the day even though he didn't believe a word of my *my arm is not broken anymore* story.

He would not have a choice to believe it when he saw it, however. In the meantime my mother and Mike had come back and brought me breakfast from McDonald's. Hospital food was nasty and the Bluepond University Hospital had a reputation for giving sunny side ups that were as rubbery as car tires in the morning.

Both my mother and Mike pleaded their case to the doctor that I was mentally unfit and that there was no way my arm could have been healed just like that overnight but I plead my case too and right after breakfast we all went to the x-ray room for the big moment. In just a few seconds an x-ray of my arm that was apparently broken showed up on a screen in a small room just outside the x-ray room and there was no indication that my arm had ever been broken.

Subsequently, the nurses removed my cast and the doctor examined my arm further, mostly fiddling with his instruments just poking around the skin because he couldn't believe what he was seeing. All I could do was smile at Adler. I didn't have to say anything, not that there really was something to say in the first place, because both my mom and Mike had a pretty good idea of what I was going to tell them regarding how my arm had just healed up.

The doctor looked embarrassed and quite frankly ashamed of himself as he paced back and forth around the room, trying to come up with some plausible explanation to what he had just seen. Dismissing it as a medical error wouldn't do the trick, because nobody would believe that I'd had only banged my head on the concrete after being thrown out of a vehicle. While everybody around me were scratching their heads, I was sitting back in a chair waiting to be discharged and move on with my life.

Finally, after examining me at length as well as checking my father from head to toe, the two of us were discharged from the hospital and were expected to make a full recovery. Because my father would need some rehabilitation after extensive healing it was agreed that I would return to live with my mother and Mike for a while not to put additional strain on his new family that hadn't even come down to see him in the hospital.

My father was somewhat disappointed that I wouldn't be coming but it didn't really make a difference to me. It also seemed that my mother was concerned that my father had become crazy too, because he seemed to be rather open-minded to keepers since the accident.

Everybody was dead silent during the ride home. Nobody could come up with something worthwhile to say. All I could do was smile at myself, and at Adler, knowing that no matter what the world thought about me or my stories of having a keeper, I knew that I wasn't crazy. I had all the proof I could ever need to believe in forces greater than me and in the afterlife, whatever that consisted of.

Neither me or my folks had ever been people of faith, but there came a time that you simply had to accept that science and research, or even logic, couldn't explain everything.

# ELEVEN

Going back to school on Tuesday morning I knew I would have to face Rosanna and confront her about what she had set in motion. My mother had begged me to stay home and rest for at least one more day but I didn't want to. I had more than enough to think about with restoring my living space and getting some new clothes from the thrift store after almost all of my possessions had been pulverized in the accident.

Thankfully, I'd left many things behind because I'd always been planning to return eventually. Although Adler had soothed my shock and my fear following the accident, I was still furious with the person that I had once thought was my best friend, my *only* friend. My only *human* friend, at least.

Mike and my mother could not comprehend how I could have just survived a horrific car crash and not have a single ache or pain in my entire body. I wasn't even on painkillers anymore once I got back home. I didn't even try to tell them that Adler had healed me either because they didn't want to hear it and after the crash they'd kind of dropped the whole *Joanie you're insane and you need help* thing.

The whole idea of my imaginary friend named Adler seemed to have vanished completely, at least for the time being. Honestly, if I had been in my parents' shoes after that accident, I most likely would have forgotten about my kid's imaginary friend too.

"I can't believe that Rosie could do something like this to me though," I muttered to Adler as we both sat on my bed before my alarm clock rang, "she *believed*."

"I know Joanie," Adler's voice was soft as usual, "but it's honestly useless to be angry. You have every right to be, but the end result hasn't changed. We're both still here and we're a team."

"You always know how to turn a crummy situation into a not-so-crummy one. But it still hasn't completely sank in to my head that she could just go right ahead and betray me like this after we shared so many special moments! She could see you and touch you and feel you, and now look at this!"

"I know how you feel, I've been betrayed too, and often. What I hope you understand though, is that anger is a very destructive emotion. It accompanies hatred, fear and prejudice in causing nothing but greater pain than a person began with if we let it sour into a self-destructive rage."

"Sometimes it feels like anger is your only friend."

"Yes, that's true, but channeled properly anger doesn't have to be destructive. I'll never tell you that you're not allowed to be angry, but I will tell you that the first step in dealing with your emotions is accepting them."

"And I don't want to be angry either Adler. I know it does something to you inside to feel this kind of anger and from now on I want you to stop replacing my emotions with peace and serenity. Stop carrying the weight of them on your shoulders. I know that you still have unresolved feelings from the war."

"Are you sure about that? You know that it doesn't hurt me to carry your emotions for you. Either way, I'll still feel everything you feel, but this has nothing to do with my residual emotions from the war."

"Let's try it and see what happens, okay?"

"Okay, I'll do whatever you request of me."

"Right now I'd just appreciate you making that ugly cut on my face disappear."

Just as I spoke those words Adler leaned over and kissed the side of my face. The nasty wound faded away like it had never existed. I knew that it would raise plenty of questions but none of that mattered to me. I had much bigger problems and much more important things to think about.

"You know, the more I learn about keepers the more they seem mysterious to me," I added, "like how one theory says that the innermost depths of my soul created you but how another says you come from a parallel universe."

"Parallel universes are said to interact with each other," Adler added, "so the two aren't necessarily contrary. In this universe I was created by you and in another I went to war. The two interacted and now I'm somewhere in the middle. How about that?"

"Well, how about that! Maybe we've just figured out part of the mystery to your existence!"

"By the way, you have thirty seconds before your alarm clock goes off."

"You're very precise."

He knew full well how I was going to react upon heading the bells of impending doom go off. I stretched out my arm to turn off the alarm before it sounded. Ironically, my alarm clock was one of the few things I hadn't brought with me to my father's house but it was the one thing I wished would have been smashed in the middle of the road.

"Heightened awareness about your environment is one of the many perks of being a keeper. You know, some days it's not half bad!"

"None of my days are bad now that you're around."

"Then I hope to be around for a very long time. I could use a boost in agape this morning though, and I promise that I won't tamper with your emotions but sometimes it's stronger than me."

"Of course Adler, and since we're up early again we could stop by a restaurant and get ourselves something fancy after breakfast this morning. I know that you're hungry, you know."

"I don't even need to eat in this life or whatever else you wanna call it, but I could eat and never stop nonetheless."

"I'll feed you, whatever you want, you know that."

Finally, I got out of bed after convincing myself that it was in my *best interest* to do so — as much as I hated those two words — and that it would be much worst if I didn't move. I got dressed with the few pieces of clothing I'd left in my dresser and put on a new plum hoodie from the thrift store and went on my way. I looked decent despite that I was still pretty banged up. I should have been in much worst shape though, so I was very lucky in that regard. Without Adler I probably would not still be alive.

I went downstairs just in time for the usual breakfast around the table. There was an awkward silence filling the atmosphere and it was obvious that I was the elephant in the room. Certainly they realized that some of my scars had mysteriously disappeared overnight but no one dared to speak a word.

I discretely dropped most of the food on my plate to Adler down on the floor and ate the rest before excusing myself and barging out the door despite that my mother had previously begged me to stay home. Honestly, I needed some air. After coming so close to death I needed to *feel* what it was like to be alive again. It seemed like for some time I had completely neglected to feel life, the most basic thing a person had.

Adler never spoke much about his own residual feelings but I knew that on many levels he felt the same way I did. My needs had also become his, just like my emotions had been for so long. As the two of us walked down the street most people took a second look at me as I still had plenty of cuts and bruises.

I deliberately limped slightly just so I wouldn't come off as suspicious because my actions didn't match my appearance. Everyone who walked passed me also caught a chill when thy passed through Adler and the expression on their faces indicated that they didn't understand what was happening because the weather was so mild for the time of year. I grinned to myself because I knew the reason why.

"You've had a mood change for the better," Adler commented as we walked up to a little bistro.

"Just getting some fresh air can make all the difference

sometimes," I replied as a gentle breeze blew through my hair, "but don't worry, I know I still have to face Rosanna today."

"I feel it in my bones that she didn't do this to hurt you even thought that's what turned out to be the end result."

"Tell me Adler, which one is the one that really matters: the motivation or the end result? Does the end justify the means?"

Adler sighed loudly before taking a few moments to think about the answer. I obviously had struck something deep inside of him that he had been struggling with. Certainly, my keeper had some residual feelings that still haunted him from the war.

"The only thing I can really say about that is that nothing changes the end result," he finally spoke in a seemingly pained tone of voice after a while, "but the motivation is what can change people's hearts."

"That makes sense," I replied, "thanks."

"But to give you a more proper answer to your question, the end generally doesn't justify the means. Only in exceptional circumstances are exceptional actions acceptable."

"Like a war."

"Yes, like a war."

"I take it you had to do some shady things in order to save people."

"Yes, a lot of which I'm not proud of."

"You're still my hero."

"Well, we're a team after all."

At the little bistro I bought the day's breakfast special and ate about half of it before giving the rest to Adler. The dish had been way too big for me even if I hadn't eaten in days and I wouldn't have been able to eat all of that by myself either way. On top of that I'd eaten a little bit at home before leaving just to satisfy Mike and my mother. Adler was delighted by the food and quickly swallowed the breakfast meal without taking the time to chew most of it. I was curious to know what it looked like to the people around us seeing visible food suddenly becoming invisible, as though it had disappeared into thin air.

"I was always bad for doing this," Adler muttered with his mouth full of food, "but the food is too damn good to take the time to chew it."

"You know, you'd taste more if it if you did," I giggled.

"My bad, I simply cannot control myself sometimes. Lucky me it's more socially acceptable now than it was when I was your age."

"Well, I'll keep on buying you food for as long as you're around."

"I'm not planning on going anywhere, but I don't know if other beings have different plans for me though."

"We'll deal with whatever results of the future when it happens, but for the time being we should focus on the present."

As the two of us left the restaurant I pointed to a bruise on my face and it disappeared after Adler leaned over and gave me a kiss on the forehead. Perks of a having a keeper. Too bad for Rosanna, she'd lost those perks when she turned her back on me.

"Are you up for school today?" Adler asked me almost like he could read my thoughts, "You know it's not too late to change your mind."

"I stand behind my decision Adler," I retorted trying to convince myself above all, "and I'm not backing out, not anymore. I'm part of the Resistance too now."

"And you know that I'll stand behind you no matter what you choose."

"I know, and that means the world to me."

"I'll give you advice and share with you my wisdom but ultimately the only person in control of what you choose to do in your life is you Joanie, and I want you to have that self-confidence required to be independent."

"Independence sounds both scary and liberating."

"Being a follower isn't always bad, but ultimately going your own way is the only way you'll ever be satisfied. It's a duty to go your own way when you're following something harmful to you or others. I wish I would have realized that sooner, maybe I could have saved more people and maybe I wouldn't be stuck like this."

"Do you like being a keeper though? I know that sometimes this wears you down even though you don't say it, but other time it's really wonderful."

"You know, I keep going back and forth because I haven't completely accepted either existence yet. I still have unresolved feelings about the other world or whichever place I originated from before your soul opened that door to the other universe, and this existence is rather restrictive. I'm invisible, for starters."

Adler and I had been exploring other keeper theories since the accident and certain things were beginning to make more sense as we sorted through the different philosophies. It seemed as though many worlds existed out there and time wasn't necessarily linear like humans believed. I had most likely created Adler at the same time that he'd served in the Wehrmacht, in two separate worlds simultaneously and the two had interacted in some way that made it so that his soul had transitioned.

Or maybe I hadn't created him and the first theory had been wrong all along. Maybe he'd always existed and some other weird mystical process had happened. Or maybe it was all a dream and none of it was real. The more time passed, the less answers we had. A new theory came along once in a while that seemed to make sense, and then it didn't, and we were still left with a big mystery.

"Your existence never seems to become easier to figure out," I muttered, "and in fact the more I learn the less I understand about the world I live in."

"I completely understand my dear, it feels like you have a piece and then you find something that sends you right back to square one," Adler responded in a pensive tone of voice, "and I don't know what to expect either."

"Too bad not more was ever written about keepers either. Finding something that's not gibberish is like finding a needle in a haystack."

"I hold on to the hope that the right answers will reveal themselves at the right time. I must believe that."

"So do I."

All the theories had their similarities, so there was no doubt in my mind that there must have been some element of truth in there as the common denominator, but the pieces still didn't all fit. Sure, atoms could exist in two places and two or more worlds could exist simultaneously and all experience time differently, but what was the missing link? Most importantly, where could we find that missing link? I was only driving myself crazy with the mystery so I thought of other things while we continued the trek to school.

The sky was a mix of sun and cloud but it was quite damp from a few millimeters of rain overnight. The afternoon forecast was supposed to be a warm one, not necessarily another record high but an El Nino was moving in and bringing with it some bizarre, but much welcomed mild weather. Everyone who'd ever lived in a coastal region knew that it rained a lot but also that it wasn't exactly the warmest type of climate around, especially at that time of the year.

"It's going to be such a beautiful day," I muttered to myself as the sun peaked through the clouds, "it's such a shame that we'll have to spend it indoors again."

"You keep saying that you want to go to school my dear Joanie," Adler chuckled lightly as he spoke, "but your emotions tell me that it's the last place you want to go to this morning."

"I'm still not used to the fact that nothing about my private life is actually still *private* now that you're around. Maybe you can't hear my thoughts but you still figure them out pretty well."

"I wouldn't be a good keeper if I didn't at least try!"

"You're a wonderful keeper, and also a wonderful person."

Once Adler and I arrived on school grounds I made sure to pass by the spot he had thrown Alana Overton up against the wall just to remind myself of his power and how he would always protect me. I didn't exactly need to be *protected* against anything or anyone at school but I was still going to need the strength, dedication and bravery of a Wehrmacht officer who saved people to face the day after the recent downfall.

Ever since the incident with Alana nobody hung out by that wall anymore, and I couldn't help but wonder what the school administrators had written in their report after hearing stories that a ghost had done that. I laughed quietly to myself at the thought.

"You don't need to do this today," Adler reassured me as he felt my emotions go downhill again, "not doing this today doesn't mean backing out and never doing it at all."

"I know," I replied as I turned to look at him, all dressed up and ready for battle, "but it's better to get this out of the way now than to leave it looming over my head forever."

"Indeed!"

"My parents and my aunt Kendra tried to get that into my head for ages but I never really understood what that meant until you came along Adler."

"That's what I'm here for."

Lieutenant Adler and I walked into a mostly empty hallway inside the school since it was still so early and most students hadn't arrived yet. I quickly raced to the vending machines to buy some chocolate bars for Adler and I before classes were to start. Everybody knew that you couldn't eat in class even though most people did anyway.

"With your keeper powers you technically could just stick your hand into the machine and take out whatever you want, right?" I asked Adler.

"Yes," he replied blankly as he passed his invisible hand through the glass and brought back three chocolate bars.

"That's amazing!"

"I still don't understand how matter becomes invisible like that when I touch it, yet returns to its original state once I give it to you."

"I have no idea, but I don't really need to know. All I know is that it's awesome and now we have more chocolate than we can eat in one day."

Adler and I both giggled as we opened our chocolate bars. Eating in the hallways was also technically prohibited but nobody enforced that rule either. Students could only eat in the cafeteria or the student lounge, yet most of us mimicked the teachers in eating whatever we wanted wherever we were at the time. The enjoyment of my chocolate bar was cut short when I heard

Rosanna's mousy voice behind me.

"Joanie," she said.

Suddenly, I felt a surge of anger in my veins and I literally wanted to grab Rosanna and shove her against the wall just like Adler had done to Alana. Adler felt that too, so he put his arm around my shoulder and surrounded me in agape to keep me calm. It enraged me so much that she could just approach me like that as if she had never betrayed Adler and I! Beyond that, the accident was a direct result of what she'd set in motion with her big mouth!

"How dare you!" I shouted angrily at her, completely oblivious to the few people around in the hallways as she approached me cautiously.

"Joanie, please listen," Rosanna pleaded as if she was about to cry, "let me explain, this is just a big misunderstanding!"

"No Rosanna, there's nothing to be said and even less to be explained! If it hadn't been for your big fat lying mouth blabbing to your mom like that, my dad and I would never have been in a car accident! Did you know that he can't even work right now?"

"I'm so sorry that this happened to you Joanie."

She began to cry but I was still too angry to show her any compassion even though I knew very well that Adler wanted me to. The look on his face indicated that I was right, but I couldn't bring myself to do it. I couldn't fake my emotions, that was nothing more than hypocrisy.

"Joanie, please," Rosanna choked up through her tears, "I had no choice but to make up a lie when I was confronted by my mom because I didn't want my parents to lock me up in the psych ward! I believe that Adler is real, I know he is Joanie!"

"Well thank you very much," I angrily snapped back through clenched teeth, "because I'm the one who is going to be locked up in the psych ward now!"

"I'm so sorry Joanie! Please forgive me, *please*. I was just trying to protect myself and I swear that I *never* wanted to hurt you or anybody else. And where is Adler? I want to apologize to him too."

Adler had been by my side the entire time, in fact he was never *not* around, but Rosanna was completely unaware of his presence. He had become invisible to her again, just like he didn't exist.

"You can't see him because he hates you! And so do I!" I snapped back before I turned around and ran out of the building only to break down crying on the sidewalk.

"I don't hate her sweetie," Adler whispered to me as he held me in a reassuring hold, "and you shouldn't either."

"I guess it's just you and me now," I muttered to him as I let my head rest against his shoulder, "and I'm gonna need a soldier in my corner."

Rosanna found the guts and the audacity to come back and find us out on the street to torment me some more. I wanted to scream at her so loudly that my voice would always resonate in the back of the brain until she took her last breath but for Adler's sake I wanted to remain civil. The two of us had made so much progress with soothing my feelings since we'd been outside and I didn't want to undo that just because my emotions got the best of my decency for a brief moment.

"You have a lot of guts coming back here," I angrily muttered through my teeth.

"I want to tell you how sorry I really am Joanie," she replied, struggling to keep her voice from cracking.

"Well, Rosanna, I'm really not interested in your apologies. I don't care how sorry you are, if you really are to begin with. You betrayed my trust and put people's lives in danger and that is unforgivable."

"And I accept responsibility for my actions, but just please tell Adler that I'm sorry and I miss hanging out with him."

"He hears you loud and clear."

"I'm sorry Adler."

Adler and I looked at each other for a brief moment but he didn't say anything. Even if he had wanted to say something to Rosanna, she would not have been able to hear him and he knew that I wasn't up for being a translator of sorts or a messenger of any kind. After a few moments of silence on my part Rosanna finally turned back and left us alone.

"You were right," I muttered to Adler, "I shouldn't have come to school today."

"You'll see that one day all of this pain will be invisible," he retorted in his eternally gentle and soothing voice.

"Are you sure that I can't die with you so we can exist in another form in another universe somewhere?"

"I'm afraid that it doesn't work that way Joanie. I don't think I would like to live forever in this state either, at least not here on Earth. There is way too much pain here."

"That makes sense, and I take back what I said earlier. I want you to take away my emotions again."

"Not a problem."

Just as he said that, I felt the overwhelming sense of serenity sweep over me again and all of my feelings disappeared. I connected to the agape deep inside of me and everything was better again. It was almost surreal to feel such an incredible sense of peace. A feeling like that was otherworldly. There was no finding it on your own without some help from a being greater than you.

"Let's go back home shall we?" I proposed, "I've decided that I don't want to go to class after all."

"Sure," Adler retorted, "it's going to be a beautiful day at the very least."

"It still hasn't quite sunken into my head yet that if you hadn't been there that night of the accident we would have all died."

"You don't know that for certain. People survive incredible car wrecks every day!"

"But you saw the picture somebody took of the crash on TV! A silhouette of you was watching over the crash site! Heck, we made it to the evening news!"

Adler grinned slightly but he didn't seem to like having attention drawn to him like that. He was a very humble man despite his heroism. One of the many perks of being invisible was that he didn't attract attention from anyone anymore. He didn't have to worry about the Gestapo finding out that he was getting Jews to safety. It was just he and I again. Adler got up after a few more moments and grabbed me by the hand to get me moving before starting the long walk back home.

As we left the school property the bell rang and I could almost hear the lockers slamming and people flooding the classrooms and pushing each other around to get the best spot. The teachers yelling at the idiots in the room and Rosanna's voice trying to justify her actions. Part of me understood why she wanted to protect herself, but that was no excuse to sink me. That wasn't a reason to inflict that kind of hurt on me. That wasn't a reason to put lives in danger.

"Do you know what's even better than having a keeper subdue your emotions?" Adler asked me with a sweet smile on his face as he walked down the street.

"Please enlighten me," I challenged him, genuinely interested in what he had to say.

"Forgiveness. When you forgive someone it's like setting a prisoner free, and once it's done you realize that the prisoner was you."

"That's deep."

"So many people have shallow concepts of forgiveness, but ultimately only *you* can freely give forgiveness. It's not about the other person deserving it or having to earn it or some other corrupt concept, it's about you allowing yourself to be set free, to be liberated."

"I agree, but sometimes that's so hard to do."

"Yes it is, and it certainly doesn't mean that forgiveness implies that what happened was okay, because it wasn't, but that doesn't mean that there is no healing or peace to be achieved."

"Your wisdom is contagious Adler, I honestly don't know what I'd do without you at this point in my life. As much as I like to make myself believe that I've got it all together, I realize that I'm a mess but you give me hope."

"The only real purpose in our life is helping others live better for the short time that we've got here because everything else is so trivial and irrelevant to living well."

"Touché."

"You know that I didn't tell you that to dredge up some painful memories of feeling abandoned or neglected Joanie. Sometimes people get so caught up in their ideologies of the good life, or at least the fantasy of what it's supposed to be, that they completely neglect to live at all."

"I know, and what I feel like my parents don't understand is that it's not about whether they have good jobs or we have a nice house and we go on vacation every year or whatever. It's about the fact that they've both basically left me orphaned now. My father was gone for what seems like an eternity to me and now he's in bad shape so he won't be doing much for a while, and my mother is completely in Mike's grip and she has no will of her own anymore. I'm all alone in this basically."

"No, you're not. You have me and you always will. You know Joanie, one of my comrades once told me that the most precious thing you can give a person is your time, and I firmly believe that to be true. On the other hand, I think that your mother is beginning to see things differently when it comes to Mike now."

"Once upon a time I was very close to both my mom and dad but now I feel like I am separate from them completely and I don't like that."

"The good news in this life is that nothing lasts forever. That can be both a blessing and a curse though."

"Tell me about it Adler."

"Have some more patience. If we want the things we are seeking to reveal themselves to us, we must first open our minds and abandon our predefined ideas about them."

"You sound exactly like my aunt Kendra again."

# TWELVE

Back at home I was surprised to see that my father and his new family were sitting around the kitchen table with my mother. They were equally surprised to see me because they expected me to be in class. I figured that they's been talking about me because the conversation abruptly stopped once I walked into the room.

Thankfully my mother didn't give me a hard time over me ditching school and I wasn't in for an interrogation either because Mike wasn't around to keep me in line. Not having anything better to do, I sat down next to my dad at the kitchen table. If they were talking about what to do with me they could at least consider my input. My father appeared to be in a lot of agony over his injuries even though he didn't want to admit it.

"You should go see a doctor dad," I told him, "you really don't look so good."

"I'll have to feed Marjorie soon," his new wife interjected like she didn't want to have to take him to the hospital.

"We'll take you," my mother added.

Eventually my mom and I convinced him to come with us to get checked out by a doctor just to make sure that there wasn't something more serious going on. Maybe my mother was worried that his injuries had miraculously healed like my arm too.

Nobody understood what had happened there so nobody dared to speak about it either because that would be opening up a can of worms but I knew that it burned at the back of the minds of a lot of people. There was really only one way to explain such an occurrence: Adler had done it. That created a big moral conflict for those who didn't believe that forces greater than the rest of us existed.

Finally, my father agreed to let my mother drive him to get checked out so I hopped in with them so I wouldn't have to be alone with his new family because I didn't get the impression that the new wife liked me too much and things were always awkward between us. At least I had Adler by my side and I wouldn't have to be alone with my thoughts aimlessly swinging all around the place. I knew that I'd have to attempt to sort them out at some point but for the moment all I wanted to do was take a deep breath of air and momentarily get away from them.

I indulged in the agape that Adler gave me and connected with the love deep inside of me to reciprocate the amazing feeling back to him and sustain the flow of energy. It seemed like even my parents in the vehicle with us were feeling a surge in positive energy too. They probably dismissed it as nothing but Adler and I knew that our fields of loving energy overflowed and affected the other people around us. That kind of positivity was definitely contagious. The two of them didn't get along so well after such a nasty divorce just because my father was seriously injured.

At the hospital the waiting room was full. That was nothing new but once I got there I somewhat wished that I'd stayed home with Adler after all. We could've gone outside or something and I could've had a two-way conversation with him instead of just having him talk to me in a crowded hospital room with a bunch of crying kids and other people making weird and unnatural noises. Both Adler and I tuned into the muted TV in the corner of the room but there wasn't anything interesting on the news so that didn't succeed in mentally distracting me from an unpleasant environment.

After a while the physician was finally ready to check out my dad and since it was the same doctor that had treated us right after the crash, he decided to check me out too. Everything was fine at my end and my dad was only feeling the normal kind of pain that came with a crash of that severity. He was still going to be perfectly fine though. The doctor wrote him a different prescription for painkillers and he sent us on our way. As the three of us were walking out of the hospital's main entrance, we came face to face with the driver of the tractor trailer involved in the wreck.

He was a big and tall bald man with a long white beard. There was a grandfatherly aura to him with his red plaid shirt and faded jeans. He seemed genuinely surprised to see us and for a moment I wondered if maybe he could see Adler. I looked up at my keeper but he gave me no indication that the truck driver noticed anything out of the ordinary. For the last little while Adler had only been visible to me.

"Oh! I hope that all of you are recovering well!" the driver exclaimed loudly in a scratchy voice, "I've never had the chance to talk to you before, and I just wanted to tell you how profoundly sorry I truly am for what happened."

"It's not your fault," my father reassured him, "it was an *accident*. The visibility was horrendous and the city should have closed down that road in the first place because the last I've heard, part of it washed out in that storm not too long after the crash."

"I shouldn't've been still driving either. I swerved onto your side of the road trying to avoid running over some freaking guy dressed like a soldier standing in the middle of the road! I saw him at the last minute and just missed him!"

"You saw him too? It was though he deliberately ran in front of my vehicle and I swore I ran him over!"

"He looked like he came straight out of a movie about the Second World War, and weirder than that, he didn't appear to be wet either but then again it all happened so fast. Nobody has seen or heard from him since. The police haven't been able to find him and ask him questions either. That is, if there was actually somebody there in the first place, that's why I feel really guilty. Maybe I was just so stressed behind the wheel that I was beginning to see things in the road that weren't really there.

I looked over at Adler a second time but there were no emotions on his face. He didn't say anything either. I got the impression that he'd known what he'd been doing and that he'd been in control of the situation the entire time.

"I had plenty of unanswered questions so I looked into this," the truck driver went on, "but I haven't been able to find anything concrete! The dispatcher who received the 911 call said that a man named Adler called and gave her the exact coordinates to the location of the crash even though his voice can't be heard on the recording."

A horrified yet mystified look appeared on my parents' faces as well as mine as the other driver kept on sharing his side of the story. They couldn't dismiss me as being crazy unless they wanted to be labeled as crazy too.

"And apparently the number he called from is completely untraceable! Nobody seems to be able to understand this but I heard the recording and I saw the guy standing in the middle of the road! I was so afraid that I'd run him over but obviously I didn't because he saved all of our lives! Maybe this is the proof that otherworldly beings do exist and that they are around. Guardian angels, or keepers, or whatever you wanna call them."

A smile had since appeared on Adler's face and he winked at me when I turned to look at him again. In moments like those I couldn't help but wonder if Adler was able to manipulate circumstances in a certain way even though he wasn't consciously aware that he was doing it. Maybe he had otherworldly powers far beyond what we knew.

"All in all I'm sorry for what happened and I hope that all of you fully recover," the truck driver went on, "please give me some updates from time to time. Take care of yourselves folks!"

The driver shook each of our hands before he went in to see the doctor himself for a checkup too. He didn't have any visible injuries but he did limp slightly. If we hadn't all been completely baffled before, we were after that encounter. The ride back home in the early afternoon after all the time at the hospital was done in complete silence. I had an urge to talk to Adler about so many things but I knew that I'd have to wait until we were in a more private setting to have an uninterrupted two-way conversation.

Back home I quickly raced up to my room before anyone could interrupt me so I could have some time alone with Adler. I needed to talk to him because even though I knew that he had saved all of our lives, I had been ignorant to the extend of the whole thing. I flopped down on my bed in my room and let everything sink into my head.

"How did you do that?" I asked Adler, completely baffled.

"Don't even worry about that Joanie," he spoke in his usual soft voice, "I only did what I had to do."

"You say that like saving people is an everyday hobby for you."

"If it's how I'll redeem myself, then I'll do whatever it takes."

"Excuse me Adler, *redeem* yourself? What did you do that requires redemption? It this still about having guilt for not having saved more people during the Holocaust?"

"This carries more implications that anyone can understand my dear."

"If I may share something else that my aunt Kendra told me, she said that you can't rip yourself apart to keep somebody else whole. You did what you could and lives were saved because of you! *My* life was saved because of you! And the accident didn't hurt you at all?"

"No, I can't feel any type of physical pain like that. I'm invisible remember?"

"You know, sometimes it doesn't sound half bad being a keeper."

"Being your keeper is wonderful Joanie, you are a wonderful person."

"So are you Adler, don't forget that."

Our conversation was interrupted by the door slamming downstairs. Mike was home and if my biological father and his family were still around he probably wasn't thrilled about seeing them but he'd put on a beautiful facade to make them believe that everything was nice and dandy. I could only hope that my father would see through all of the lies and see that something was wrong.

"I know that everybody realizes that there's an elephant in the room here but nobody seems to be willing to do anything about it," I told Adler.

"Your folks will have to stop denying my existence at some point and accept the fact that you're not crazy. You're not seeing people or hearing voices."

"Maybe I should go talk to them while they are all under one roof."

"I don't think that will be necessary."

Just as Adler said that I heard a slight knock on my bedroom door. It was my dad who wanted to have a talk with me before having to leave. The original talk that we were supposed to have had been interrupted by a transport truck smashing into us and we hadn't really been able to talk like we'd wanted to afterwards. There had been much more important things than ghosts after a car accident like that.

I invited my dad to come and sit down next to me on the bed so we could talk and he caught a chill when he sat down where Adler was sitting. Adler immediately scooted aside and put his arm around my shoulder like he usually did when I needed a mood boost. I already knew what my dad came to talk to me about, but unfortunately for him I didn't have much to say about the subject.

"I'm sorry that I've failed you in the past and had a hand in your current pain," my dad seemed to be struggling to find words, "but now I see things differently and I'm ready to do things differently. Once I'm back on my feet and everything is fixed I still want you to come and live with us. I don't exactly know what all of *this* is right now that is happening, but I can no longer deny that it exists. There's something more, that I know."

"It's fine dad," I muttered, "I believe that the right answers will come at the right time."

"I don't understand this whole realm of keepers, or frankly anything about spirituality, but I know that it's real and that something is among us."

"The possibilities beyond this world are endless."

"Maybe I should have listened to Kendra more when she was giving me some pre-marital spiritual blessings. Maybe if I'd listened my marriage to your mother wouldn't have ended the way it did."

"It's not too late to open our hearts and our minds to something more."

"I wish I could understand what has been going on lately, maybe it would clear up a million of my questions but I'd still like to hear what you have to say my dear. My heart and my mind are open now and I know that I have a lot to make up for."

"And I'm open to telling you dad, but not all at once. I didn't figure this out all at once and quite frankly, neither did Adler. In fact, we don't have much figured out at all!"

"I know I'll have a hard time understanding but all the signs point to keepers being real and I *want* to believe now more than ever."

*I want you to believe too dad, and I want you to help mom and I get out of here.*

"So your keeper Adler," my dad went on, "he's a flesh and bones person or is he kind of like a ghost or something else?"

"You saw him outside the other day," I replied, "that's him, a Wehrmacht officer with flesh and bones and heartbeat and everything."

For a moment it seemed like my dad looked straight into Adler's eyes but in reality he was just looking into the distance. He couldn't see my best friend, nor could he touch him or interact with him. Adler was invisible to him as well.

"I have a hard time believing that keepers actually exist, and that he's actually here," my dad muttered after a moment of contemplation, "but I have an equally hard time believing that he isn't here as well, and that there isn't something more at play here."

As he said that, Adler leaned over closer to him and blew in his face. My father's hair moved slightly and his eyes opened wide. He had definitely felt that. His heart and mind had opened up to the possibility of Adler's existence and it seemed like that had allowed the energy to move up a level.

"That's Adler's way to say hello dad," I told him.

"Hello Adler," my father whispered, mostly to himself, as he extended out his arm to touch the void in the distance.

"It's nice to finally meet you," Adler smiled as he met my dad's hand and my father caught a chill.

My father seemed to be frightened more than anything as he recoiled his arm after catching the chill. He was was only scared because he didn't know what had just happened. There was nothing scary about Adler, unless you were afraid of otherworldly spirits of course, but once people experienced the amazing sense of peace that keepers carried around with them there was absolutely no reason to be afraid of them.

"Honey!" my father's new wife called out, "I need your help down here!"

"You've been summoned," I giggled as I smiled at my dad.

He reluctantly got off my bed and slowly went back downstairs, being careful not to aggravate his injuries, to help out with whatever was wrong. I figured that the woman was just beginning to feel uncomfortable around my father's former family because my dad couldn't be of much help since he was still quite battered up from the accident. Eventually he'd still be handy around the house like he'd always been, but he would have to be a couch potato for a little while.

"He's not going to forget that any time soon," Adler commented after my bedroom door slammed shut.

"Sometimes I wonder if it's not just because he feels guilty about abandoning me," I muttered in response.

"To some degree, something like that will always stay with a person, regardless of if they were the one inflicting the pain or if they were at the receiving end of it. If you drive a nail into a piece of wood because you're hurting and then take it out when you've healed, there is still going to be a mark there."

"The wounds will heal but the scars will still be visible. Do you think he's guilty or sincere though?"

"At least the good part about that is that when you look at the scars, you'll always be reminded of how far you've come and not just how far you have to go. You'll be reminded of how strong you are because you've endured hell and you've survived to fight another day. You'll look at your scars and you'll know that you're not a victim. As for your father, I think that maybe he feels a little of both, but I believe that he's learned a valuable lesson and gained valuable wisdom from this entire experience."

"Why do you speak with so much regret in your voice sometimes?"

"Residual emotions from the war Joanie, don't worry about that. I'm the one taking care of you, not the other way around."

On the other side of my room a hologram opened up on the wall. Two men in Wehrmacht uniforms were working in a dimly lit office, one was Adler, but I didn't know who the second man was. They were both printing documents and filing paperwork, looking stressed, like they were working under duress. Then there was a knock at the door and Gestapo officers were on the other side. Their Jew rescue operation had been busted by the Nazis and the two of them had been caught red-handed. Then the hologram disappeared before I could see what happened next, but I had the feeling that it wasn't pretty.

"I didn't know that somebody else was involved to that degree," I spoke in a shaky voice, "what happened to him?"

"His name was Erich Fischer," Adler spoke in a voice filled with agony, "we were in the same unit and once I had my rescue operation up and running smoothly I asked him to help me after he approached me to help a Jewish woman get out of town. He ended up being sent to the gallows."

"I'm so sorry Adler, I'm sorry that your fellow comrade gave his life to save people."

"So am I."

"But you're still my hero. You're still my hero even if things ended badly for you. You'll always be my hero Adler."

"It warms my heart to hear that, Joanie, thank you."

I hugged Adler the same way he hugged me when I was feeling under the weather. Adler's energy soothed me despite that I was the one who wanted to comfort him. I let my head flop over his shoulder as I closed my eyes and let the world around me disappear. We were a team, Adler and I were in this journey of healing together.

"Share with me some of your incredible otherworldly wisdom and you'll see that *you* are the one who is going to feel better in the long run."

"You are not your age or the way you look to the outside world. You are not how intelligent others may perceive you to be without knowing the depth of your heart. You're more than these clothes we got you from the thrift store or your socio-economic status in a particular society. You are so much more than what happened in the past."

"And I've been told so many times what I can't be that I have no idea what I *can* be."

"You aren't a single moment in your life Joanie. You're not a single action, a single event. Your life is made up of so many things so do not ever let anyone single something out about you and tell you that it determines the outcome of your life. This storm, too, shall come to pass."

"Someday you *really* need to meet my aunt Kendra. Gosh, I miss her now."

# THIRTEEN

Even after all the times that Adler had healed my physical injuries, I was still just as mystified by his abilities each and every time. With each kiss the scars and the bruises from the accident vanished one by one. After just a few days I was completely healed. There were no traces that I'd ever come so close to death. The only scars were the ones left in my memory.

Part of me wanted to completely forget the pain and the fear and completely have to bypass the healing process that came after such a thing, but the bigger part of me always wanted those things to be on my mind so I could always be reminded of Adler's greatness.

I never wanted to forget how he put himself in between that truck and I to save my life and how he had healed my injuries. I never wanted to *not* appreciate him as much as I possibly could. Even after all the weeks and the months that I had spent with Adler, his existence still mystified me just as much. The more time I spent with him, the less I was able to comprehend his mystical existence. He seemed to understand it even less than I did as he was stuck in it, and I was only on the outside.

I was still in my original human form, I was still normal, but he was trapped in something he didn't understand. There were no *Keepers For Dummies* manuals at the bookstore and anybody with a head on their shoulders knew not to believe everything that was on the internet. Some theories were complete gibberish, others were completely farfetched, but some appeared to make sense for a while and then we discovered something else that seemed to make more sense but contradicted what we previously had believed. Maybe keepers weren't meant to be understood, they weren't meant to be figured out.

Obviously there was some surreal aspect when it came to Adler's existence in this realm but I still found no half-decent theory that could explain everything. Not knowing all the answers, neither one of us could see or understand the full scope of things. Many worlds, atoms, energy fields, parallel universes, souls, wars, life, death. Who would have known that a person's existence could be so complicated and hard to understand! My life sucked sometimes, but I was certainly happy to be human after racking my brain to figure out a realm beyond my own.

"How are you feeling?" I asked Adler as the two of us were sitting on my bed early one morning, "Lately you've been much quieter than usual."

"I don't know," Adler seemed to be deep in thought as he spoke softly, "I haven't been feeling quite like myself lately, whatever that's supposed to mean now."

"Tell me, I'm listening Adler. We're a team and we're in this together."

"I don't expect you to understand because I don't understand much of this myself, but I have some weird feeling of urgency. Like time is going to run out or something."

"Did you feel like that in your human life, like during the war?"

"Oh yes, but it still wasn't like this. On the Eastern Front I knew I was going to die, and I accepted that, but this is different. I can't say that I'm *human* like I used to be anymore, and I also don't know what will be happening after this, if it does come to an end."

"Tell me, I'm listening."

"What's really been getting under my skin recently is that I've never been able to come to terms with my residual emotions since I've been here. It's quite hard not feeling them to begin with, and now with this new feeling I'm confused. I know it's not coming from you, that's about all I can say."

"And you don't know where it's coming from, that's why you're worried."

"Exactly. It's like some sickness inside that I don't know how to explain. It feels like some metaphysical paradigm has shifted. That's as best as I can describe it."

"Are you afraid that you're crossing into another dimension and becoming human again?"

"That's impossible!"

"*This* is possible."

Adler smiled sweetly at me but I knew that he wasn't convinced. On my end I was trying not to get worried about him or to begin overthinking about what life would be like without my keeper. I didn't want to think about that. I needed Adler.

"Why don't you just tell me the whole story?" I continued, "That way I could at least have all the pieces to form a point of view as I'm on the outside looking in."

"If I told you the truth," Adler's voice was filled with pain, "would you stand by me?"

"Of course Adler! That's not even a question! We're a team. You've always stood by me like a good soldier, and I'll stand by you no matter what."

"My honor was *not* my loyalty during the war."

As he said that, Adler let out an exasperated sigh. He knew that burying your problems and unresolved feelings didn't make them go away. It did nothing but create bigger problems and as I saw the worn out look on his face I got the impression that the whole story was much greater than any of the logic involved in the situation.

"Joanie!" I was surprised to hear Aaron's voice call from the other side of the door, "I need your help with something."

"Unbelievable how this happens!" I muttered angrily under my breath, "It's just like when you watch a soap opera and the episode ends right at the climax!"

"It's not always the time Joanie, it's the timing."

"And I guess that this is my time and not yours."

I got out of my bed and went to see what was wrong with my step-brother. I knew that it was something serious because the guy never spoke to me. He probably didn't even know that I existed as far as I was concerned! Adler trailed behind me as I tiptoed on the floor of my room not to step on the dirty clothing and other trash littering the floor to reach the door.

As soon as I swung it wide open my step-brother's face drained of blood and he looked like he was about to pass out. Adler and I both knew that he had seen him and the thought of seeing a ghost greatly frightened him, as it would anybody not expecting it. He turned back without saying a word and went to sit in the stairs to catch his breath.

"He saw me," Adler muttered to himself, "and he's probably thinking that I'm a monster. I mean, why else would you have a grown man in your room right? That poor guy might never sleep at night for the rest of his life by the look on his face!"

"You're not a monster, and there's a perfectly good reason why I have a grown man in my room," I muttered in response, "and Aaron's just scared because he doesn't know what he saw."

I approached Aaron cautiously, hoping that he wouldn't make a scene and attract attention or worst, go tell my mother and Mike that I was doing something weird with an adult guy in a military uniform. Aaron looked at me with a blank stare as I sat down next to him. I too had a stone-faced expression on my face but I wanted to comfort Aaron, or at least try to, nonetheless.

"Please tell me that I'm mentally ill or that that's a ghost," he said in a low, confused voice, "and that you seriously didn't bring home a grown man."

I looked up at Adler standing a few feet behind me where Aaron couldn't see him but he did nothing but shrug. His existence was out of his control and nobody could do a thing about it. A person could put an end to their own life, but keepers couldn't. There was little Adler could do except ride out his existence for however long it would last.

"You're not mentally ill," I tried to reassure Aaron, though being mentally ill probably would've brought him more reassurance, "the man you saw is my keeper Adler."

"It's nice to meet you Aaron," Adler took a leap of faith and tried communicating with my stepbrother, "and I'm not here to scare you or to hurt Joanie. If you can hear me, turn around a wave at me."

Aaron turned around, his face still as white as the North Pole, and waved at Adler. Aaron slowly stood up, fighting both fright and curiosity as he extended his hand towards Adler. He was within reach and Aaron wanted to know if he was indeed real, probably hoping that he wasn't and that he was hallucinating.

"Don't do that Aaron," Adler gently warned him, "you might catch a big chill or possibly an electric shock."

Aaron had either gathered up all his courage in an instant or acted on an irresistible impulse because he walked right up to Adler and grabbed a piece of fabric at the bottom of his tunic and squeezed it into his hand for a few moments but he caught a chill and recoiled his hand. In response, Adler cautiously took a step forward and took Aaron's hand into his. The second time around the effects of the chill were much milder and as he held his hand for a few seconds the negative side effects of being touched by a keeper completely vanished.

"What did you need my help with?" I asked Aaron after a moment.

"The police are looking for me," he replied, still in awe at Adler's presence, "and I need you to cover for me."

"Okay," I replied emotionlessly, not knowing what else to say.

"But for now I think I'll just go back to my room," he replied suddenly seemingly in a daze as he got up to go back down the stairs.

Aaron must've been intoxicated by a lot more than experiencing the supernatural powers my keeper had because he only took a few steps before he tumbled the rest of the way down the staircase. Both Adler and I raced down to see if he was alright and were met by my mother and Mike at the bottom. All eyes shifted to me as I knelt down next to my step-brother like I was the culprit who'd pushed him down the stairs. It wasn't my fault if he was high and fell down or that there was a warrant out for his arrest!

"What the hell's going on here?" Mike grumbled.

"The police are looking for him," I said in a mousy voice despite having just promised Aaron that I'd cover for him.

"Have you been taking those cheap counterfeit pills again?" Mike muttered through clenched teeth as he grabbed Aaron by the collar of his shirt and jerked him to his feet.

"He's not intoxicated," Adler interjected although Mike couldn't hear him, "for some reason it's my energy doing that to him. Ever since he entered the energy field he's been feeling sick. It seems like some atoms might be decaying."

"Joanie's story of her keeper is real dad," Aaron choked out, "he's standing right there next to her!"

Everyone looked at me but nobody else seemed to be aware of Adler's presence there. Only Aaron and I could see him. Mike let go of his grip on him and Aaron slowly walked towards Adler, cautiously holding out his hand as everyone looked on waiting for something to happen. Adler pushed some of Aaron's messy hair out of his face and for a moment being touched by a keeper seemed to soothe my step-brother but as soon as Adler let him go he returned to feeling sick.

"I don't understand what's happening," Adler said to himself as he looked on.

"What do you see Aaron?" my mom asked in a shaky voice.

"I see Adler," Aaron slurred, "and he's not scary actually."

"What in the world did you put inside his head?" Mike angrily shouted at me.

I knew it. I was once again going to be blamed for something I had absolutely no part in. In defiance to Mike's anger, Adler walked over to him and put both of his hands on his shoulders. As he did so there was a spark of electricity that ignited in the air and Mike got the zap of his life. He jumped back in a mixture of both surprise and pain.

The look on Adler's face indicated anger and the usual soft glowing aura that surrounded him hummed with electricity. I'd never seen him like that before, and he probably also hadn't been aware that he was capable of doing that. The more I tried to decipher the situation the less anything made sense.

"I don't understand," my mom's voice was filled with fear.

"They say that those who don't believe in magic will never see it," Adler whispered to himself with a hint of anger in his voice.

The moment was interrupted by two police cars pulling up in the driveway. I didn't want to be around to see my step-brother be arrested, or possibly committed to a mental institution if he told them that he could see Adler, so I went back up to my room. I didn't feel like being berated by my mother and Mike over the entire situation either because who else could put in his head that Adler was real, right? The atmosphere in the room seemed to deflate with the arrival of the police officers, and the hum of electricity coming from Adler subsided.

My keeper followed me faithfully has he always did and sat down next to me. He didn't say anything but I knew that thoughts were spiraling around inside his head in an incoherent and confused fashion, the exact same thing that was happening inside of mine.

At first I had thought that maybe over time the answers to my questions would reveal themselves to me, but the exact opposite was happening. There was no making sense in anything when where was nothing to be made sense of to begin with. Mentally tired, I let my head flop down on my pillow and rubbed my eyes as I tried to figure out what to do next.

"We're gonna prove to them that you're real," I whispered after an extended moment of silence.

"How do you plan on doing that?" Adler was curious.

"I'm going to make a slight cut on my hand, and you're to heal it in front of everybody. They won't be able to deny your existence any longer."

"I don't think that's a good idea Joanie."

"Why not? It'll prove that you're real. And yeah, my folks will accuse me of mutilating myself because I only want attention but that's not why I'm doing this."

"Are you sure about that?"

"What are you implying? That it's okay for my folks to treat me like I'm insane and manipulative like that? My life has been nothing but a living hell recently!"

"The night I came to you, your hurt was real. But now you're angry, it isn't about pain, grief or confusion anymore."

"If you're not here to help me or uplift me just leave."

"Joanie, please listen to me. I didn't say this to hurt you."

"I need you right now Adler, we all do, so you need to be here with me and you need to help me please."

Memories of the first night Adler stayed with me came flooding over me and with them came feelings of loneliness and desolation. Was it really just a ghost that was in my corner? Could I really patch things up with Rosanna? What about my father and his new family? Would he ever love me again? My mind began to race with a million doubts about my own existence.

"I'm right here Joanie, don't you worry now because I'm right here," Adler's voice was gentle and compassionate as he pulled me up next to him and put his arm around my shoulders, "I'll do anything you want, just say the word and I'll do it."

"I'm sorry I treated you so badly earlier," I apologized as I thought back to all that Adler had done for me since we'd met, "please forgive me."

"Already done."

"Can you share with me some of your keeper wisdom to make me feel better?"

"Sure. You cannot erase hate with hate. Love is the only cure."

"Oh that burns. There's so much hate in this house."

"Be like a tree and let the dead leaves fall off."

"That's deep."

"And it's much easier said than done too, but trees are notorious for weathering the harshest of conditions and still growing taller and stronger."

"This world will try to bury you, but what these people don't know is that you're a seed."

"Now *that's* deep Joanie."

The two of us looked at each other and smiled. He knew that deep down inside I knew most of the things he told me but sometimes I needed a gentle reminder. We all did. I looked over at my clock and saw that it would soon be time to start the day but as usual I didn't really want to leave my private space with Adler. In fact I didn't want to do anything at all.

"I can't stop thinking about Aaron," I spoke softly.

"Aggravated burglary is a serious crime," Adler spoke in his usual calm voice, "but the physical sickness I caused him worries me."

"What do you think it means? Is your time running out or something?"

"I don't know Joanie, but just in case my time does run out again sometime in the near future, I just want to know that you'll be okay."

"Of course. I'll be lonely for a while but you've taught me so much that I'll never forget for as long as I live."

"If there is anything that's still left for me to do here, just let me know."

"Let's go down to the park by the boardwalk again just like we did before or go back down by the water where I buried the doll of you. If this feeling doesn't leave you then it's because it means something."

"What is your mother going to say about you skipping school?"

"What can they say? They can't stop me from hanging out with you."

Adler flashed me that amazingly beautiful perfect otherworldly smile and signaled me to get up and follow him. I turned off my alarm clock before it rang, put on whichever clothes that were the first on top of the pile and followed Adler. My mother and Mike were both arguing in the living room about Aaron's upcoming day in court. It was awkward to be up that early but it felt good.

"Off to the boardwalk we go!" Adler cheered happily as we

walked out of the house.

"It might be a little cold," I replied as we walked down the driveway, "but let me guess, you have some incredible warming powers too."

"I guess we'll just have to find out for ourselves!"

"Rock and roll!"

"We should grab you some breakfast on our way to the boardwalk since you won't be eating at home."

"There are plenty of tasty treats *at* the boardwalk."

And with that we went on our way through the streets of Bluepond that were slowly filling up with morning commuters and kids going to school. The sun was out but a few clouds were still floating around in the atmosphere. The seasonal temperature was nice with no cold breeze so it made for a truly beautiful day once again, if only it could stay that way. It wasn't particularly warm but it was comfortable considering I enjoyed the cooler weather over the usual hot and humid temperatures. Adler of course had a warm aura that surrounded me and made everything warmer than it actually was.

Adler's eyes shined in the sunlight like diamonds and his perfectly placed hair did not move an inch. His beauty and perfection was otherworldly. He'd been around for quite a long time but I could never get over that. I was still in awe every time I saw him no matter how many times I did. I admired him from the corner of my eye for a little while before he began to notice and started to playfully tease me about it.

"I've never seen anything like you," I muttered out in embarrassment at being caught redhanded.

"I've never seen anything like me either," Adler joked as he giggled.

"You've never ever had any experiences with keepers or angels or ghosts before?"

"Never, but it's true that I never really believed in keepers or even knew about them to begin with. Well, not until *this* at least."

"And you've never encountered other spiritual beings here, I mean, in this form?"

"Nope, it's nothing other than the real world as I remembered it. The only difference is that it's a heck of a lot more modern!"

"Either way, you're incredible Adler."

"This *is* incredible! My eyes weren't nearly as radiant when I was human and my hair wasn't as shiny nor as soft. For some reason this existence also comes with a bunch of wisdom and reason. It has both its perks and its drawbacks, much like everything else in life it seems."

Once we arrived at the park by the boardwalk I bought a double portion of candies and sweets and other stuff that was terrible for your teeth and that might as well give you diabetes for Adler and I. Afterwards we immediately hopped onto the ferris wheel and waited to be elevated all the way to the top so we could see the city skyline. The morning sun was beautiful as our pod slowly went up to the very top and we had a spectacular view of everything. It was just as breathtaking as the very first time.

The second time around was probably even more magical because Adler and I had grown to be so close and the bottom line was that I owed him my life. Looking at his radiant and perfect features against the skyline in the backdrop took my breath away on more than one level. It was such a shame that I was the only person who could see him all the time.

"Do you think it's naive to want my parents to get back together?" I asked Adler after a long period of silence as our pod went down.

"No, dear," he replied softly, "it's not wrong to grieve for what you lost, but I hope you realize that it's highly unrealistic that your parents will ever get back together. The most you can hope for is that they get along for your sake and that they'll both give you the absolute best version of themselves."

"It's weird that it's just now that my dad woke up, now that I'm apparently insane and seeing dead soldiers that served in the Second World War."

"I'm sure that your father has experienced worst than his daughter's invisible friend. Look on the bright side though, you might just get your dad back."

"I hope so, I'm kind of bummed that I won't be able to go stay with him for a while but I guess if you're by my side I can survive until then. I survived a tractor trailer thanks to you."

"I only did what I had to do. No differently than I did in 1943."

"Give me a random piece of your epic wisdom please?"

"You can't set yourself on fire to keep someone else warm."

"Wow, that's a little deep for this early in the morning."

"Alright, let's talk about something lighthearted."

I couldn't help myself so I reached out and grabbed Adler's big strong hand. He squeezed my little hand into his to reassure me as he felt my emotions shift slightly and adjusted the serene energy he gave off accordingly. Both of our energy fields merged and it wasn't long before positive agape was radiating all over the place.

"It's funny how you seem to glow in the darkness but in the sunlight you look completely normal," I continued.

"Are you implying that I'm not normal?" Adler responded in a playful tone of voice.

"Yes! As a matter of fact I am! There's nothing normal about you, and that's a good thing! I just figured that maybe you'd glow more in the sunlight, or sparkle, I don't know. Not that it matters because I'm the only one who can see you."

"Those who don't see me but who feel me must be kinda freaked out, especially those who don't believe."

"Those who don't believe definitely are missing out on some pretty amazing things!"

"I agree, but I guess that maybe they aren't at a point in their lives where their hearts are open to belief. I think of your father and the wakeup call the accident gave him. Some people won't understand something or believe in something until it happens to them, or at least until they witness it."

"Speaking of witnessing, you must've seen many terrible things during the war."

"More than I'd like to share that's for sure."

"Since I've met you I've come to realize how precious life really is, and how important it is to both reach out to others and have someone by your side. It only takes one push to fall off the edge and only one helpful hand to pull you back. To give life or to give death, it sounds grand but in fact it's very simple."

"You are right about that. Printing fake documents didn't seem like much to me at the time but it did save hundreds of lives."

"I'll never understand how some people can have hearts filled with such hatred that they ostracize, abuse and kill people like that. I was always told at school that we shouldn't look down on others just because they are different."

"The only time you should look down on a person is when you're bending over to pick them up off the ground."

"Out of all the fancy things that my aunt Kendra told me, I've never heard that one!"

"Well, she's got to leave some to the ghosts!"

"Angels."

"Keepers."

"Dead members of the German Resistance."

"Expired people who... uh... are not gone. Okay, that was pretty lame."

The two of us giggled as our pod went around the ferris wheel for the third and final time. The sky began to get darker and darker as more and more angry clouds moved into the atmosphere. Bluepond was usually a very rainy and humid city but in recent days the sun had been out and shining bright and overall it had felt more like California weather. As Adler and I got out of the ferris wheel pod my stomach grumbled and I knew that my keeper wouldn't let me *not* eat so I let him take the lead and decide what he wanted to eat. I was content with just about anything either way.

Since we had both the rest of the morning and the entire afternoon to kill we decided to take our time, stopping here and there for a few bites to eat until I was full. Adler didn't feel fullness like humans did so he literally could've eaten all the food in the universe. Ironically, he didn't feel hunger in the first place either.

We then rode around the city buses for about two hours to get away from the drizzling rain but it didn't seem like it would let up and after a while my butt was getting sore from sitting on those uncomfortable seats. There was only so much looking at the buildings flying by through the bus window you could do for fun in a single day.

Despite the rain Adler wasn't wet, but I was completely soaked by the time we made it to the place where I'd buried my doll. The wetness didn't bother me though, because the general rule was that after the rain came the blazing sunlight and heat that would make everything dry again in no time. And a bonus for me, Adler would probably only have to touch me to make me dry again. The rain came with the territory in Bluepond but I could almost see the sunshine waiting to speak through the behind the clouds.

Sure enough the sun started peaking through the clouds as the two of us walked over to the small clearing by the side of the water and looked at the civilization on the other side. The clouds had thinned out and just as I'd expected it was going to be a sunny couple of hours. I was happy to see the clear blue sky revealing itself more and more as the dark clouds dissipated, but above all I was happy to dry off in the sunlight.

Adler put his arm around my shoulder upon noticing what I was doing and within an instant I was completely dry. All he did was grin at me without saying a word. I latched on to his arm as I took a moment to simply appreciate the beauty that was in front of me.

The seagulls flew around looking for food and the cars sped by going Nascar fast on the highway behind us. To the rest of the world I was soaking up the sunshine in solitude but in fact I was standing right at the spot where I'd buried who would later become my best friend, as odd as it sounded to put it like that. I looked at the dirt under my feet for a moment, wondering if Adler was still in there or if the water had washed him away. I was afraid that if my keeper left for reasons out of his control I wouldn't have anything left of him.

"No Joanie," he said like he could read my thoughts again, "I'm right here. I'm not buried in the dirt, I'm right by your side."

# FOURTEEN

Adler's existence never got easier to understand. Sometimes people seemed to feel his aura while others were completely oblivious. According to some websites about keepers that weren't complete gibberish, visual manifestations to others depended on a long list of factors. It depended on the level of energy that Adler had recently absorbed and maintained, at what level of energy I was vibrating at, the energy of the other living beings in the room and the energy of the surrounding environment itself.

Considering that most people had not reached a state of heightened awareness to consciously propagate the agape from deep inside of them, it was often impossible to get the synchronicity required for an apparition, despite in many cases this rule didn't seem to apply at all. The bottom line seemed to be that if all the required components weren't in sync, you couldn't see Adler. Something like that. Something else had obviously happened with Aaron though, and that weird sick feeling had never left Adler either.

My aunt Kendra hadn't been able to see him either when I'd finally gotten around to visiting her, but she did say, however, that she felt a strong aura of love and goodness around me. Both Adler and I were incredibly happy to hear that she felt something and that she believed in greater things at play but I chickened out and didn't tell her about my keeper. I couldn't get my mom's meltdown out of my mind and all the chaos that had taken place after she'd gotten wind of my keeper.

I knew that my aunt Kendra was different but my flawed human insecurities still got the best of me. Those doubts at the back of my mind had come creeping in again and had managed to shut me inside of myself. I *wanted* to tell her so badly but when the time came to do so, I didn't find myself feeling so strong and bold.

I had no trouble connecting with Adler in the agape, but I had a hard time connecting to the overwhelming sense of peace and serenity that had once consumed me completely. I knew that my keeper had a hard time feeling it too and something was definitely eating away at him from the inside out, it was becoming more and more obvious.

Over the subsequent weeks things were as they'd always been in my area of Bluepond. Aaron was in jail, Mike and my mother had periodic blowouts but they always got back together. My father's injuries had healed and although we spoke on the phone from time to time he was still more preoccupied with his new family than with me. My eventual move into his house was in limbo much like the rest of my life but Adler helped me take it one day at a time.

There always seemed to be an elephant in the room wherever I was concerned because nobody had ever dared to make the first move to have a conversation about keepers after the accident. It was something like the topic of drunk driving or suicide, people *need* to talk about it if anything is ever going to be done to resolve those issues but nobody likes talking about such things.

Which was the lesser of two evils? To ignore the problem and move on with our lives but suffer the disastrous consequences? Or to face up to the hard facts, own up to your failures and open up the lines of communication? As much as I would have liked to pick the second option, considering the current atmosphere in my house it was probably better to stick with the first.

"You've been distant lately," I muttered to Adler as we walked to school in the rain one morning, "what's going on with you?"

And it was true, Adler had been unusually silent and reserved. The chivalrous lieutenant who was usually very talkative, animated, funny, witty and bright had been reduced to merely an imaginary friend. It seemed like everyone around me had unresolved issues that they didn't want to talk about. It was eating away at everybody's peace of mind, one that had been fragile to begin with.

"To tell you the truth Joanie, I don't really know. I'm feeling quite lost," Adler's voice was bleak and emotionless, "and this is going to sound really screwed up but I feel like I'm becoming human again."

"There's nothing screwed up about the way we feel. We don't get to choose how we feel and it's by ignoring our emotions that they end up consuming us completely. You're even the one who taught me that."

"I know."

"And by the way, if you care about my two cents on the subject, I don't think it's possible to become human again in your situation if there's any comfort in that for you."

"I'm thinking that maybe my soul is becoming loose from this body and is becoming ready to transition into the next world for yet another time. It's definitely strange because I didn't feel like this prior to my death on the Eastern Front."

"Or maybe you're just not dying. The thought that maybe you'll have to leave me soon makes me very sad but I don't think you'll be going to a bad place."

"I just don't want to leave things half-finished again."

The puddles on the ground quickly became the size of lakes as we stomped through them on the journey to school one morning. My exams were looming over my head but I had done well in all of my classes thus far and I had Adler to help me out when I got stuck. The weatherman had forecasted mild weather so that was definitely welcomed because I'd seen on TV that many places were being blasted with snow!

A little snow on the ground was beautiful but usually along with the snow came the frigid weather and that was really what I disliked the most. I was over playing in the snow with the neighbors' kids despite that I'd loved snowball fights when the snow was sticky, or making a snowman with my dad in the front yard. Those were all happy memories but I'd outgrown that kind of childish fun and I preferred to busy myself with other hobbies.

I arrived at school just in time for the first morning bell to ring and as I walked into the lobby I came face to face with Alana Overton. She gave me some dirty looks and then went on her way down a hallway far from where I was going. Obviously she hadn't forgotten what had happened, but then again, something like that was hard to forget. As far as I was concerned the school had written in the incident report that she had been trying to perform a stunt with other students at the time of the accident because, quite frankly, there wasn't any other plausible conclusion to the matter.

I chuckled under my breath and went up to my first class for another boring review before exam time. In my opinion I had navigated well the waters of my first year of high school and all that entailed. The one and only persistent annoying problem at school was Rosanna. She knew better than to try to speak to me again, but I always saw her glancing in my direction from her corner of my eye. I had come to blame her less for everything that had happened as time went by but that didn't change my distain for her.

She had betrayed me and although I hadn't driven a nail into a plank of wood and then pulled it out, the scar still remained. I hadn't made any new friends throughout the entire semester because I didn't want a repeat of what happened with Rosanna and I knew that she was lonely too because she always sat by herself in the cafeteria and I had never seen her hang out with other people during the daily morning break.

"Why don't you go talk to her?" Adler proposed as he felt my emotions during morning break.

"And say what?" I asked as Rosanna passed by in the distance.

"That you don't hate her for starters."

"Yeah."

"Forgiveness is the only real way you'll ever be set free of the negative emotions that you still carry around."

"I know Adler, I'm just not sure that I'm ready to take this step right now. I don't know what it's going to bring and I really need to focus on passing my classes. I'm not sure how I'll handle additional stress."

"I understand, and your success in school should absolutely be your priority right now but don't forget what I told you. Most of all though, don't let this feeling of not being able forgive sour into something that you cannot control."

"I know that you won't let me not forgive her when the time comes. Just one more week of class and one week of exams and I'll actually have a life again."

"I completely understand Joanie, and remember that forgiving Rosanna doesn't mean being best friends again. If you don't want a friendship with her that's completely fine, but at least for your own sake bring yourself to a place where there's not this tension in the room when the two of you are near each other."

Rosanna shot me a look as she passed by but quickly looked away when she saw that I was looking at her too. Deep down inside I wanted to be friends again because I missed her. The two of us had been so good together, she had been like the sister I'd always wanted but never had. I resolved to wait until the exams were over because I wouldn't be able to handle additional stress while I was already under so much pressure just in case something went awry.

The rest of the school day was highly uneventful and with hours upon hours of studying looming over my head I preferred it that way. Nobody gave me dirty looks and Adler didn't have to zap anyone or shove them up against a brick wall to defend and protect me. I didn't even get any new homework! My only task for the rest of the week was make sure that I had actually learned something during the past five months.

Back at home I found a note left on the counter written by my mother telling me that she and Mike would be out for the evening. I figured that the two of them had had another big fight and he was now taking her out to make it up to her. I'd given up a long time ago on trying to break the cycle because it was obviously too big for me to handle. The most I could do was stay out of their way and hope for the best.

Going to see another adult was out of the question because if Mike got wind that I did that I knew there would be hell to pay and it was probably safer to stay silent. I trusted Adler and I trusted that in due time he'd stand up to Mike if he ever tried to get physical with one of us. I looked over at my keeper in awe and gratitude but Adler seemed to be somewhere else. I knew that residual emotions from the war were bothering him but all I could do was respect his choice to not want to share them with me.

I was happy that I had the house all to myself because I was tired from my day and it wouldn't do me any harm to stay inside with Adler and be able to have absolute peace and quiet for what seemed like the longest time on earth. Maybe I'd get to watch TV in solitude or take a super long shower because there wouldn't be anybody to complain about the lack of hot water for the rest of the evening. Indeed, being home alone was definitely nice.

"I don't know what I want out of life," I muttered as I flopped down on the living room couch and Adler sat next to me.

"Most people your age don't," Adler replied in his usual soft voice, "and there's nothing wrong with that. Nobody says you have to pick out a profession now and be stuck with it for the rest of your life."

"That's true, and I should make making a *life* my priority instead of making a *living*. I don't want to waste my youth and my health accumulating material wealth and then be old and realize that my entire life has passed me by and I'm left with nothing but a pile of money and no health and no youth and no one."

"Those are the wise words of a person with a head on their shoulders."

"I'm not interested in the high life, I'm interested in a fulfilling life after I'm done school here, but I'm not quite sure what that's going to be yet."

"If you ask me, when the right thing comes along you'll feel it in your heart."

As I flipped through the TV channels I came across The Movie Network that was playing *Schindler's List* so I decided to tune in since I could probably learn something valuable for class at the same time that I was relaxing. I'd missed about twenty minutes of the film but considering that it was so long I probably could be fine with just the rest of it.

I knew a great deal about Oskar Schindler's story from both school and my own obsession with history but I'd never seen that movie before. He was one of the most notable members of the German Resistance during the Second World War and had saved over a thousand Jews by employing them in his factory in Krakow, Poland and subsequently prevented them from being deported to death camps like Auschwitz.

Adler's face immediately fell as I tuned into the movie. His body became rigid and he swallowed hard. I knew that he still had many unresolved feelings about the war, especially being a German who had to fight against his own country, but who doesn't react negatively towards something like the Holocaust? Adler's reaction indicated emotions more powerful than most and I knew that it bothered him to watch that film with me but he didn't protest to change the channel or anything of the sort.

"This is obviously something extremely painful for you," I said as I gently placed my hand on my keeper's shoulder, "did you ever see the camps?"

"Oh Joanie, you don't even know," he replied in an exasperated tone of voice, "there's something I haven't told you and it's been eating away at me constantly."

"You should let it out, whatever is bothering you, Adler. There's nothing easy about a situation like this but you can't keep it all bottled up inside either. Schindler saved a lot of people but I'm sure that he struggled with not having been able to save more too."

"That's the thing Joanie, people didn't just live because of me.

A lot of people also died because of me.”

Adler immediately broke down in an uncontrollable sob on the couch next to me. I didn’t understand what he meant by saying that a lot of people had also died because of him, but to me he was still my hero and I took him into a hug to console him.

“What I left out of my story of saving Jews is that I also turned some in to the Gestapo,” he spoke in a shaky voice.

“What?!” I asked in complete shock and disbelief at what I was hearing.

“When I was caught I was given a choice to either face an SS court or go to the Eastern Front but in exchange for letting me go I had to give the names and addresses of many of the people who hid the Jews after I got them out of the area. Well, I did.”

If I had felt betrayed by Rosanna when her mom called mine to whine about my so-called imaginary friend, it was a drop of water in an endless sea compared to what I felt as I stared blankly at the TV screen in front of me. All emotions left me and I was left in a blank, empty inside state. Had everything just been based on a lie? The whole time had it been nothing more than a lie?

“Why?” I muttered in a shaky voice after an extended moment of silence on my part.

“I thought I used to know, but now I’m not so sure anymore Joanie,” Adler choked up through an ocean of sorrow, “I thought that once the Gestapo was off my case I could go back to saving more but I guess I was just a coward.”

“How dare you?! I don’t blame you for having unresolved feelings about the war! You ought to be ashamed of yourself for turning your back on the people you vowed to help!”

“I put it off as long as I could but you have no idea what kind of torture the Gestapo was capable of. I gave them only a few names to downplay the scale of my operation, hoping that the rescued Jews would all be gone by the time they got there but they caught fourteen and along with the host families two dozen people were sent to the camps.”

In my blank state of shock, confusion and disbelief I wasn’t able to utter out a single word. A million and one things were swirling around my mind and clouding up my logic, whatever little logic was involved in something like that in the first place. I couldn't think. I couldn't feel. I could only barely breathe.

"On the Eastern Front I tried to make myself believe that my rescue operation had been a success, that hundreds of people had still escaped to safety and even that I'd save some more once I was on leave, but I've never been able to forgive myself for my actions. I should've faced that military judge, I'm the one who should've perished in Auschwitz, at least I would have died a martyr and not a traitor of the German Resistance. I envy all of my comrades who died an honest soldier's death."

I didn't speak. In fact I couldn't speak. I was numb. Out of all the things that Adler could have told me, that one hadn't been on the list. The man who had been my hero and who had saved hundreds of people had also betrayed the entire human race by collaborating with the Nazis to save his own skin. Maybe one couldn't blame an ordinary person for doing something like that under duress, but Adler had put everything on the line to save these people. How could he turn his back on them?

"Just a few more minutes and you'll never see me again," Adler whispered after his tears had dried up, "so I guess this is the part where I say thanks. Thank you for your wonderful company and I'm sorry that I've failed so miserably for a second time in doing what I was sent here to do."

Just like Adler had predicted, within a few minutes of having the agape energy cut off his aura began to diminish until it completely faded into thin air. The beautiful colors of his face faded out to nothing as well and a few seconds later he began to dematerialize completely. First you could see right through him and then he disappeared entirely, leaving nothing behind, just like he had never been there in the first place. The look on his face as he faded away indicated that he had a good idea of what was going to come next.

I turned off the TV and walked up to my bedroom on the second floor because I needed to lay down comfortably and in a private place because my mother and Mike were bound to come back at any moment. With only the ticking of the clock and my heavy breathing, the silence was haunting. My heart was racing out of my chest but I was still too shocked to even cry.

As much as I would have liked to fall asleep and wake up and find out that it had been nothing but a bad dream, I was restless. I kept tossing and turning for what seemed like an eternity but as I looked at the digital clock in my room, I saw that only a few minutes had went by. The only thing I could think of doing was to get online and look up stories and interviews about the German Resistance and Holocaust survivors and at least educate myself more on their stories. It seemed like all that was left to do was use the tragedy as a teaching tool after all.

"These kinds of books are nothing new as many Holocaust survivors, as well as survivors of other genocides, have written them before," a survivor spoke to Larry King in an interview about her newly published memoir, "but I felt like I owed it to the good people who have suffered unjustly to tell my story but I also owe it to the people who have helped me recover from this. I cannot remain silent in the face of rising political radicalism around the world and I hope that this book is the first step to mending the hearts of people and empowering them to *do* something *before* situations get to the point that the Nazi regime did. People are not blameless in this, we are the ones who elect these politicians and it's the most vulnerable who pay the biggest price."

After that lengthy interview was over I watched another one about a Jewish family telling their story of being saved by members of the Dutch Resistance who kept them in hiding for over two years until the Canadians arrived to liberate their town. A lump in my throat formed and tears filled my eyes as I listened to their words.

"The host family who took us in are all heroes," one of them said, "they risked their lives for us. Had they been caught helping Jews they all would've been sent to the camps along with us. I can't blame those who didn't want to get involved or who refused to let us stay in their house, I don't have a single ounce of anger towards them, but those who did help are all true heroes. It's important that the stories of these people are never forgotten."

Listening to the many stories of the survivors was both heartwarming and heartbreaking at the same time. I'd always found it interesting how there could be so much love and courage yet so much hurt and destruction happening simultaneously. The bravery and strength of not only those who survived but also those who helped them left me in awe. All of those people were *my* heroes.

"The scariest part in all of this is that once upon a time the monsters we call Nazis were just ordinary men no different than us," another survivor went on, "they weren't born with the idea that they wanted to wipe out an entire race of people. Somewhere along the way they all *became* monsters and that's what's scary because the capacity to do exactly as they did is present within each and every one of us."

"Yes, that's true," a third person added to the conversation, "prior to the rise of Nazism the men who would die in the camps and those who'd carry out the exterminations were no different. We were all just average people, engineers, merchants, journalists, parents, students. Political extremism is more dangerous than I can describe but if there's one thing that I hope people understand it's that you cannot use hatred to take out hatred. The only way you'll remove the hatred from the equation is by adding love. To combat extremism we must use love, compassion and understanding. We need to build bridges between different communities, not walls."

As I watched endless news clips in my room I broke down in an uncontrollable sob too. I cried for the innocent victims, I cried for their families, for all that was lost and never had the chance to be, and I cried for Adler, but I also cried for myself. I cried because I had recoiled my hand judgmentally to an honorable man that had only done his best under the most impossible of circumstances.

Intellectually I knew that he hadn't given up the names and addresses of a few individuals to the Gestapo out of malice or hatred. He'd done it in good faith, believing that these safe houses would've been vacant by that point and that the Nazis would come back empty handed. He hadn't tried to save himself selfishly, he had tried to get out of that situation so he could eventually go back to saving even more people.

He could not have continued to run his Jew rescue operation if he was dead after all! The world worked in mysterious ways and sometimes we had to do a little wrong for the greater good. In his case maybe things hadn't worked out but I knew that his heart had always been in the right place.

And then I thought about Rosanna. She had no more friends because of *me*. I had been the only person she had but I had shoved her aside in favor of my own ideologies and negative emotions. During his time with me Adler had also been battling his own residual emotions about something gone wrong in the past and now I understood what he was going through inside with greater clarity. It was now my turn to try to make things right with my former best friend.

I wanted so badly to call Rosanna but it was almost eleven o'clock when I looked at the clock the second time. There was no more waiting until after exam time. That had been such a foolish and selfish idea in the first place. I was still furious with Adler but I was furious with myself too. How could my mind have been so blind and my heart so unwilling when I was seeking the same things they were?

While debating with myself whether or not I should call Rosanna despite that it was late I decided that I had to call her immediately after all, regardless of what time it was, so I punched in her number on my cellphone and waited. After only a few rings she picked up but to me it had still felt like an eternity with my heart pounding out of my chest and struggling to find the right words to say.

"Hello?" she answered in a tired and confused voice.

"Hello Rosanna, it's me," I spoke softly as I didn't know how she was going to react, "I hope I didn't wake you."

"No, I was just about to head to bed, what's going on?"

"I'm so sorry Rosanna, please forgive me."

"Please forgive *me* Joanie! I never meant to hurt you!"

"You're forgiven, absolutely forgiven. I came to a series of realizations tonight and a big one that I made is that it was wrong of me to shun you like I did. I want to be friends again. We don't need to talk tonight if it's too late and we're all tired anyway, but I'd like to sit down and talk."

"I would like that too. I'll meet you in the cafeteria in the morning since I can't really talk tonight. If my parents find me talking on the phone at this hour I'll be grounded for the rest of my life."

"Okay, that's perfect, thank you Rosanna. I hope you have a good night and I'm sorry if I bothered you."

I hung up before she could say another word. My throat was so tight and I didn't want her to worry about what was wrong with me because there was no doubt in my mind that my voice had still sounded pretty awful. I was still so overwhelmed with a thousand different emotions and I no longer had my keeper around to soothe them. Knowing that I'd brought that upon myself by making him disappear was the worst feeling in the world.

My only consolation was the fact that the situation with Rosanna was on its way of being fixed but I had another big problem that I needed to figure out how to solve too. Where had Adler gone? Was he okay? Was he suffering or was he in a state of non-existence? Was he in another parallel universe perhaps? If it was true what they said about existing simultaneously in parallel universes that could interact with each other maybe he was facing his day in an SS court.

I swallowed hard. I didn't want that to be true. There would be hell to pay for such a good and kindhearted man at the hands of the Nazis. My keeper had just disappeared on me when I had cut off the energy he required to exist and I hadn't been able to connect with him since. No matter how much I tried to connect with the agape inside of me like I had done nearly automatically each day, I couldn't sustain the energy. I could barely produce it.

I didn't know what I wanted to say to Adler but I knew I had to at least tell him that I was sorry for passing judgment the way I had done earlier. I didn't know how I was going to apologize, but I at least wanted to try. At the very least, I wanted a chance to show him how much I loved him for not only what he had done for me, but for all he had done to make the world a better place since he came into it.

His mission hadn't failed. He was still my hero. He would always be my hero no matter what because he'd saved me, guided me and loved me when nobody else did. After everything he deserved to know that his life had at least meant something to me even if the greater part of the rest of the world had forgotten about him. No matter what I could never forget him.

Since I couldn't sleep I decided to sit down in the chair in the corner of my room and think back to the many conversations and wisdom we'd shared in that very space. I could almost hear his voice echoing in the room and for just a moment I looked around just to see if he was there, but he wasn't. Nonetheless, I could still hear his soft voice and his wise words resonating inside my brain.

"Some people think that strength is never feeling pain but in reality the strongest people are those who understand and accept their pain in order to be able to move forward from it," I could still hear him say.

And oh boy, was I ever in pain! What would I do without my keeper? Yes, he'd taught me so much and filled me with so much wisdom and clarity but I wasn't ready for him to leave me so suddenly. I was still crawling and I wasn't ready to walk on my own!

"You must be the change you want to see in the world," I remembered Adler telling me, "because the most dangerous thing we can do as a society is think that somebody else will save the world."

I swallowed tightly because those words echoed exactly what one of the survivors had said in the interview. More tears escaped from my eyes as I tried so hard to connect with the energy deep inside of me to get my Adler back. It felt as though a being greater than me had blocked it because no matter what I did I could never get to it.

*"You know Joanie, my soul longs for a place that I don't even*

*know exists. I long for a place where my heart is whole, my soul is understood and my spirit is at peace."*

He'd given me absolutely everything I needed but I obviously hadn't been able to return the favor.

NO ACT OF KINDNESS
no matter how
SMALL
EVER goes to waste
so if you can't
find a nice
person in
this world
you can at least
be one <3

# FIFTEEN

Loneliness was the only thing with me in my bedroom. It was another one of those times where the loneliness wouldn't leave me alone. What had I done? Things had been going so well! But Adler was gone, seemingly forever. No matter what I did, I couldn't reach him. He was gone to a place somewhere far away from Bluepond and I feared that it wasn't the kind of place in which he would find what his soul had been longing for desperately.

I still clutched my cell phone in my hand after I finished talking to Rosanna and buried my face in my pillow. The only thing I could do was cry. You could say that I felt the very same way that I did the first night I met Adler, the only difference was that he wasn't around to comfort me. Ironically, he was the one who had needed such comfort.

The sound of his exasperated voice echoed at the back of my mind. And now he was gone. I was haunted by the look on his face during the last few moments of his existence before he faded away into thin air. His eyes begged to be held and to be comforted but I had turned away judgmentally. All the times that he had selflessly helped me — *saved my life* even — and all I had to offer him in return was condemnation without mercy or understanding.

My heart broke for him, it broke for the innocent people he'd worked so hard to save and their folks, as well as the population at large but most of all I felt for all the brokenhearted individuals out there seeking something to hold on to but never finding anything. I felt like I had joined them in their quest for unfindable answers.

I was breaking inside asking myself what if my best friend had gotten a second chance but I had done nothing but destroy him all over again. All the times that we had told each other that we were a team and that we'd lift each other up no matter what happened! He had kept his end of the bargain but I hadn't!

Eventually I fell asleep out of nothing other than exhaustion but I was tormented by nightmares. I had a dream in which I was falling down to somewhere dark and I was reaching out to people who were up high someplace safe above me but I couldn't reach. I was begging them to grab on to me to save me but we were too far apart. Eventually I fell to the very bottom and the darkness consumed me completely.

And then I woke up in a cold sweat. I had slept for only a few hours. The sky outside was still pitch black and I knew I couldn't get up without making noise and waking up somebody but I wasn't about to fall asleep in the near future either. I did the only thing I could think of doing and that was logging onto the computer and looking at some more postings about the Holocaust and the Second World War.

I broke down crying after the second interview with a survivor. I quickly shoved my face back into my pillow so no one would hear anything because the last thing I wanted was to attract some attention and be faced with another question period that I really wasn't up for. I especially didn't want to worry my mother because she had to travel three hours up north for a business conference and I knew that Mike wouldn't be thrilled either way.

The last thing I wanted was for my mom to have to cancel her plans just for me, just because I had lost something I never really had in the first place. I needed to go meet up with Rosanna anyhow, she was about the last person who could help me. She was possibly the only person who could help me.

Fast forward a few hours and a few rivers of tears and everyone in the house was up and getting ready for a big day. I called up Rosanna as soon as I thought that she'd be awake and told her I needed an emergency meeting at Clancy's Diner not too far from the school because I couldn't wait for the cafeteria and she agreed to meet me there so I got dressed in a jiffy and flew out the door.

I dismissed my folks, telling them that I needed to attend a study club with some other people before my first class and I didn't want to miss a thing. I quickly wished them well for the day before I left without eating and without leaving anyone the chance to respond. I raced to the nearest bus station and took public transit down a couple of blocks where Rosanna was already waiting for me.

She already had a table by the window and was eating some bacon and eggs, Clancy's signature meal. I didn't really know what to say to Rosanna after so many months had gone by and we hadn't spoken a single word to each other. She seemed to be open-minded and willing to forgive though. I needed that. I realized the mistakes I had made with her and I wanted to make things right.

I knew that Adler had wanted to make things right but he hadn't gotten the chance because I had cut off his energy and it seemed like there was no coming back for him. He was gone forever, and I had a part to play in that. He carried around so much guilt for doing what he thought was best at the time and I carried around guilt for not seeing that earlier.

"What's going on Jo?" Rosanna asked me in a mousy voice, unsure of why I seemed so messed up.

"Everything," I muttered, "but first of all I want you to know that I am honestly very sorry for how things ended up between us. I understand your reasons now, and I reckon that back then you felt the same way I do now."

"I know, and I've forgiven you a long time ago. I'm responsible for the part I played in ruining our friendship and I've wanted this back for a very long time and I'm grateful for this opportunity. You were my best friend! Now please tell me what's going on with you? Why is your face so troubled and downcast?"

"It's Adler."

"Oh! What's going on with him? Is he alright?"

"No, he's gone."

"Where? I don't understand, what happened to him?"

"I guess you could say he died again."

"I'm so sorry Jo! I know that he was a wonderful person and an absolutely wonderful keeper! Is there anything we can do to make him come back?"

"I don't know, but I think I'm the one who killed his soul this time!"

"Joanie, listen, I know you're not the one who killed him or made him disappear, so please tell me what happened."

Tears filled my eyes as I swallowed hard. The previous night replayed in my mind, especially the part where Adler trusted me enough to tell me the truth and I condemned him for it. While I didn't necessarily agree with his choices, I knew that his heart had been in the right place when he had decided to do that.

"Well, the two of us decided to watch Schindler's List on TV last night," I told Rosanna once I had composed myself, "and that was particularly painful for him. It's hard for anyone to watch a movie like that but for him there was something more and when I finally got him to open up to me all hell broke loose. I totally flipped out when I found out and I cut off the agape he needed in order to exist."

Rosanna listened attentively as I told her the whole story, just like a best friend would do in a time of need. Unlike how I'd reacted to Adler opening up to me, Rosanna didn't judge me. In fact all she did was offer me compassion and that probably burned more than anything.

"And then he told me that I would never see him again. I've been trying to connect with him ever since but to no avail. He's gone."

"So he just disappeared? Just like that? After everything?!"

"Yes."

"But is it really because you judged his actions? I mean, how can you not be furious upon finding out something like that? I know that his heart was in the right place and I understand that it was probably the toughest choice of his life, but it's still a shock!"

"I don't know, that's what I don't understand. It all ended so suddenly and you're like the only person who saw him that is also my friend. By being without him I realized how you must've felt being all alone too and even though it seems like there's nothing I can do for him now, I can at least patch things up between us."

"Thank you for this opportunity Joanie, I appreciate it, I'm just sorry that Adler had to suffer this way for us to fix our friendship."

"I know, me too, but I don't want to lose this too. You're all that I have left."

"And I'm not going anywhere, but right now we need to figure out a way to get your keeper back!"

Was there really a way to do that? I had tried and tried and tried and actually felt the agape but Adler hadn't come back. Nothing had happened. I was sure that he was gone forever but there was a part of me that still believed in things unseen, and I chose to believe that I'd see Adler again.

I chose to believe that it wasn't over. I dared to seek something I wasn't sure was even out there and I dared to believe that I was going to find it. I wasn't going to screw things up twice. I was going to get Adler back, but convincing myself of that was a lot harder than it sounded.

"What do you have in mind?" I asked Rosanna as it was obvious she was thinking hard.

"Build a shrine?" she muttered, unsure of herself.

"I don't think that's gonna work," I retorted, "because Adler was never a deity. As a person who believed strongly in God I think he'd been highly offended if we started worshiping idols."

Rosanna and I seemed to debate endlessly without being able to come to a sensible conclusion. Or was it just me overthinking again when the answer was right in front of my face? The more I tried to think the less I seemed to be able too. Was I slowly fading away too? Had I ever been whole in the first place?

Rosanna did her best to help me out but the bottom line was that nobody could help me. I'd failed Adler at the most crucial point of his keeper existence. I'd sent him right back to that same place before I created him. Then it struck me, maybe I'd find him by digging up my doll! I didn't know if it was still there or if the water had washed it away but I had to try so when Rosanna had to head to school I decided to skip yet another day, a very important review day, but I had better things to do.

The first thing I did was decide to go home to change into some old dingy clothes because I'd be digging around in the dirt for a while. As I hopped onto the bus I made mental notes of everything I thought I might need like a small shovel and some gloves perhaps. Back at home the house was empty. You could even hear the clock ticking on the wall.

Adler wasn't there next to me to breathe gently. I couldn't hear his heartbeat. It didn't beat anymore and I knew it. In one last attempt at holding on to something that was already gone I went up to my room and sat on the edge of my bed and stared blankly around the place. His presence still lingered around.

"I can still feel you but I know I can't have you anymore," I choked up through a spontaneous river of tears, "so just go away. Gosh, I there is still so much left unsaid!"

I looked at my other dolls standing on other pieces of furniture around the place, the good guys and the bad guys. The only one that was missing was the best guy.

"Adler, I'm calling out to you now," I whispered in a hoarse voice as I did my best to compose myself, "we all need someone to help us make it through. God had blessed us with each other and I can't believe that it's already over so please just give me a sign!"

With that said I leaned back on my bed and connected with the agape deep inside of me. Once I found that place of serenity I let all of my emotions get washed out by the feeling of peace until I came to a level where I could sustain it nicely without exhausting myself afterwards.

That was the level of vibration that Adler and I usually spent our quiet lazy days at. I closed my eyes and thought back to the good times we spent together on the boardwalk, on the ferris wheel, walking to school, walking back home, taking the bus, watching the stars, looking out at the ocean.

Then I thought back to the time that he had pushed Alana Overton up against the wall, and when he put himself between that truck and our vehicle when my dad and I were out for a drive. How I could I *not* love him? How could I *not* be thankful? Maybe it didn't change his regrets being faced with the Gestapo but in my opinion his goodness greatly overshadowed his mistakes.

After at least nearly an hour of quietly meditating in the agape I began to feel a change in the energy and so I opened my eyes in response and saw that there were a pair of boots next to me on my bed. A pair of black jackboots with *blood splats* on them. Of course I was afraid but I knew too well who those boots belonged to so I sat up and looked behind me.

I screamed when I saw what Adler looked like. He was in terrible shape. He was a soldier about to pay the ultimate price on the bloody Eastern Front. There was no more life in his eyes, his lips were cracked up and dry and the rest of his skin was nothing other than a dead person's skin. It had no color. Just like the soul inside of him, it had faded away to almost nothing.

Adler wasn't breathing and as I reached out for him my hand went right through him. Not only was that what he probably looked like right before he died, but I couldn't even physically have him with me anymore. I inhaled loudly and gave it all I had to amplify the agape and the energy field around me as much as I could. After a few moments of having my entire being vibrate at a higher level, I reached out to touch Adler again.

I could touch him, he had materialized, but his body was cold and his heart was no longer beating. I was devastated by what I saw. He had once been so beautiful, so sweet, so loving! But he was dead, literally *dead* yet forces greater than the two of us kept him around to prolong his suffering. I did the last thing I could do and that was hold him tightly in my arms.

"I'm so, *so* sorry that I didn't give you compassion and understanding when you asked me to," I muttered in anguish, "when you most *needed* me to."

"You can tell me that I should stick around for you but the truth is Joanie, I'm only here for a little while."

"Where did you go last night? And most importantly, why do you look like this now?"

"I went to some places, I saw certain people, but they obviously weren't aware of my presence next to them. And my darling, I'm dead."

"But there's got to be *something* we can do for you to not end like this!"

Before I had the chance to say anything else there was a weird shift in energy in the room. For a fraction of a second it seemed like multicolored lights flashed in the room but I couldn't be sure because it all happened so fast and tears were still escaping from my eyes. Almost immediately after the flashing lights thing, Adler's body became rigid for a few moments and he blankly stared into the distance seemingly seeing something that I wasn't, almost like he had been momentarily transported to another dimension before coming back.

"It's your mom," he muttered in a worried voice when his soul came back to where we were sitting.

"What?" I asked in confusion, "What's wrong with my mom?"

"You need to call her and tell her to stop the car or turn around!"

"Why? Do you sense something?"

Once again Adler momentarily went somewhere else for a lack of a better way to describe it. Just a split second later he was back with me again and still in the same condition.

"You need to help her, I'm not strong enough to do it myself."

"Okay, tell me what to do and I'll do it."

Adler instructed me to pick up the phone and to call my mom's cell. I knew that she was still on the road and about halfway to her destination so I prayed that she was in a service area and could answer my call. I waited impatiently as the phone rang a couple of times but then I heard her voice on the other end of the line.

"Hi honey, what's going on?" she sounded genuinely surprised, "Is something wrong for you to call me like this at this time?"

"Yes!" Adler exclaimed, "Tell her that she needs to pull up on the side of the road right now because a tanker truck is coming up the hill and it's going to explode as soon as it gets to the other side."

"Yes mom," I tried to remain as calm and composed as possible, "you need to pull over to the side of the road right away."

"There's a truck stop just over the hill honey, hang on a few minutes," she replied, seemingly annoyed and concerned at the same time.

I looked over at Adler who had a look of urgency on his face. He looked beat up and exhausted as he kept on going back and forth between me and somewhere else. And then it hit me. The other place he was going back and forth to was my mom's car! That was the only possible explanation to how he knew exactly where she was and most of all that a tanker truck was coming up the hill on the other side.

"Mom, I don't expect you to understand this," I went on in a more urgent tone of voice, "but there's a tanker coming up the hill on the other side and it's just about to flip over and blow up so please *stop the car* right now!"

"Joanie what's going on?" her voice seemed to be more confused than ever, "And how do you know there's a tanker here?"

"I don't have enough energy," Adler whispered as he closed his eyes in exasperation.

I opened up my texting app while I was still on the line with my mom and told Rosanna that I needed as much agape as possible for a few moments. I had no idea if it was going to work but I at least had to try. I also honestly prayed to God for the first time in my life because I still had so many things to say to Adler before it was all over and I needed divine help at that point!

"It's now or never, the truck is coming up over the hill!" Adler whispered at me as he was beginning to fade out again.

"Mom! Just pull over please!" I shouted through the telephone in a panicked voice, "I need you to do this for me now!"

"Oh my goodness!" my mother exclaimed as she gasped.

She must have dropped the phone as I heard some screeching and tapping noises and then I could only hear her voice in the background. And then I heard what was nothing other than an explosion. My mother screamed and I screamed for her at my end. A few moments later she picked up the phone from off the floor or wherever it had landed and I heard her soothing voice again.

"Oh my goodness Joanie! I need to call 911! The truck did explode exactly like you said it would! I'll call you back in a few minutes!"

"Mom! Are you okay?!"

"Yes! Yes, honey, I pulled over just in time when I saw the truck swerving across the road. I'll talk to you again in five minutes!"

And with that she hung up the phone. I exhaled excessively loudly and let my head flop on Adler's shoulder. I let my phone drop on the bed as I tightly held on to Adler, just trying to sort out my emotions and to keep my cool. Just a few moments after my phone rang again and I saw that it was my mom calling as she had promised.

"Hi mom," I answered her call in an exhausted voice.

"Oh Joanie!" she was obviously distraught, "I've just turned the car around and I'll be back home in about an hour and a half."

"Oh thank goodness that you're okay! I'll be right here waiting for you mom."

"Okay, we'll talk as soon as I get back. I have so much to say to you right now but I'll be home as soon as I can!"

After that there were no more flashing lights and no more temporarily going into other dimensions for Adler. He stayed with me but his condition hadn't changed. His time was still running out and I still didn't know what I was supposed to do about it. I knew that keeping him around was selfish because it prolonged his suffering, but I wasn't finished with the man.

"Soon I've gotta go," he whispered to me as I looked into his dead eyes, "I'll fall asleep and be transported somewhere far away from here."

"Forgive yourself Adler!" I pleaded with him, "Forgive yourself! It's the only thing missing! You are a good person, in fact you are the best person that I've ever met, so forgive yourself for your failure and be at peace!"

For a moment it seemed like I was about to lose him forever when he appeared to take his last breath but then another breath of air came out from deep within him and he began to breathe normally again. His color and warmth returned and so did the glowing aura around him. The blood had disappeared from his boots and my Adler looked the same way he always had.

"That's what I needed," he said to me in his usual calming voice.

"I'm so glad to still have you," I told him through another river of tears as I hugged him tighter than I ever had before, "and I'm so sorry."

"Don't you worry about a thing my dear," he retorted in a reassuring tone of voice.

Despite that it was Adler who had just gone through a traumatic experience, I was the one who needed his otherworldly reassurance. I felt protected and safe from everything in his strong arms and so I remained there for well over an hour until my mother returned. Once I heard her coming through the door I ran downstairs as fast as I could and jumped into her arms.

We both sobbed as we held each other, simply thankful to be alive. I hadn't been able to have a moment like that with my mother in what seemed like the longest time. Despite the stress of the situation I felt like I had my mom back even for just a fraction of a second.

"I felt him Joanie," my mom muttered in a tone of voice plagued with a mixture of anxiety but also relief, "I felt him with me in the car on the side of the road!"

"Mom," I muttered in response, "you felt Adler?"

"Yes! I felt him just like Rosanna's mother said that the two of you felt his presence and now everything you've said and everything that's happened makes more sense to me."

"Lucky you, because I don't understand anything anymore."

"Honey, I want to apologize for everything and I want you to know that I had a wakeup call today. I'm so sorry for all that I've put you through since the divorce and I know that by now you probably don't believe me or trust me but I promise you that it's over between Mike and I this time."

I didn't speak. She was right that I didn't believe her or trust her anymore because I'd heard that so many times. I'd heard something of the sort after every fight she had with Mike and before I knew it they were right back in each other's arms. I looked over at Adler who didn't say anything.

"Most of all I want to say thank you and thank Adler for me for basically saving my life today! The way that truck swerved and blocked off the entire road before it exploded today, I would never have made it out of there! Where is he honey, your keeper or whatever he is?"

My mother looked right at him but she couldn't see him. Adler stood there emotionless, probably still trying to come down from the all the stress of recent events. I told my mother to reach out and touch him but her hand went right through him. She caught an enormous chill but nothing else happened.

"I think I need to sit down," my mother muttered in an exasperated tone of voice as she sat down at the kitchen table.

Meanwhile, I checked my phone and saw that I had a thousand text messages from Rosanna asking me if I was okay, what had happened to Adler and apologizing for the fact that she had no more energy to help me sustain the agape. I sent her a single text message thanking her for her efforts, reassuring her that everything was fine and promising her that I would explain everything later.

I took out a few snacks from the fridge and sat down next to my mother at the kitchen table. Adler sat across from me and next to her, eyes fixated on my crackers and fruit tray. I set some aside for him and slid the plate across the table over to him. My mother watched in awe as the food became invisible to her once Adler touched it. She didn't know what she was seeing but based on the look that covered her face she thought it was amazing and beautiful.

Our moment of peace was disturbed when we all heard the screeching tires of Mike's truck pulling into the driveway at high speed. It was still early in the afternoon, and much too early for him to be back from work, so we knew that something bad had most certainly happened and that he would be belligerent and angry once he set foot through the door. Sure enough, that was exactly what happened.

"What are you doing home so early?" my mother asked him, trying to be as calm as possible, "Did something happen?"

"Yeah, something did happen alright," he grumbled angrily, "you're not where you said you'd be! That just proves what I suspected that you've been cheating on me with that Italian at work!"

"What? No! I was on my way to the conference when a tanker exploded in the middle of the road and I turned back to come home!"

"Liar! I've caught you in many lies before and I've had it with your lies and fooling around behind my back! I never should've allowed you to get that job!"

I'd seen Mike angry before but I'd never seen him furious like *that*. I hadn't previously noticed that Adler's keeper powers hadn't been soothing the atmosphere because I had been so mentally caught up in other things that I was numb inside but in that moment I was struck with absolute fear. Fear for my life. Fear that the moment I'd always dreaded was finally happening.

"Go grab your emergency bags and all the important documents that you think you might need," Adler ordered authoritatively, "then get out of here as quickly as you can and go to a safe place."

As my mother and I got up to go upstairs and get our previously packed things Mike lunged towards us with fury. Adler once again put himself between us and the danger and sent Mike flying across the room and landing on the shoe rack with one effortless push. He groaned in both anger and pain after a very hard and noisy landing and for a moment I froze on the spot before being able to run upstairs and grab my things as quickly as I could.

I heard some commotion downstairs but I knew that my mother wasn't in the middle of it so I drowned it out and rummaged through the closet to get my emergency bag and a few other things from my room before having to gather my courage and make my way downstairs. One couldn't go outside without having to pass through the kitchen that had become a war zone but I trusted Adler. As terrified as I was I knew that he wouldn't fail me. He never had before.

Once my mother and I got down we looked around the room to make sure we had safe passage to the door and saw no trace of Mike. Only Adler was there, seemingly struggling with energy as an odd low-pitch humming sound filled the atmosphere. I walked over to him to make sure he was okay while my mother reached for her car keys over the table when Mike came out of another room holding a loaded shotgun.

I became frozen in place. I could not move a muscle. I couldn't even scream as I watched him coming towards me in slow motion, pointing the gun at my mom and me with nowhere to run. My hands and feet became numb but I was still aware of my surroundings enough to hear my mom on the phone with 911 and to see Adler shielding us with his body.

My legs gave out and I fell to the floor after the earth-shattering shotgun blast that was followed with the worst ringing in my eyes. Hitting the hard floor jolted me back to reality and the first thing I noticed was a puddle of blood on the floor. I looked around me and neither me nor my mother had been hit. That left only Adler.

As I got up and moved to another corner of the room with my mom we heard sirens approaching in the distance. I also noticed that Adler had been shot in the chest and he was bleeding real blood. He looked incredibly *human* instead of having perfect keeper features. My mother screamed as he became visible to her and Mike seemed equally terrified to see a soldier in the room.

The bullet wound didn't appear to hurt Adler, in fact he didn't seem to be able to physically feel anything but he was definitely surprised. He pulled out his army pistol from its holster and pointed it at Mike's face. His hand was shaking as he tried to keep it steady. Horrific memories of the fighting on the Eastern Front obviously came flooding back into his memory.

"Drop the shotgun right now and surrender peacefully," Adler's voice shook as much as his hand, "or I swear to God that I'll shoot you!"

Mike was probably more terrified of Adler's existence that the threat of being shot or possibly killed but nonetheless he complied with Adler's orders and gently put the shotgun on the floor in front of him. He raised both of his arms and put his hands behind his head as he walked outside just in time for a flood of police cars to show up.

Time appeared to *literally* have paused after that because everything was frozen and there was no more commotion anywhere. Several holograms popped up all over the room showing a variety of different things including several versions of myself in the future, some of Adler during the war and other worlds entirely. I'd previously heard of several theories pointing to many different versions of ourselves in other worlds happening simultaneously and I was now seeing it up and close.

In between all of those holograms a blank portal of glowing light appeared. It had the same glow keepers had but I couldn't see where it lead to. I knew that it was the transition portal into one of those other worlds in the holograms for Adler to walk through once he was ready. It was bittersweet to see. It was beautiful because I knew that a bright future, or several, was waiting for me but at the same it was bitter because I knew that Adler wouldn't be part of it.

"Wow," was the only thing I could say.

"It's breathtaking to see it like this," Adler added.

"So, which one of the theories pertaining to keepers was true after all?"

"They are all true in their own way, in their own worlds, because everything is happening simultaneously across several universes, each with different natural laws and different concepts of time."

"That's amazing!"

"If it gives you any consolation Joanie, your conscious self exists in the best of all these worlds. Even with its flaws and dark times, this world is the best of them all. The beauty of this realm exists everywhere, but not everyone can see it. Trust me, but more importantly, trust God. "

Adler stuck his hand through the hologram of me creating dolls in my room and pulled back the one I'd made of him. He gave it an approving look before handing it to me. It was indeed the same beautiful creation that I'd put together months and months ago.

"Don't let me go," Adler whispered before walking straight through the glowing portal and disappearing.

Just like that he was gone and everything else disappeared after the biggest flash of the purest light engulfed the entire room. The next thing I saw were police officers walking into the room. I let out a deep breath as I held on tightly to my doll.

There were still so many things that I wished I could have told Adler before he abruptly left but deep down I was convinced that he could still hear me. At the very least I believed that in some other world, in another form, in another time we were still together. We had never really been apart to begin with, and I'd have plenty of time to tell him everything.

# EPILOGUE

I tied up my hair into a ponytail since it had been a victim to the wind by the shore during the last few hours and went into my room to work on a doll I'd started a few days ago. I was almost done but couldn't really decide which military uniform he was going to wear. I knew he was a soldier and I instinctively knew that he was a good man but I kept on going back and forth on other details.

Was he going to be an American or a British soldier of the Second World War? Or maybe a German. If so he would've been part of the German Resistance. Or, alternatively he could be half British and half German, I already had a few American soldiers standing twelve inches tall. I didn't really know what I wanted to do with him so I went downstairs and got a snack before resuming my work on him.

Eventually I decided that he would wear a Wehrmacht uniform and gave him the rank of lieutenant. I added a few finishing touches to his face and gave him sparkling stereotypical blue eyes and sandy hair. I also put some miniature 1940s round glasses on him to give him an extra touch of elegance and to stand out from my other soldiers standing on my shelf.

One of them had a missing hand that I hadn't been able to

repair after finding him in that condition at the thrift store so I'd added an eyepatch to him to give him more of a hero returning from battle type of look. He had been my favorite until I'd just finished my first German, a good German. He had been a savior to the most vulnerable during one of the worst times of their lives. He was sort've a metaphor for what I wanted in my own life, or more like who I wanted to enter my life.

"Welcome to the world Adler," I whispered to him as I placed him on the night table next to my bed, "welcome to war."

# READING QUESTIONS

Why do you think it was Adler and not someone else who became Joanie's keeper?

What parallels can you draw between your own life and Joanie's life, or the life of another character?

Which theory about keepers do you think best fit the narrative of this story?

Why did Joanie's parents repeatedly refuse to believe in or acknowledge Adler's existence despite the constant and overwhelming evidence that he was indeed real?

Can you identify parallels between the blowout Joanie had with Rosanna and the one she had with Adler? What can you conclude from this?

Did the themes present in this novel reinforce or oppose certain notions or ideologies in your current life? If so, which ones? How did they change?

Do you think that there are greater beings at work in our lives (God, angels, spirits, etc.) that influence the course of it in one way or another?

Why do you think that despite all the talk about the social issues happening in society and initiatives to make things better the number of lost and hopeless youth keeps steadily going up?

if you're looking for that person who can have an impact an impact LOOK in the mirror YOU MUST BE the change you wish to see in THE WORLD even if you change just one person's life, it was totally WORTH IT

# COMMENTARY

Unfortunately keepers are not real, though life would certainly be easier if they were, and are not based on any actual spiritual teaching. They are solely a product of my imagination but serve as an important metaphor for the lack of guidance and stability in the lives of young people, and not just in a family environment (or lack thereof) either. I know this for a fact because I've lived it, and although this book is 100% fiction the inspiration was largely drawn from my own personal experiences.

This book has been a long time in the making and actually started out as a 15 000 word short story written in 2014 as a writing prompt about a supernatural being and it took on several different forms in the last four years. You can now read the original *Keepers of Me* in a free short story compilation book in the fourth volume of *Lost Thoughts* on my website. For the expanded edition of this book I've included the original text of *Keepers of Me* immediately after this commentary without any additional editing or polishing because a lot of people have been curious to know what my "raw" writings look like!

In 2015 I wrote a "novel length" version of Keepers of Me but it never went very far. After publishing my first book *Innermost* in early 2018 I decided to revive this project and completely rewrite it while still maintaining the original plot line. I hadn't gotten very far when my grandmother suddenly became very ill and passed away shortly thereafter. She was the only person who had never given up on me and finishing this book is probably what kept me alive after her death.

Her passing was a very spiritual experience though I've stuck to fantasy and sci-fi in this novel because pushing a particular belief or ideology on a person usually only further contributes to the problem and not the solution, and that's why this book was kept faith-neutral and inclusive to all. The purpose of writing this was both to heal and to entertain, not to preach or impose.

Nonetheless, the themes presented in this book still highlight very real and very important social issues that plague an epidemic of young people today. Teen anxiety is on the rise everywhere and suicide is the *second* leading cause of death among young persons aged 15 to 24 and the numbers only seem to be going up. More teens and young adults die by suicide than from cancer, heart disease, AIDS, birth defects, stroke, pneumonia, influenza, and chronic lung disease, *combined*.

It's a phenomenon that's spread out across all demographics from suburban to rural, from wealthy to barely making it by, from those who seem to have a bright future ahead of them to those who don't. While I don't have all the answers to the growing epidemic, I definitely know that it can't be ignored. It can't be brushed off as "it's just a phase" or "things will get better" because the suffering of *now* is not something that young people can get away from anymore.

Being a teenager is basically a draining full-time job that includes doing schoolwork, keeping up with the social scene, fretting about the future, and then throw in global uncertainty, economic instability, discrimination and prejudice and you still don't have someone who is trapped in a disadvantaged situation on top of that.

We all know what effects that domestic violence, poverty, hunger and homelessness have on an adult who is a fully mature and independent person so imagine what these same things do to a young developing mind, and these too are all horrific circumstances that young persons are often faced with on top of their already heavy load.

So many teens and young adults feel alone and have no one to turn to. Everywhere you look people tell you to get help from a trusted adult if something is wrong but I also know from personal experience that sometimes these same people are precisely the ones who end up failing us in the most miserable of ways.

While I definitely don't advocate for people to suffer in silence, I know it takes tremendous courage and strength to speak up and the conversation will have to shift from "tell someone about it" to actually having a plan in place to do *something* about it when that talk does come because we'll never get to the root of the problem otherwise.

I have no easy answers as to how everything can be remedied and I never pretended to inside the pages of this novel but I do know that we must all open our eyes to what's going on around us and do something about it. Irrespective of what you thought of this story, I hope that you took the message of this book to heart and most importantly that you'll do something when you see something because saying something just isn't enough anymore.

Now on a lighter note, for those who enjoyed the more more mysterious aspects of this book, I definitely recommend reading up on actual quantum mechanics and philosophies about our universe and what lies beyond it.

As a complete science geek and philosophy nut, I've dedicated many hours pondering life and death, contemplating my own existence and alternate realities, among many other things. This final version of this story was really the culmination of those pondering mixed in with my wild imagination and my passion for human rights and social justice.

If this book contributed something meaningful to the world in even the smallest fashion I've successfully completed what I came here to do.

Heal the broken
Have mercy on
THE LOST
Show compassion to the
misunderstood
Befriend the lonely
Hug those who are
HURTING &
love everyone
let the flame of kindness
inside of you burn
brighter
THAN THE DARNKESS
AROUND YOU

# KEEPERS OF ME

*Keepers are said to be departed souls who return to the metaphysical world to provide guidance for fellow humans. Keepers are not guardian angels; they have not ascended into heaven. Keepers are souls who have once been human, whether it was 1000 years ago or yesterday. The legend says that keepers can come in many forms; a faint presence, a glowing orb, or even in the form of a human being with flesh and bones. Not much is known about Keepers apart from ancient legends written thousands of years ago. It is said that every human has a keeper, but many are unaware as keepers manifest themselves in various different ways.*

*The legend says that keepers come back to Earth to guide us but are able to retreat to their vortex beyond this universe since their souls are free. Since the atomic energy that composes their souls can vibrate at two places at one time, they are free to come and go as they please. Energy cannot be created nor destroyed, and our human bodies are nothing but a transition phase for the soul; we come from nothing and we are nothing when we die. But not all souls become keepers, nobody knows why some are somehow selected to return to Earth, but for some reason they do. Keepers keep many secrets and are a mystery to earthly beings, but they only feed off two things; love and truth.*

I was lying on my bed crying, with only the street light down below illuminating parts of my room in the dark night. The street lights generated enough light for me to clearly see the fresh wounds on my arm and the bloody razor blade on my night table next to my bed. As tears escape my ears everything became a blur of faint colors as the dim light could not penetrate through the tears. My body ached with stress and despair, my mind felt like a bomb about to blow and my heart was crying out for help. I wished that the sheets could just have suffocated me in my wake. My whole world seemed like it was coming down, crashing hard as it hit the ground. My soul shattered under the fire of pain and the absence of momentary hope.

Each vertebrate in my spin seemed to throb, begging my mind to cease the pain and my heart seemed to shake my entire core. The cuts on my arm burned as the blood coagulated and sealed my skin together again. I thought it would've helped me forget the emotional pain but it didn't; my whole body was declaring a state of emergency. One by one all my hopes had vanished just the same. My erratic breathing seemed to slow as my mind gradually shut down. I felt like my pain resonated throughout the entire universe, maybe it did.

I let out a sigh of relief as my tense body seemed to relax. It was almost like a hand touched my every aching bone and filled it with the essence of serenity. I couldn't move onto my back, but I felt a presence behind me. As my mind became more aware of my surroundings I realized that something was indeed touching me, it wasn't just in my head. But I wasn't afraid, I felt a sense of calm and pure bliss sweep over me. I eventually managed to sit up in my bed and look at what was behind me.

A young man about my age was sitting there right next to me with one hand on my shoulder, easing up the tension. Needing comfort, I latched onto him and he took me in his arms as I kept on crying. His body was warm, and he had a heartbeat! His gentle touch relaxed my racing mind and brought it to a peaceful place. The rhythm of his heart soothed me and brought me to a place almost beyond this world. He was a godsend! I clutched onto him, never wanting him to leave.

"Please, please don't go!" I whispered in a hoarse voice. "I never will," he whispered in a soft voice.

I wrapped my arms around him and caressed his soft skin the same way he caressed mine. His body was warm against mine and I completely indulged. I tilted my head up to look at him and grabbed a strand of his long hair. The young man had long sandy wavy hair and pale blue eyes on pale white skin. He had a long face and little pink lips with no distinctive features other than his long grunge-era hairstyle. He looked at me with sad yet sympathetic eyes and softly stroked the skin of my face, wiping away my tears. Eventually, I fell asleep in his hold and woke up a few hours later, still in his arms with my head on his chest listening to his steadily beating heart. I climbed up over him and let my chin rest on his chest as I looked deeply into his eyes in awe.

*My keeper.*

"What's your name?" I ask him in a soft whisper.

"Kevin," he whispered back to me in a gentle tone.

"Are you my keeper?" I ask.

"Yes I am," he replies with a gentle smile and his hands caressing my face," I am always going to be here for you."

I rested on my side and he positioned himself behind me and wrapped his strong arms around me. I placed my little hand in his and closed my eyes.

"Can you stay with me tonight?" I ask him.

"I will be with you every moment of every day," he reassured me, "now get some sleep."

He held me close and I drifted away to a far away world to the sound of his breathing. I woke up the next morning some ten minutes before my alarm clock. Kevin was still there, hold me. I turned over to face him, filled with exhilaration at the thought of my very own keeper. I was so relieved to have someone there to hold me and love me unconditionally like only a keeper could. His body was so warm and his touch so gentle. It was everything I needed, and I never wanted Kevin to leave.

He let go of me and sat up on my bed and I sat up next to him. He wore some black cargo pants and a plain back shirt. His unruly hair was gold-like in the sunlight coming through the window of my room. He looked so sublime, he was perfect. He took my arm into his hand and turned it so he could see my scars. He pressed it to his lips and each cut disappeared with every kiss. I watched in awe as the scars all faded away. I touched where they used to be because I couldn't believe what I was seeing. I didn't even know Kevin but I already had so much reverence for him because he loved my so passionately and so purely. My skin was soft, there was absolutely no evidence that I had ever cut myself there.

"Are they going to come back?"

"Not if you don't make them come back."

"How is that even possible?"

"It's possible in my world."

Kevin gave me a tender kiss on the forehead.

"Are you like my guardian angel?"

"No, I'm just a keeper. Angels are from a completely different world. I don't know exactly how they come about their business, but angels are not human. I am."

He took my hands into his and I leaned over and put my head on his shoulder. I closed my eyes and clutched onto him. My keeper. I was so grateful to have him by my side. I knew nothing about keepers or much about life in the first place, but the young man next to me made me see a whole new facade of it that I hadn't been able to appreciate before. I had given up but he had given me that faint glimmer of hope that I had been so desperately needing.

"So you were human before?"

"Yeah, I was a creature of the earth before this, just like you."

"Do all dead people become keepers?"

"I have no idea dear. I don't know why or how I got here. I don't know much more than I did back when I was still human. I don't know if this is a punishment for what I've done or my chance to redeem myself."

"What did you do?"

"I did something bad and I guess now I'm paying for it. But just know that I love you."

My alarm clock went off to disturb our perfect moment and Kevin patted me on the shoulder, indicating that it was time to get up and get ready for the day. I reluctantly got up and picked out some clothes out of my closet. I grabbed some faded blue jeans and a purple shirt with black stripes. When I turned around to talk to Kevin I noticed that he was no longer in my room. I looked all over but he wasn't there. He was gone. I was disappointed and frustrated that he had disappeared just like he had never came in the first place.

"Hey don't worry, I'm still here!" he said as he came up behind me and pulled me into a tight embrace.

I put my arms around him in return and instantly found relief. He kissed my neck and I went back to getting ready for school.

"Am I the only one who sees you?" I inquired as I was brushing my long brown hair.

"Well, not really," Kevin replied, thinking hard, "you see, keepers feed off energy humans give us and if it's needed we can appear to others but that's rather rare."

"What kind of energy are you talking about?"

"Love. Right now I'm replenished on energy but to have me around like this in the future you'll have to emerge yourself in agape.It is the purest form of love, unconditional love. Feel agape from deep inside your heart and soul and I'll be here, always."

I closed my eyes and let the love flow from inside of me for a short while but I couldn't sustain it.

"Don't worry, it'll come." Kevin reassured me, "For the moment just focus on the now. I'm not going anywhere."

"Kevin?"

"Yeah?"

"Can you hear my thoughts?"

"No, but I can feel everything you feel. That's where the agape energy comes in. No matter what, I will comfort you if you want me around."

I touched his hand just to remind myself that he was real and smiled to myself. I felt so much relief from the inside out. I felt like I could take a breath without it burning like fire deep inside.

"How long will you be here?"

"I don't know, but don't worry about that alright?"

I smiled at him and finished getting dressed, putting on some light eyeliner to compliment my hazel eyes and tied my hair up in a ponytail since I couldn't get it to be the way I wanted it. I walked downstairs into the kitchen where my mother was making breakfast with my two younger sisters. Ever since my dad had died when I was seven, things were awkward at the table. There was a piece of the family missing and even after nine and a half years, the pain was no less. I had always been daddy's girl, but my daddy was gone. My youngest sister Carrie wasn't even born when he died so she was lucky to escape the pain I was constantly feeling.

"Well you're up early!" my mother commented as I walked into the kitchen.

"Yeah I'm gonna walk to school and grab some breakfast at Gilmore's on my way there."

We said goodbye to each other and I walked out the door. Kevin walked with me and grabbed a hold of my hand as we neared the end of the driveway. He held my hand as we passed over the bridge and headed over to Gilmore's. We both walked into the small restaurant and stood in line behind a few other hungry customers.

"Do you eat?" I asked Kevin.

"I can," he replied looking at me with tender eyes, "but I don't have to." "Do people know you're here with me?"

"No, they don't. They aren't aware of anything."

I ordered one of Gilmore's world famous bacon and egg sandwiches and headed back out with Kevin following me. We walked hand-in-hand all the way to school as I ate my breakfast sandwich with the other hand. Despite the frigid morning air, Kevin kept me warm with his overwhelming presence.

"Do you know what happened here?" I asked Kevin as we walked into the school's parking lot.

"No," he whispered to me, "I don't know anything."

I swallowed hard and clutched his hand tightly.

"Well, I guess you'll find out."

The two of us walked in and made our way down the halls to where the memorials were set up on the wall.

"What went on here?" Kevin asked me in a soft whisper.

"Two girls got killed in a drunk driving accident two weeks ago." I replied in a shaky voice, "I'm the one who was supposed to be the designated driver but I bailed early."

Kevin put his arm around me and comforted me greatly as the memories of that night came back to haunt me.

"While they were bleeding to death in that car wreck I was goofing off with a homeless man at the corner store on the end of the street here. I stopped in to buy a snack on my way home and I ended up giving it to him. He was a cool old dude you know. We sat there as he ate his chips and told me about his life before his daughter got killed in a drunk driving accident."

I broke down crying and Kevin hugged me tightly. I couldn't shake that thought out of my mind. I bailed on my friends to hang out with a homeless man who told me some heartbreaking story of how he lost his precious daughter while my friends were actually dying in the same kind of nightmare.

"Don't blame yourself for this, this isn't your fault."

"I know it isn't, but some people blame me anyway."

Kevin looked at me with compassion in his eyes as he stroked my cheek with his big hand. I remembered that he could feel everything I felt too. He hurt just as much as I did. Kevin's loving hand calmed me down and comforted me like he had promised me he would. I held him tightly in my arms and indulged into the serenity his aura gave off.

"I know it wasn't my fault that they got behind the wheel drunk and I know that they could've called a cap or someone else could've taken them home but there's just this part of me that hates myself so much for not being there when my friends needed me the most."

Most people didn't blame me at all, but some of the girls' closest friends needed someone to blame for their poor judgment that night and that person ended up being me. While the majority were supportive, the few who gave me harsh words really got to me. They made sure to remind me every day that both of them were dead and it was because of me. They really made me believe that if I hadn't bailed early, things might have gone differently. At times, I believed it too. I wiped my tears and walked to my first class holding Kevin's hand. I squeezed it as it brought me comfort to know that I was no alone. I walked around the classroom aimlessly before finding a seat.

"Does this mean you can give me all the answers?" I jokingly asked him trying to lighten the mood.

"Only the ones I know," he replied laughing, I'm good in language and science but not so much in math."

"You don't have supreme understanding of the universe now that you're dead?"

"Not here. I only know what I learned on Earth and what I can currently observe."

"Do you believe in multiple lives, you know, considering you're still here?"

"It would be inappropriate to say that I don't, but this isn't exactly my idea of the afterlife."

"I guess that makes you the perfect companion for me because this isn't exactly my definition of a life either."

I finally picked out a seat at the back of the room at sat down. Kevin sat next to me and reassuringly placed his hand on my knee.

"That's why I'm here," he replied as he leaned over and kissed me in response to my feelings.

"Do you see other people's keepers too?" I inquired to make conversation before the bell rang.

"No, it's just you and me."

"That's kinda cool. I guess we both have a lot to learn about life."

"I'll make sure you have a good one, that's my promise to you. I know that I was sent to you for a reason and I won't screw this up. I know you have a lot of questions and I don't have a lot of answers, but just know that I love you and you are not alone."

I placed my hand into Kevin's and let his love and strength wash over and guide me for the rest of the day. My school day went without incident. I stayed away from most people except this freshman girl named Rosanna, who asked me for directions in the big school. The two of us ended up sitting together at lunch with Kevin sitting behind me, completely unnoticed.

"Man, sometimes I wish I was invisible like you," I muttered to him.

"No you don't. Life is something to be cherished and

celebrated. I wasted mine. Heck it hadn't even started yet, but it's gone."

"So does that mean that I will get old but you won't?"

"That's right, I'm always going to be seventeen and I'm always going to carry around regret."

After Rosanna and I finished eating, I sat down in a deserted hallway to spend some time alone with Kevin before my next class.

"What is it that you did that could possibly be so bad?" I ask him, "Did you commit suicide or something?"

"Yes I did." Kevin's voice was nothing but a soft whisper.

I took him into a hug and held him tightly.

"How long ago?" I asked him.

"Longer than you've been alive. But I'm here now and if I can make things right for you it will have made it all worth it." he replied in a sympathetic voice.

"I love you already Kevin." I whispered in his ear and squeezed him tightly.

I could see that he was a broken young man but that he had a big heart. He wanted to make things right and I desperately needed someone to comfort me and to help me deal with the pain of losing two of my closest friends. I hated myself for what happened to them instead of being grateful to God that it wasn't me. My parents said it was some sort of survivor's guilt or something but I didn't really understand my own emotions anymore. Why did I feel the way I did? I didn't know.

After school I walked home with Kevin and sat down on my bed next to him. I slouched my head over his shoulder and cried. He held me close and his presence was very comforting since nobody had really been there for me. My dad wasn't around and my mom worked long hours plus she had other children who were still young to take care of. Kevin and I laid down on my bed and I let my head rest on his chest. He ran his gentle fingers through my hair and serenity swept over me. I indulged in the love and comfort he gave me. I didn't know him but I already loved him. I knew that a keeper's love was infinite, even though my limited human understanding could never comprehend it.

"Does everyone have a keeper like you?" I ask him as I looked into his deep blue eyes.

"I don't know how it all works," he admitted, "but I do believe that everyone is watched over whether they are aware of it or not."

"Did you watch over me before this?"

"No, all of this is new, I've never done anything like this before. I died nearly two decades ago but it's only now that I've come back so to speak. I don't know where all that time went, because I don't remember it."

"Well you're here now, don't ever leave."

"I won't."

During the first few weeks of school after the accident, Kevin was always there by my side in each moment, but after that he only came by when I gave him agape. The trade of energy between us was overflowing and it was easy to sustain. During the hard moments I only had to think of him and his loving arms were around me. I spent every night with him and brought him everywhere with me. I spoke to him at length before I went to sleep and he became so much more than just someone to watch over me. He was my best friend, my protector and my lifeline.

"I love you Arlene," Kevin whispered to me just before I went to sleep.

"I love you too Kevin," I whispered back, "I'll see you in the morning."

"Honey, who are you walking to?" my mother asks as she was passing down the hall.

"Nobody," I replied in an absent-minded tone.

"You were obviously talking to somebody," she pressed on as she walked into my room.

"I was talking to myself," I dismissed.

She didn't make too much of a big deal out of it but told me that I should get help to deal with my grief. What she didn't know was that I did have help, he was holding me in his arms. I also ended up forming a friendship with Rosanna. She was my only real friend left after Sabrina and Melanie died. Their friends didn't like me because they blamed me for their deaths but Rosanna was very understanding and supportive. By the end of the school year we were best buds. She had just moved to the community during spring break, during the same time as the accident, and I was the only person who had really welcomed her.

I ended up spending my summer with Kevin and Rosanna at her grandparents' farm in upstate Wisconsin. My mother thought it was a good idea and she was right. It gave me a new perspective on both my life and the tragedy as well as giving me a good opportunity to get my emotions in check. Rosanna's grandparents had a beautiful antique-style home and warmly opened its doors to me. Rosanna and I had to share a room and each night after she fell asleep I had my nightly conversations with Kevin. He was always faithfully by my side with his head resting on the pillows and his sandy-colored all over my face. I had been the happiest since the accident.

"Who is that Kevin guy you talk to at night?" Rosanna asked me one evening before we went to bed.

I was taken aback that she knew about Kevin but I also realized that it was my own fault that I hadn't been more discrete about it. Not wanting her to think that I was crazy, I decided to tell her the truth about Kevin.

"He's my keeper," I told her.

"Do you really believe in all that keeper stuff?" she asked me, seemingly confused. "He's real real Rosanna, he's been with me ever since the accident."

"Good for you, I'm really happy for you."

She didn't seem to believe me at first but she was fine with it. She embraced Kevin even though she couldn't see him, touch him or interact with him. At night she even gave me an extra pillow and an extra blanket for him even though he didn't need it. For a while I acted as some sort of mediator between Kevin and Rosanna so they could communicate with each other. After some time Rosanna came to believe that Kevin was indeed real and that the legend was true. I told her about agape and all the valuable lessons about life and love that Kevin taught me. She was just as amazed when she heard my stories as I was when Kevin shared them with me.

At the end of the summer we both returned home to our normal lives and returned to school in September. During that whole time Kevin never left my side. During one hot afternoon we got a spare in our last class so Rosanna and I decided to hang out outside in a nearby park and that's where she saw Kevin for the first time. For the first time she could see him like I did, complete with flesh and blood and everything. The three of us were equally mystified and overjoyed at the same time.

"I'm so happy to finally meet you!" Rosanna exclaimed once he appeared to her.

"Me too!" Kevin exclaimed too as he wrapped his arms around her.

I could tell by the sparkle in Rosanna's eyes that the transfer of energy because Kevin and her was amazing. I smiled as I watcher her grab a strand of his hair and stroke his cheek. The three of us revealed at being able to finally all be together in a way that we could equally enjoy ourselves. Rosanna didn't seem to be in touch with her own keeper though, but Kevin was always with us when we were together. Kevin and Rosanna loved each other as much as I loved them, it was nothing short of wonderful to be always surrounded by such love.

All that wonderful love was dampened when my mother got a call from Rosanna's parents saying that Rosanna and I had some weird obsession over this imaginary boyfriend we both had and that they didn't want me to hang out with her anymore. I felt so betrayed that she would do something like that to me after having believed to the point that Kevin actually revealed himself to her. And not to mention the months we spent together making memories of the three of us! I was so hurt by what she did that it felt like that car crash all over again. Maybe she hadn't died, but she certainly felt dead to me. Even Kevin seemed to be heartbroken over the situation.

"This Kevin person, was he the one you've been talking to when you said you had been talking to yourself these past few month?" my mother asked me.

"Mom, Kevin is real," I insisted, "Rosanna sees him too!"

"No she doesn't honey, she only went along with it because she's concerned about you and your wellbeing."

"What are you talking about mom? The three of us spent so much time together!" "After the accident happened you were grieving and you made up Kevin to help you cope with your loss."

"No I did not!"

"It's good to turn to spirituality to help you cope with your loss and to hold on to a future hope but sweetie, Kevin isn't real."

"Yes he is mom! He's real, he's right here!"

Kevin was faithfully by my side during the whole ordeal but he told me not to defend our relationship. I didn't listen to his advice and my mother ended up telling me that I was delusional and that I needed therapy. The next morning at school Rosanna approached me just like nothing had happened, like she had never betrayed Kevin and I.

"How dare you!" I shouted at her in front of everyone as she approached me in the hallway.

"Arlene, listen," she pleaded, "let me explain, this is just a big misunderstanding!"

"No Rosanna, there's nothing to explain."

"Arlene please, I had to make up a lie so my parents don't lock me up in the psych ward! I believe Kevin is real, I know he is!"

"Well I'm the one who is going to be locked up in the psych ward now!"

"I'm sorry Arlene, please forgive me, I was just trying to protect myself. And where's Kevin? I want to apologize to him too."

Kevin had been right there the entire time but Rosanna seemed to be oblivious to his presence. He was invisible to her again.

"You can't see him because he hates you!" I snapped back before I turned around and walked out of the building and broke down crying on the sidewalk.

"I don't hate her sweetie," Kevin whispered to me as he took me in his hold, "and you shouldn't either."

"I guess it's just you a me now," I whispered to him as I buried my face in his chest.

He held me tightly as he always did and I ended up ditching my first class that morning so I could spent time alone outside with him. He advised against it but I wanted to be with him in the cool morning air to collect my thoughts. My mother was called since I had skipped class and I got in trouble again because of it. In defiance to my mother asking why I skipped class, I told her that I wanted to spend time alone with Kevin. I knew it wasn't going to help anything but I wasn't going to give up on Kevin over some hypocrites and unbelievers.

Rosanna still wanted to be my friend after the whole thing but I no longer wanted anything to do with her. Kevin encouraged me time and time again to forgive her and take her back but I was too hurt to do so after the betrayal. Rosanna didn't really have any friends other than me but I had Kevin and he was all that mattered. I loved him so much and I wasn't about to give up after all that he had done for me. My parents sent me to therapy and I told my therapist all about how wonderful Kevin was because I did not want to forsake him over a lie any longer. He told me on numerous occasions to deny him but I loved him too much for that and I made sure to show him that his endless love for me was reciprocated.

I spent long nights in my room by myself with Kevin since I had no more friends and things between my mother and I were hostile. She had convinced herself that I had some mental illness that made me crazy because I was seeing people who weren't there and that I needed therapy. It hurt me deeply but it was comforting to know that Kevin was there. I could clearly see in his eyes that he was hurting too since he could feel everything I felt but a keeper's love was infinite and he wasn't about to give up on me. I wasn't about to give up on him either over some notion that I was completely crazy.

"You should forgive Rosanna," Kevin whispered to me one night while he was holding me tight.

"I know I should," I replied tiredly, "but I'm still so hurt Kevin."

"I know you are, but remember that I'm here for you and I'll help you heal. That's why I'm here in the first place! And make peace with your mother, dear."

"She's the one who's going to have to make peace with me!"

I cried thinking about all the hurtful things she had said to me. Not only had I just lost two friends in a freak drunk driving accident, but I had lost Rosanna and ultimately her as well. Kevin was all I had left and people treated him with such hostility and accused me of being completely insane. Sometimes I came to believe them even if Kevin was nothing short of very real to me. The news of my "imaginary boyfriend" somehow spread to school and people began making fun of me too, and Rosanna was one of them. I couldn't understand why she would do those things to me. Not only did we spent countless nights together in the company of Kevin but she even had the audacity to ridicule me in front of everyone.

After one particularly horrible day at school, I came home and locked myself up in my room and took out that same razor blade that I had cut myself with the first time. I had left it in my night table and I proceeded to create twelve bloody lines on my arm. My soul shattered under the fire of pain and the absence of momentary hope. In the middle of that crisis I called to Kevin in agape and he was there in a heartbeat. He took me into his gentle hold and was about to press his lips to my bleeding scars before I stopped him.

"Don't," I whispered to him, "let me show my mother first."

"Why would you want to do that?" he asked me, seemingly puzzled.

"Let me show her my scars, and then kiss them away and I'll show her my arm again." "And what exactly are you trying to prove by doing this?"

"I'm going to prove to her that you're real."

"Do you think that's a good idea?"

"Do you?"

"No, because I'm afraid she's going to do something drastic because you cut yourself." "She can't do much worst than shun me like she already is."

Kevin advised me to just cover up my arm and not show her since I wouldn't let him erase them but I went right ahead and made my arm visible during breakfast the following morning.
"You're not going to school like that!" she sternly told me after my siblings had left the table.

"Kevin is real mom, "I told her, "I'll prove it to you."

"And how do you think you're going to do that?"

"He's going to kiss my scars and all of them will fade away like they never were on my arm."

She looked at me defiantly, not believing a single word I said. I gave her a defiant stare in return before I went up to my room and handed my arm over to Kevin. He tenderly kissed every scare and one by one they vanished and my skin returned to it's soft pink state. I went back down and showed my mother. She didn't know what she was seeing, and she even touched my arm to make sure they were really gone, but she still didn't believe that I had a keeper named Kevin. To her the scars were just another crazy stunt for attention.

"She thinks I only want attention," I whispered to Kevin in a sad voice. "Do you?" he asked me.

I grimaced at him, hurt at the fact that he thought that I was just doing that for attention too.

"The night I came to you I know the hurt was real," he went on, "but now you're angry. It's not about grief or confusion anymore."

"Go away Kevin," I dismissed him before laying down on my and wishing that the sheets would suffocate me in my wake again.

Dead silence filled the entire house up until I heard my mother dial a number on the phone. I didn't pay too much attention until she told the person on the other end that she was calling about me because she was afraid for my safety. I grunted loudly and slapped my head on the pillow next to me. I started to cry again and called on to Kevin to comfort me. He was there in the blink of an eye to make everything okay again just like he had the first time we met.

"Are you aware of what goes on in my life when you're in the other dimension?" I ask him as I put my head on his chest.

"Yes," he replied in a soft whisper, "but I can't see or hear, I can only feel."

"I'm so sorry I treated you so badly earlier. Please forgive me."

"Already forgiven."

He kissed my forehead and I traced his soft lips with my index finger afterwards. He kissed my finger and smiled at me like he always did. I caressed his soft cheeks with my hand and traced the beautiful features of his face. His face was only inches from mine and I could feel the tingle of his warm breath on my skin as I looked deeply into the sea of his eyes.

"Why did you commit suicide?" I whispered to him.

"I just couldn't live with myself," he replied as he closed his eyes, seemingly hurting.

I kissed his left eye as I put my fingers in his sandy hair and stroked it gently. I loved him so much, it was impossible for me to picture him hating himself so much that he thought suicide was the only way out. I kissed him and reveled at the amazing love he gave me any time I asked for it. I began to imagine that we had been sent to each other so we could help one another and fix each other. My fingers ran all over his scalp as my lips gently pressed against the skin of his face.

"Ain't I the one who is supposed to kiss you?" he whispered to me grinning.

I grinned back at him and he took a hold of me and shifted our body positions so he was the one who could kiss me and stroke my face just like I did to him. I put my hand on the back of his neck and pulled him down towards me and we both kissed each other passionately. The feel of his hands on my neck and collar bone was enough to really make me crazy.

My breathing rapidly accelerated but his slowed down since he didn't need to actually breathe. Our perfect moment was disrupted when I heard my mother's footsteps coming up the stairs. She then barged into my room without knocking and began to talk apprehensively about this apparent mental illness that I didn't really have.

"I know you've been hurting a lot Arlene," she told me, "but you need some help and I've arranged for you to live with your aunt and uncle in Portage. They have some good facilities to help you there too, so pack your bags."

"You can just send me away!" I angrily shouted back, "I am not your property! I have a say in this!"

Kevin put his warm hands on my shoulders and softly whispered to me to comply with my mother for my own sake but I pushed him aside and had a screaming match with my mother. Kevin begged me to hear him out about the whole thing but I didn't want to.

"No Kevin!" I shouted at him, "I'm not going!"

"Yes you are!" my mother shouted back at me, "And you're going to get rid of Kevin!"

"I'm gonna get rid of *you*!" I angrily and defiantly shouted back at her, "I'm gonna pack my bags and go on *vacation* far away from you with aunt Marie and uncle Bill!"

She didn't know what to reply to that. I looked over at Kevin who was still standing by my closet and grinned at him, knowing that we'd spend all our days together at aunt Marie's and uncle Bill's. My mother's plan didn't sound so bad after all and I more than willingly packed my bags with Kevin's help.

We smiled at each other the whole time and I marveled at how he could turn an awful situation into a pleasant one. Spending some time alone with him at my aunt's and uncle's house, I couldn't have asked for better! And the timing was perfect too. I climbed over the bed and smooched him to say thank you and I grinned to myself in delight.

That same afternoon my mother decided to make the eight-hour trip to Portage with me to get me out of the house as soon as possible. I was riding shotgun while Kevin was faithfully behind me in the backseat with my luggage. He reached out his hand and began to play with my hair during the long and boring ride. The skies were overcast for a while before it began to rain heavily.

The big raindrops were more than the windshield wipers could handle and it became very hard to see the road ahead. The streetlights were nothing but a distant blur until we hit the highway. Everything was black in the late evening and neither my mother or I could see anything. I turned around to ask Kevin if he could see anything more than we could but he was just as human as the rest of us and he was no help.

"When are you going to leave Kevin alone?" my mother was nearly shouting at me, "He isn't real! Get over him!"

"Mom! Watch where you're going!" I yelled back as she was swerving on the slippery wet highway.

Another fight broke out between us again and my mother ended up slapping me in the left temple area when the back of her hand. I quickly glanced over at Kevin in the backseat but noticed that he wasn't there so I didn't hesitate to slap my mother back twice as hard on the side of the face too. It caused her to swerve violently again on the wet road but she had time regaining control of the van as we kept on going from side to side in the rain.

Ahead I saw a white dot in the distance as it quickly got closer I realized that it was a set of headlights headed straight in our direction. The vehicle ahead was serving too and I quickly called on to Kevin in agape for him to comfort me but nothing happened. I screamed his name much to the frustration of my mother but nothing happened, he wasn't there.

I could clearly see the truck headed exactly for us in a head-on collision despite all the rain. I braced myself for whatever was to come and silently pleaded for Kevin to come rescue me in my time of need. As the truck was about to hit us, I saw Kevin standing in front of it with his arms stretched out on the front of it, seemingly trying to push it in the opposite direction. And then everything went black. All I remembered was something cold surrounding me completely. I didn't feel anything else other than cold. It was almost like a dream-like state.

Bright lights were all around me and I could hear faint voices in the background, possibly coming from another room. I focused more on what was surrounding me and I could hear a constant, steady beeping sound. The beeping sound like on those hospital machines. The thought didn't sink in immediately, but then I realized that I was in the hospital and I was hooked up to those machines! The beeping then increased as I was hyperventilating. Doctors quickly rushed to me and gave me some sort of sedative. I woke up a short time later and I could feel something on my head, like a hand. I opened my eyes to the bright lights again but my eyes slowly adjusted and the hospital room became clear around me.

On my left Kevin was sitting on my bed and had his gentle hand over my head, calming me and keeping my blood pressure down. I examined him from head to toe to make sure he was okay after the accident but he didn't have a scratch. Only his hair was messier than usual, but apart from that there was nothing different about him. He still had on the same dark clothes and the same look on his face. He was just like he had always been.

"Everything is fine darling," he whispered to me, "you're going to make a full recovery and so will your mom. The other driver is going to be fine too."

I smiled softly at him and he gave me a tender reassuring kiss. He stayed on my bed until I fully aware of my surroundings and my condition. I didn't have any serious injuries, but I was pretty banged up. Kevin then walked around my room talking to me and eventually turned on the TV. The six o'clock news had just come on and I tuned in since Kevin seemed to want me to watch them. The first thing they showed on the large TV screen was a picture of an awful car wreck with a white silhouette in the form of a man standing next to it. There were no details or features on the silhouette, but it was obviously the one of a young man. The wreckage was something to see. Both the vehicles had been completely destroyed, there was *nothing* left.

*Here's an update on yesterday's devastating car accident near Portage. A small family van collided head on with a freight truck heading in the opposite direction. First responders on the scene said the crash was due to poor visibility during yesterday's storm. In this photo you can clearly see what's left of the wreckage in the middle of the highway along with a mysterious white silhouette seemingly looking over the crash site. Everyone survived.*

I couldn't believe what I was seeing! How was it possible that I survived that crash? Both vehicles were totalled! I looked over at Kevin who had returned at my side. I looked deep into his diamond eyes with such admiration and gratitude. He kissed my forehead as tears escaped from my eyes as the full scope of the situation sank in. Kevin had saved my life. He seemed to be overwhelmed with emotion too as he took me into a tight hug and took a series of heavy breaths even though he technically didn't need to breathe. His touch calmed me down and relaxed my stiff, aching muscles.

"You saved my life," I whispered to him through my tears.

He didn't say anything. Instead, he leaned over and kissed me again.

"Can you *die*?" I asked him.

"I'm already dead," he replied chuckling, "I don't think I can die again."

"Are you hurt though?"

"No sweetheart, I didn't feel a thing. Don't worry about me, it's my job to worry about *you*."

A sweet gentle smile appeared on his lips as he said those words. It was another perfect moments until a doctor and some nurses walked in to check up on me. They all smiled broadly when they saw I was awake. They told me I had only been out less than twenty-four hours, which was quite something considering the severity of my injuries.

I had broken nearly every bone in my body and had a severe concussion as a result of a skull fracture on impact. As horrible as my injuries were, I was grateful of just being alive after such a horrific crash. I also knew that no matter what happened, Kevin would always be there by my side to help me get through it all. And he was. It took over a year for me to walk again, but eventually I did. My mother had only crushed one leg in the crash but it took her multiple months to walk again too. I never got any updates on the other driver, but I knew he was alive.

My mother had never seen the photo of the crash site they had shown on TV until over a year later, when I showed her on the internet. She was in awe as she looked at Kevin's silhouette and the pieces of the wreckage scattered all over the highway. She still couldn't believe that we had both survived the crash, it was nothing short of a miracle.

"Kevin is real mom," I whispered to her as we both looked at the picture.

She didn't speak. She didn't seem to know what to believe. She could no longer deny that Kevin was real since she had experienced his presence and seen his aura. However, she still didn't seem to believe that he was my keeper. On the good side though, she left Kevin and I alone. She no longer made a big deal about my friendship with him. I didn't need to go to therapy and I wasn't sent away after all.

The whole ordeal just made me love Kevin even more. I owed him my life! We only grew closer and closer. At school I eventually made more friends, with Rosanna not in the picture. I wondered if she had gotten in touch with her own keeper if she had one, but since Kevin had no interactions with other keepers the only way to know would have been to ask her.

Eventually my mother met another man through a mutual coworker in whom she was interested. I encouraged her to pursue it and she did. I was happy for her that she had found someone after my dad and she seemed to be happier than she had ever been in a long time. Kevin and I were both elated that she had found someone and could finally be happy. I had Kevin so I didn't anybody else, but my mother had never been able to get in touch with a keeper.

In the summertime when I finished my school year my mother wanted to travel to Ohio from Wisconsin where Jeffrey, her boyfriend, had been transferred after getting a promotion. She wanted to bring my siblings and I but I didn't want to go and decided to stay home instead. I was going to spend some time with Kevin and some friends I had made in school instead. I helped my mother pack up her bags to go spend two weeks with Jeffrey out of state with a smile on my face as big as hers but at the last minute Kevin told me to stop her from leaving.

"Why don't you want her to go?" I asked Kevin, confused because he had been so happy that my mother had found someone.

"I have this awful eerie feeling about it Arlene," Kevin had a sharp edge in his voice, "just don't let her go."

"What's wrong?"

"I can't tell for sure, but I just know it's not good."

I didn't want to damped my mother's happiness but Kevin had never been wrong before and I decided to put my trust in him again. I trusted him that he truly knew what was best for my family and I so I listened to what he had to say and did what he told me.

"Don't go mom," as she was finishing getting ready.

"Well come with me!" she told me with a warm smile.

"No mom, please don't go."

"Why not? What's wrong?"

"Kevin told me something bad was going to happen."

She let out a loud sigh and gave me the *not-this-again* look. I begged her to listen to me and to not blow me off after the horrific car accident Kevin had saved us from. All she did was get angry though, and give me that lecture about how Kevin wasn't real. I looked over at him and he kept telling me to not let her go. I lost the argument though and she ended up leaving and slamming the door in my face but not before giving me some harsh words about my relationship with Kevin. I dismissed the whole thing but Kevin was obviously distraught and kept on begging me to call my mother and convince her to turn back.

"I can't Kevin," I tried to calm him down, "her mind is made up."

"There's gotta be something you can do!" he pleaded with his spiritual body shaking like a lead in the wind.

"What's wrong anyway?"

"I don't really know, I just have this deep feeling from deep inside of me that's telling me that something's not right."

"Is there a way that you can go watch over her even when she doesn't see you? I'll give you all the energy I have."

"I don't know, but we can try."

Kevin disappeared from my presence but I kept on giving him all the energy I could manage. I prayed that wherever he was, he could somehow help my mother or help me help her that something bad was going to happen. After a few minutes I was no longer able to sustain the agape and the energy field crashed. I was afraid that because I couldn't sustain the energy that I wasn't going to be able to help Kevin. I was anxious for him to come back and give me some news on what went on. Time seemed to tick forever before he appeared next to me at the kitchen table. I was so relieved to see him but he still seemed so tense.

"Call your mom, *right now!*" he commanded in a tired voice.

I immediately grabbed the phone on the kitchen table and dialed my mom's cellphone. I was barely able to breathe as I waited for her to answer. I heard a few too many rings before I heard her voice. I looked over at Kevin, not really knowing what to say after she answered.

"Tell her to pull over," he told me.

"Mom," I began, "please pull over."

"Why sweetheart?" she asked me in a confused voice.

"Tell her there's a tanker up a head on the other side of the hill and that it will hit her if she doesn't pull over."

"Mom, there's a tanker coming your way and..."

I could no longer speak.

"Tell her Arlene!" Kevin almost shouted at me.

"What's with the tanker? And how do you know that anyway?"

"Do you see it mom?"

"Yes I do, it's right here. How did you know there was a tanker coming my way?"

"Kevin told me mom, now pull over right now!"

For a few moments I heard nothing but dead silence. I shouted my mom's name over the phone until her blank voice told me that she had just seen the tanker explode right in front of her.

"Are you okay?!"

"Yes honey, I pulled over."

I collapsed to the floor in relief that she had listened to me. Kevin was still with me but I could no longer touch him. Every time I reached for him my hand would go right through him.

"I'm running out of energy," he told me, "don't worry. You rest for now and I'll come back later."

I nodded my head as he disappeared from my sight. I stayed on the line with my mother until the first responders arrived on the scene. Somebody had called 911 and the police officers on site were rerouting all the traffic. She told me she was returning home before she hung up and I patiently waiting for her until I heard her insert her keys into the lock of the front door. I quickly rushed over to her and hugged her tightly. Both us let out a massive sigh of relief as we held each other. My rigid muscles finally relaxed as she held me in her arms and thanked me endlessly for having convinced her to pull over on the side of the road. When she let go of me she looked at me with such a horrified look on her face.

"What is it?" I asked her.

"Kevin," she whispered.

"What about him? Do you see him?"

"No I don't, but he was with me on that highway wasn't he?"

"Yes he was, he's the one who told me about the tanker truck." Chills ran down her spine as she thought about it.

"Only a keeper would know something like that," she whispered, "only a keeper could predict that the truck would explode right next to me."

We looked at each other for a few moments before she threw her arms around me again. We were both overwhelmed with emotion and began to sob in each other's arms. Kevin showed up a few moments later and put his loving arms around us too. I grabbed a strand of his hair before I stroked his face. After a few moments our tears dried up and the three of us sat on the couch and talked for a while. My mother was mystified that she had just been saved from another accident. She seemed to finally understand that Kevin was indeed real and that he was looking out for us.

"He's real," she whispered to herself in a barely audible voice.

"Yes I am," Kevin whispered in her ear as he put his arm around her but she didn't seem to notice.

"Is he here?" she asked, still seemingly oblivious to his presence.

"He's right beside you mom," I whispered to her.

She looked over at her side but she still didn't seem to see Kevin. However, she lifted up her hand and reached out where Kevin was sitting and although she couldn't see him, I could perfectly see that her hand was caressing his face. He smiled softly at her and then looked at me with that same smile. He put his hand over hers and she seemed to be overwhelmed with the same feeling of inner serenity that I felt from being in Kevin's presence. My mother then looked at me with a blank, mystified expression on her face. I hugged her again and we both wept some more. Kevin put his arms around the both of us and we both felt his amazing presence.

"Who is Kevin?" my mother asked me.

"I'm just a kid who screwed up," he replied to himself.

"He's a teenager who committed suicide," I whisper to her.

Tears escaped from her eyes as she listened to me telling her how Kevin took his own life before I was born and how he came to me the night I contemplated taking my own life as well.

"What's his last name?" she asked me.

"I don't know mom," I replied, "he never told me. It doesn't really matter anyway."

"No it doesn't, but you say he was human before?"

"Yeah he was, it's cool isn't it?"

"It's nothing short of amazing. I love the young man although I've never met him."

"Maybe one day you will, Rosanna saw him."

My mother was taken aback. We had completely put the Rosanna story behind us a long time ago and both forgotten about her completely.

"I remember you saying that," my mother whispered, "gosh I hate myself for what I've put you through."

"But Kevin was there to get me through it all," I reassured her.

"I should've been there for you after the drunk driving accident but I wasn't! And on top of that I've put you through so much with Kevin."

"That's fine mom, we're all still alive aren't we?" We hugged each other again.

"Do you want to come out to dinner Arlene? Just you and me?"

"Sure, of course!"

"And Kevin, does he eat?"

"He doesn't really, but he's coming regardless."

We both laughed at once and went on our way to the restaurant. My mother and I enjoyed a good meal and Kevin sat next to me across from my mother. Once again I was the mediator for the two of them to talk and my mother was in complete awe as she got to hear his thoughts and opinions. After our meal was over, just as we were heading out the door we came face to face with the driver of the freight truck that totaled our van. It took all of us by surprise to see each other, but at the same time everything was relieved. He broke down in tears and hugged us all, so thankful that we had made all out alive and in one piece. For a moment he looked in Kevin's direction but he ended up looking past him.

"Are you the one who called 911?" my mother asked the freight truck driver.

"No," he replied, "they told me a boy named Kevin did."

My mother and I looked at each other with tearful faces. I then looked at Kevin and he gave me a kiss on the cheek. I hadn't previously known that he's the one who had called for help, I had never really thought about asking because it's not what concerned me.

"Kevin?" my mother chocked out, wanting not to cry.

"Yeah, nobody knows where he called from," the driver replied, "or how he knew about the crash in the first place. His voice isn't even on the audio recording but the operator was speaking to him!"

My mother and I knew. We grinned at each other before saying goodbye to the freight truck driver and going back home.

"He never told me he's the one who called," I told her.

"How in the world did he do that?" she asked me.

"I don't know, I don't think he even knows himself how it all works, but we're never alone as long as he's around."

"And he knew about the tanker going to explode in the ditch too."

"Yeah he somehow did."

Kevin and I were always together and our love for each other only grew deeper with each and every day that went by. He was still evasive about my questions regarding his past and his human life. He was obviously ashamed of it and confessed to me that he had remorse, but he still refused to tell me. I eventually just let it go since it really wasn't important.

His old life was gone, he had a new one with me and that's all we both really cared about. My mother was never able to see him but despite that she always made sure to somehow include him in the household. He even had his own room in the house! It was also obvious to me that he loved her just as much in return. He helped all of us heal, and there came a time that the pain had completely vanished like it never came.

One night I was watching the news by myself with my mother and my siblings out in town and Kevin resting from energy in another dimension when Kevin's picture suddenly appeared on the TV screen. I immediately turned up the volume and tuned in to the newscast to see what they were going to say about him, especially since he had died before I was born and apparently nobody except me could still see him! The photo soon switched to the mugshot of another young man named Nate following by Nate in an orange jumpsuit being led out of a courtroom.

*Nate Anderson, 18, and Kevin Hegarty, 17, were responsible for three murders in Nashville in 1993. Amelia Sinai, 13, and her sister Natalie Sinai, 18, along with her boyfriend Gregory Sims, also 18, were savagely shot to death right in their*

I didn't know how to react to what I saw. My breath left me completely as I listened in horror to what Kevin had done with his friend Nate. I threw the TV remote across the room and broke down crying. I screamed and hit the end table with my fists as it sank in that Kevin was nothing but a murderer! *My whole world seemed like it was coming down, crashing hard as it hit the ground.* My body shook uncontrollably to the point that I eventually had to lie down because I was so upset.

I had never felt to betrayed. I had shared everything with a murderer, a teenage killer. I had let him into the most private and sensitive areas of my life, told him all my secrets and let him sleep in my bed at night. He had saved my life and healed all my pain, but he had committed murder and that was unforgivable.

I was so hurt and angry at myself for having loved a murderer the way I did. I truly hated myself for having let him into my life the way I did. I hated the entire realm of keepers for having sent me a *murderer* as a keeper. I went up to my room and cut myself again. It wasn't for attention or to prove to anyone that Kevin could heal my scars, but to try to lessen the immeasurable pain of betrayal and loss that I was feeling. Conflicting feelings went round and round inside my head. I still loved Kevin, but I couldn't accept loving a murderer. I yelled out to the sky that Kevin and the entire realm of keepers better not ever come into my life again. At the same time I was so angry at Kevin for leading me on the way he did and not being forthcoming on the multiple occasions he had the chance to tell me the truth.

I felt lightheaded from being in shock and cutting myself so I let myself drift into a dreamless sleep. I woke up again a few hours later to a still empty house. My cuts burned as I passed them under hot water. Kevin was no longer around to kiss them away. I broke down crying again as I thought of all the memories shared with Kevin and all the time I spent with him. I owed him my life! I owed him a lot more than just my life.

Deep inside me I felt sympathy for him and eventually compassion too. His bad choices obviously haunted him profoundly and it saddened me deeply. I was even angrier at myself for having disowned him the way I did instead of trying to understand first like he had begged me to do with Rosanna. I had lost her and I ended up losing him too. As angry as I was with him, I still wanted to talk to him and try to understand the full scope of the situation before passing any more judgments.

I tightly closed my eyes and left myself be overcome with agape but I just couldn't do it. I was too angry at Kevin and hurt by his actions to immerse myself in pure love for him. I put my hand over my bloody arm and begged for him to come back and erase my scars but nothing happened. I had never felt so alone. After two years of always having him by my side, I ended up alone. In between my hatred and my tears, I tried to sustain the agape to talk to Kevin one last time before I decided whether he was worthy of being forgiven for his crimes or not.

I took a deep breath and let my mind drift off back to that first night I met Kevin. I remembered how his gentle touch comforted me and how serene it felt when he held me in his arms. The agape came flowing over me again just like it did on that night. I turned over onto my back and saw that Kevin was there. I was overjoyed and went over to him.

He looked at me with a blank stare and I saw the gaping head wound in his left temple area. Some of his hair was soaked in blood and his left ear was soaked in it. I gasped in shock and reached out to touch him but my hand went right through him. I looked at him in pure horror, that's what he looked like after he shot himself! My heart broke for him and I reached out to hold him again, focusing especially on sustaining the energy. His body was cold in my arms and although I could interact with him, he wasn't breathing.

The features on his once-beautiful face looked tired and worn out. His blue eyes weren't as bright anymore, and his overwhelming peaceful aura had faded away. I held him tightly against me and poured my love over him just like he had done to me in the past in hopes that it would heal him the same way it worked on me.

"I've failed my mission," Kevin whispered in a bleak, tired voice.

"I'm so sorry Kevin," I muttered through my tears, "please forgive me. I never meant to hurt you."

"Of course I forgive you Arlene, I love you, and I always will long after I'm gone here."

"What do you mean *gone*? Where are you going?"

"I've failed Arlene."

His voice was just a soft whisper filled with angst as he told me to stop giving him agape since it no longer did anything for him. As much as I begged him to stay, he didn't have a choice but to say goodbye. He expressed regret and sorrow before he slipped out of my hold and disappeared from me. He hadn't been able to heal my scars no matter how much he tried and was no longer able to sustain his own energy. There was no way I could reach him, he was gone. I buried my face in my pillows and pleaded to higher powers to send Kevin back to me so I could properly make amends. Nothing happened. I thought back to what I had seen on TV, that Kevin had shot himself next to Amelia's body seemingly regretting what he and Nate had done.

I called on to Amelia in agape just like I used to call on Kevin in hopes that she could give me answers to the missing pieces of the puzzle since Kevin was no longer around and I never got the chance to ask him why. When I reopened my eyes, I saw this teenage girl standing at the edge of my bed. It was Amelia!

She came over to me and sat next to me on my bed. She was a beautiful young girl with long shiny brown hair down passed her shoulders and deep green eyes that complimented her small round race and a few freckles. Her little pinks lips were out of the way to reveal a perfect set of white teeth and a welcoming smile.

"You came!" I exclaimed.

"The keepers heard your prayer," she told me in a gentle voice, "whatever you request of me, I'll do my best."

"It's about Kevin Hegarty."

"What about him?"

"Why did he shoot you like that?"

"He's not the one who shot me, he didn't even know I was in the house. Nate wanted to kill my sister for leaving him but the three of us ended up being in the house."

"So Nate's the one who shot you?"

"Yes, he's the one who shot everyone. Kevin didn't even fire his gun before he shot himself."

"I presume you were already dead when he committed suicide?"

"Yeah, Nate had already shot me point-blank in the face but I do know that Kevin didn't know I was even in the house. When he stumbled across my body on his way out he just couldn't live with himself so he decided to put an end to it right there."

Amelia spoke in a very sympathetic tone of voice towards Kevin and Nate. The glimmer in her eyes showed that she understood their actions and she didn't show any kind of anger or resentment towards either of them.

"Do you forgive them?"

"Yes I do, it's a part of me having peace of mind, even here."

"I just don't understand why it all ended the way it did. I mean, we loved each other so much and then he was just gone! Do you think it's someone not forgiving him?"

"I wouldn't know, but it's definitely something plausible."

I sincerely thanked Amelia for her insights and her time away from eternal bliss and proceeded to speak with Natalie and George. Natalie had come to forgive Kevin, but not Nate and George hadn't forgiven any of them. That's where they problem was, Kevin had not been able to get the proper closure and forgiveness he needed and ended up wrecking his relationship with me. I understood why he wasn't able to forgive him, what

Kevin had done was unforgivable but I loved Kevin enough to try to reach out to George and help him move on from the tragedy.

"You're not able to move on aren't you?" I made conversation with George who had appeared in front of me.

"No," he muttered back, "I can't."

"You can't forgive Kevin."

"What he did was unforgivable!"

I felt his pain. I had felt so betrayed when I learned that Kevin had helped his friend murder three innocent people and never though I was going to be able to look at him again but as I looked deep inside of myself I realized that nothing changed my love for Kevin, and I wanted to forgive him and fix our bond. It also saddened me deeply to see even the departed stuck in limbo because they weren't able to let go. I realized at that point that I needed forgiveness too. I had never truly forgiven myself for the drunk driving accident. I shared my feelings with George and he listened attentively just like Kevin had done.

"It wasn't your fault," he told me in a gentle whisper, "they aren't dead because of you. It wasn't anything you did."

"And it wasn't anything you did that made Kevin and Nate kill you!" I replied doing my best to hold back tears.

George sighed deeply and looked up at the ceiling, deep in thought. It was true, what happened wasn't George's fault and he shouldn't have to be the one who constantly suffers for it. I knew from the look on his face that he understood that. I closed my eyes and took a deep breath myself, letting my mind drift away into limbo.

Somewhere along the way I decided to let go of my guilt regarding the tragic deaths of Sabrina and Melanie. What happened wasn't my fault, it was an accident. For the first time I felt like I was actually able to take a breath, a real breath of air. A feeling of calmness swept over me and consumed me for the short moment it lasted. I had lived with guilt for some two and a half years, but I was finally free.

"Feels good doesn't it?" George commented.

I let out a sigh of relief and as I opened my eyes I saw Kevin standing at the edge of my bed. His face was very pale and his eyes were dark and lifeless. The gaping head wound was no longer visible but Kevin was no longer vibrant and full of life like he had once been. He was formally dressed with his hair neatly combed back, he looked like a person who was about to attend a funeral. I sent him agape but nothing seemed to happen. He still stood there like a walking corpse. George left my side and walked over to Kevin's side of the room where the two of them looked at each other, each seemingly waiting for the other to begin.

"Forgive yourself," George commanded Kevin with a somewhat sharp edge in his voice.

"I can't do that," Kevin replied in a soft whisper as he bowed his head.

"I'm done with this. I'm not going to let this dictate the rest of my eternal existence!" George went on. "I'm letting go today!"

In that very moment when George forgave Kevin, a show of lights sparkled around both of their auras. George's aura stayed bright but Kevin's faded away. He was still dark and lifeless while George was radiant and lighting up the whole room. George commanded Kevin to forgive himself again but there was no visible reaction in Kevin.

I soon saw Amelia and Natalie join in with both of their auras shining bright too. I crawled over to the edge of my bed and joined them too. The five of us were standing in a circle in the middle of the room with each person's aura helping to illuminate the rest. I looked up at Kevin with compassion and sympathy in my eyes and threw my arms around him. His chin was pressed down against my shoulder when he let out a deep sigh too and I felt a surge of energy all around me.

His aura engulfed me and the biggest sense of pure bliss came sweeping over me like a hurricane. Kevin's aura had always been very comforting but it had never been quite like that. I got out of his hold and looked up at him again and saw that his eyes had become shiny and radiant again. His heart was beating again and he had regained all of his color. His golden locks of messy hair were softer than they ever were and a gentle serene smile appeared across his lips. It was finished.

Kevin had forgiven himself and had received the forgiveness of the people he had hurt along with Nate. The five of us looked at each other with smiles on everyone's lips. I had never felt so much love in my entire love, I was completely surrounded by it. In a flash of white light the Lord joined us and I got to stand right there in the midst of his amazing glory.

I watched in complete awe as one by one George, Amelia and Natalie were taken up to heaven. Only Kevin and I were left in the awesome presence of the Lord. We looked at each other for the fraction of a second and hugged each other one last time. We said our last goodbyes and Kevin gave me one last kiss on the forehead before the Lord took him up to heaven. As he ascended he waved down at me with a big smile on his face.

He was so happy, he had finally gotten his wish after almost twenty years. He was forgiven, he was free. After they had all ascended into heaven all signs of their auras and their overwhelming presences dissipated like they never existed in the first place. I sat on my bed and let my mind go blank. I had just witnessed the most amazing thing in the world but I already missed Kevin terribly.

Reality came back crashing in when my mother knocked on my bedroom door. I was startled after still reeling from my recent experiences but managed to compose myself as she walked in and sat next to me. She asked me what I had been doing up in my room all alone on such a nice day but I dismissed her and told her that I was tired and that I simply needed a little rest from time to time. I didn't tell her anything about the Lord making things right between Kevin and the people he had wronged in his human life but I did slip up and mention that Kevin was gone. My mother was taken aback at my comment and asked me what was going on.

"Kevin was taken up to heaven," I whispered to her holding back tears.

She wrapped her arms around me and held me into a tight hug as we both cried. I eventually confessed to her the whole ordeal with Kevin in the last moments of our relationship and how the Lord had redeemed him. I was comforted that he was finally in his happy place where there was no more pain but I still missed him terribly and grieved for him because I had loved him so much for the two short years that we had spent together. I felt like I was the luckiest person in the world to have gotten the chance to know him like I did even though he was gone.

"I hope he knew that I loved him before he left," my mother whispered to me as she grieved for Kevin too.

"I know he did mom," I reassured her, "he's with dad now and we'll see both of them again one day."

The mood was sober in the following few days but I reminded myself of how much Kevin and I really loved each other when the thought of being without him was unbearable. His voice always remained in the back of my mind to somehow comfort me and give me advice when I felt alone and didn't know where to turn. I eventually rekindled my friendship with Rosanna and the two of us were able to reminisce and comfort each other with the good times we both spent with Kevin. With his help and his love I became a new person and I always wanted to honor his memory by being the change I wanted to see in the world and by giving others what he gave me, hope. It delighted me to share his wisdom with others who were willing to listen.

As summer came to an end I was getting ready to move away for college in the next few weeks and was aimlessly wandering around the basement while my mother was doing the laundry. I watched her take my clothes out of the washing machine and shove them in the dryer. She then looked down to see if there were any clothes left in the washing machine and bent down over it to pick up something. In her hand was this small stainless steel link bracelet that I had never seen before. We were both puzzled since it didn't belong to either one of us and it didn't belong to any of my siblings. She gave it to me and I decided that I might as well wear it since I had it!

The morning before I left for college I decided to pull up some pictures of Kevin, Amelia, Natalie and George to carry around with me in my wallet so I would never forget the convictions and values all of them had taught me since I knew that it would be too easy to get caught up in my new life and lost in the great big world out there. For some reason I wasn't able to connect to the internet to get some so I texted Rosanna and told her to send me some when I got to college. She agreed to print some and send them to me once I got settled. A few days after I arrived there I got an envelope addressed to my name with four pictures in it. As I looked at them I couldn't help but notice the bracelet on Kevin's arm. As I looked more closely it became clear to me that it was the bracelet my mom found in the washing machine!

"How can this be?" I exclaimed to myself alone in my dorm.

I opened the window of my room and looked up at the cloudless blue sky in awe. I smiled to myself as I traced each link with my finger. I knew that Kevin hadn't left me and that he was always going to hold a very special place in my heart. I closed the window and immediately called my mother to tell her what had just happened. She just as flabbergasted as I was when I found out but we both rejoiced at the thought that Kevin was still very much in our lives. The bracelet became my little memento commemorating our time together and with it came all the sweet memories of him being there when I had no one else and him saving my life *twice*.

I proudly wore the bracelet wherever I went and never took it off. I only seemed to have to poke it around with my finger and Kevin's overwhelming presence was still with me. I couldn't see him or talk to him but his aura still lingered around my dorm and the classroom. My mother commented that she sometimes indirectly sensed someone there in the house with her when she was alone, and I simply smiled to myself as the thought that even though Kevin's work might have been done with my life, it would never really be over. I stayed in touch with Rosanna but she never mentioned Kevin's presence still lingering around her like my mother did. I didn't tell anyone else other than my mother about the bracelet or my experiences with Kevin but the things he taught me were my motivation for everything I did.

I ended up putting his picture along with the other three on my night table so they were the last thing I saw when I went to bed at night and the first thing I saw when I woke up in the morning. Seeing them made always me smile. It might have been better for the world if Kevin had never existed, but it would not have been better for me.

# LETTER TO THE READER

Dear Reader,

I humbly thank you for reading through this book that was a true labor of love for me and I sincerely hope that you enjoyed it and that you'll leave me a good review. Even if you didn't like it or if it could've been better I would still appreciate an honest and constructive review on Amazon, Goodreads and/or another platform of your choice.

All reviews, both the good ones and the bad ones, help both readers pick books they might like in an ever-growing market but they also help up and coming authors write better books. I thank you again for your time and hope to hear from you soon! Happy reading!

*Jamila Mikhail*

# ABOUT THE AUTHOR

Jamila Mikhail (Жамийла Михаил), or simply Mila for short, was born in British Columbia, Canada in 1996 and now lives in Ottawa, the city of her dreams, with her cat Squeaker. In 2018 she was one of the people who received the title of *Top Writer* on Quora and over the years she has also received several awards for her poetry and short stories ever since she started writing on a serious basis in 2011.

In her spare time Mila also enjoys various hobbies including photography, gastronomy, building toy models of various sizes — including the action figure that inspired Adler's character — and studying a variety of things including history, philosophy, quantum mechanics and foreign languages. She thinks that it's strange to write (and brag) about herself in the third person.

# BOOK READER MAGAZINE INTERVIEW

*The following interview was published in Book Reader Magazine on June 1st, 2018. The original interview can be read online here:* http://bookreadermagazine.com/featured-author-jamila-mikhail/

**Tell us a little about yourself. Where were you raised? Where do you live now?**

My name is Jamila Mikhail, I'm 21 years old and I'm a Canadian writer. I was born in British Columbia but lived here and there, even moving seven times in five years at one point! Finally, now that I'm an adult I came to settle in Ottawa, the capital and also the city of my dreams. We aren't quite halfway through 2018 yet and I've already accomplished most of the dreams I've had for the last ten years! I share this dream with my cat Squeaker who has been my number one buddy for the last three years. She doesn't meow, she literally squeaks the sissiest noise I've ever heard come out of a cat, and I've had cats my whole life.

I'm currently a student in law and human rights, which is my other passion aside from writing. The two merge more often than not though, because somewhere in my stories there will always be a character or situation that deals with real life contemporary social issues. Aside from this I'm a lover of snail mail letters, a postcard collector, a real foodie and a maker of toy soldiers. I've made myself a little army with old and recycled parts and they keep me in line in my writing!

**At what age did you realize your fascination with books? When did you start writing?**

I've loved books for as long as I can remember. Growing up I didn't have cable TV or anything like that (I didn't get my own until

I was 19 years old actually) so books, and also the newspaper, were my connection to the rest of the world. Nowadays I love books both to escape reality for a little while, and to educate myself about pertinent and important topics in my society and the world at large. You can learn anything from a book, that I believe.

I've also loved writing for just as long. I first began steadily writing in 2004 (I was seven years old) and actually still have all the old notebooks with my scribbles and two-page stories in them. It wasn't long before writing became my way to cope with life, but most importantly it was the only socially acceptable way to express myself and my grand ideas. I tend to be bold and writing enabled me to make that side of myself shine.

I began writing on a serious basis in 2011 on the advice of my therapist who was treating me for PTSD at the time, and my first completed manuscript "The Distant Factory" was born. It's actually available for free on my website along with several other books. I didn't publish anything until this year though, because it is no small task and I had to get my $#!& together before venturing out into that. It turned out to be one of the best things I've ever done.

**Who are your favorite authors to read? What is your favorite genre to read. Who Inspires you in your writings?**

This is probably the hardest question for me to answer because I literally drive all over the road here (and often drive all over the real road in my car too). I particularly love reading non-fiction about the Second World War and the Korean War since my own grandfather served in both of them and that's also what inspired me to get into the human rights field. My favorites are definitely the autobiographies of the people who lived through the darkest days in humanity, these otherwise ordinary men and women are not only my favorite authors but also my heroes.

I also love reading true crime and psychological books that seek to explain why people turn into war criminals or serial killers and other things like that. I am fascinated by people and love being able to observe both the humanity in them and the horror in them. My grandmother has inspired many of my writings through the years and was always pushing me to write some more. Sadly she passed away on March 11th of this year and writing is what has probably kept me alive since she's been gone. Otherwise, my own life and the things I witness and hear about happening around me are generally what inspire me to write. That's also what makes my stories easy to relate to.

**Tell us a little about your latest book?**

My latest book is called "Don't Let Me Go" and it is young adult fiction, geared towards readers from age 13 to adults. It actually began as a short story writing prompt in 2014 and turned into a novel-length manuscript by 2015 (the original short story can be found on my website) but it didn't go much further than that. It remained dormant on my computer until National Novel Writing Month last year. I knew that I wanted to revive it, but also rewrite it because it was pretty awful in the beginning. I won't lie, I totally flunked out during NaNoWriMo after rewriting only about 10 000 words. The manuscript remained dormant again for several months until my grandmother's passing.

After that it only took me about a week and a half to complete the final draft of 78 000 words. It wasn't hard for me to sit in front of my computer and type thousands upon thousands of words during the worst time in my life because it made me feel better and gave me purpose. Getting the whole thing 'publication pretty' so to speak took another two months but I'm very satisfied with how everything turned out. I think my grandma would be very proud of me even though she wouldn't be able to read the book either way because she only spoke French.

"Don't Let Me Go" mixes contemporary issues and situations (in this case, a teenage girl named Joanie who is reeling from her parents' bitter divorce and struggles with school) with a little bit of fantasy, history and science. Joanie decides to pass the time by making military action figures and much to her surprise, one of them comes to life! Adler is a soldier straight out of the Second World War (but Joanie is the only person who can see him) and helps Joanie navigate rough waters that include depression, domestic violence and bullying but what she doesn't know is that Adler also hides a secret…

THE ONLY WAY TO
STOP THE
HATE
is to
replace it
with love
TAKE A STAND
that means *even if*
STANDING
ALONE

# READ WRITE CLUB INTERVIEW

*The following interview was published on the Read Write Club website on July 19th, 2018. The original post can be read here:*
http://www.readwriteclub.com/jamila-mikhail-author-interview/

**Tell us about yourself and what inspired you to start writing.**

My name is Jamila Mikhail and I'm a 22-year-old Canadian author of several books. I'm a polyglot and a human rights student with a passion for writing about important (and often controversial) topics and social issues. With whatever I say and wherever I go I manage to cause a stir but that's something I enjoy, and that's part of the reason I'm both a human rights student and an author!

Although I've always loved writing and it's always been my way to cope with life, I was inspired to go big and actually publish these writings because I know for a fact that books can be revolutionary. I don't expect to change the world with my books, but I know that the stories I have to tell will leave a lasting impact on the reader. My inspiration to write and publish is precisely to inspire others much of the same way I've been inspired by books ever since I was a little girl. I guess you could take that as paying it forward being a source of inspiration to write.

**Tell us about your books.**

I currently have two published books available for sale and several more available to download for free on my website. My first published book was "Innermost" which is a collection of poetry that I've written and compiled over a period of about half a dozen years. To me poetry is one of the most beautiful art forms in the world and several of my poems have won me local awards over the years.

My second published book is called "Don't Let Me Go" and it's fiction aimed at teens and other young people. It's a little mix of fantasy, history and philosophy with contemporary social issues that young people face today including bullying, domestic violence and mental illness. Tough themes are presented in an uplifting fashion to promote a message of hope for the future. This is the kind of book I wish I'd come across as a teenager facing many of the things written about in the book.

As for the many free ebooks available on my website, they are a wide range of short stories (funny ones, weird ones, depressing ones, touching ones, a little bit of everything really), more poetry and more full length novels about contemporary issues. "The Distant Factory" is a contemporary crime novel told from the perspective of a street kid wrestling between wanting to fix her life and get revenge on a particular person who wronged her in the past. "The Florence Nightingale Effect" is exactly what the title implies it is: a nurse who develops inappropriate feelings for a patient. This novel also deals with other issues in the background, such as crime, redemption and the justice system.

**How did you go about getting published?**

Going down the self-publishing route was an easy choice in my case for several reasons, but the biggest one being that I retain complete control at all times. If I ever decide to change something, delete something or unpublish a book entirely I don't need anybody's approval or permission to do so. I don't have to answer to anybody and that enables me to hire (or fire) anyone that I please at any time. It's a lot of hard work but it's been 100% worth it because I get to carve out my own path instead of being put on one that may not have been right for me.

While I have no doubt that there are many perks to using a traditional publisher, it's just not what's right for my vision as an author. I have some fellow author friends who ended up losing the rights to their precious works going down that route and that's actually my biggest fear as an author. I've also met people who have certain books self-published and others traditionally published depending on their vision for that book and I don't believe that you have to pick a single route for your entire career.

Nowadays you have a legitimate chance of being very successful at self-publishing with the wide reach of the internet and the many tools available out there so for me this was also a safe way to dip my toes into the publishing waters and it turns out that I'm completely comfortable in these waters.

**What is your writing process? Do you have a time, day or place you like to write?**

The writing process just sort of happens for me. I have to let it come naturally otherwise it doesn't come out right. Inspiration can strike me anywhere at any time and I always bring a notebook to take down notes when that lightning strike does happen because otherwise it's gone forever. To put something together "officially" I always sit in the living room, sometimes at my desk and most often in the rocking hair because my desk is a junk magnet for everything except the laptop.

**What do you like to do when you're not writing? Full-time job, pets, hobbies?**

When I'm not writing I'm usually busy with school or other classes that I take part in to learn a new craft or refine an existing skill and that can be pretty time-consuming even as a part-time student on top of daily responsibilities. I now also have two cats living under my roof and my newest addition is quite the handful! Squeaker and Carling don't allow me to sit still and get bored I can tell you that! I also keep my mind down to earth with various hobbies including collecting postcards, writing snail mail letters, participating in community events, doing activist work and lurking around thrift stores and flea markets looking for old or neglected action figure parts which I then recycle and turn into brand new creations. This doll-making of mine is in part what inspired "Don't Let Me Go" and I actually made the doll of Adler's character too!

**Any advice for authors about book covers?**

The only thing I would tell other authors is to look at the covers of other books in the same genre. This will give them an idea of what is mainstream but I would also advise them to not be a carbon copy of others. There needs to be a balance of both your book fitting in to where it belongs and standing out enough so readers will be drawn to your novel instead of another. For those with some experience in design there are many beautiful pre-made cover templates that you can edit and rearrange to your taste but for those who have no experience I would suggest getting a cover made by someone who knows what they are doing. You don't have to pay a lot of money for something beautiful either!

**Any marketing tips you'd like to share with other authors?**

First off, authors should make their books available in as many formats as possible (for me that's paperback, ebook and audiobook) and distribute them to as many retailers as possible too. It may be tempting to capitalize on a single big market by going exclusive, but you also lose a lot of potential customers this way! I've personally sold books on very small and often ignored channels, plus I generally don't buy from some of the biggest names in the business either. I want readers more than I want money and if you put people before profit you should be successful in creating a solid fanbase!

My second tip is to not underestimate the power of in-person marketing! Get cards, bookmarks or posters promoting your work printed and be loud and proud! Give these materials to people you know, your local library, academic institution, bookstores and other places where people might be interested in what you have to offer. Offering someone something tangible, even just a small business card, can go much farther than we think!

**What's your favorite book?**

It changes just about every single day, but right now it's the Diary of Anne Frank.

**What are you reading now?**

I'm currently reading "A Mother's Reckoning" by Susan Klebold and although I'm not very far into it yet, I already recommend it to anyone who wants to read one of those books that will stay with them forever.

**What's your next book project?**

I'm currently about ten thousand words into "After Anderson" which is my latest attack on social issues expected in 2019. Like my other writings, this won't be a book for the faint of heart or those seeking to escape the real world. It's a hard to swallow story about a school shooting and the people whose lives have been turned upside down in the aftermath. Having witnessed much violence at school, including gun violence (though thankfully not a massacre), this is a topic that is particularly important to me. This is a book project that I also hope will help me in healing from those experiences at school. You know when they talk about whether you write for yourself or write for others, "After Anderson" is definitely writing for myself.

THE EYES ARE
utterly
useless
when
the
mind
is
blindless
TAKE A STAND
against the blind
leading the blind
OPEN YOUR HEART

# EXTERNAL LINKS

Log on to www.jamilamikhail.com to find contact information, get official links to all social media pages, stay up to date with new releases, download half a dozen free ebooks and other online-only content.

Both readers and fellow writers can unlock a world of services and exclusive content by becoming a patron of mine at patreon.com/jamilamikhail for as low as $1 (USD) a month.

Fellow independent authors needing reviews can also visit https://www.jamilamikhail.com/get-a-review.html to submit a query for a free book review posted on various websites and social media pages to gain more exposure.